# SINISTER
# HEIGHTS

BY LOREN D. ESTLEMAN

THE AMOS WALKER NOVELS
*Sinister Heights*
*A Smile on the Face of the Tiger*
*The Hours of the Virgin*
*The Witchfinder*
*Never Street*
*Sweet Women Lie*
*Silent Thunder*
*Downriver*
*Lady Yesterday*
*Every Brilliant Eye*
*Sugartown*
*The Glass Highway*
*The Midnight Man*
*Angel Eyes*
*Motor City Blue*

THE DETROIT NOVELS
*Thunder City*
*Jitterbug*
*Stress*
*Edsel*
*King of the Corner*
*Motown*
*Whiskey River*

THE PETER MACKLIN NOVELS
*Any Man's Death*
*Roses Are Dead*
*Kill Zone*

OTHER NOVELS
*The Rocky Mountain Moving Picture Association*
*Peeper*
*Dr. Jekyll and Mr. Holmes*
*Sherlock Holmes vs. Dracula*
*The Oklahoma Punk*

WESTERN NOVELS
*The Master Executioner*
*White Desert*
*Journey of the Dead*
*City of Widows*
*Sudden Country*
*Bloody Season*
*Gun Man*
*The Stranglers*
*This Old Bill*
*Mister St. John*
*Murdock's Law*
*The Wolfer*
*Aces & Eights*
*Stamping Ground*
*The High Rocks*
*The Hider*
*Billy Gashade*

NONFICTION
*The Wister Trace: Classic Novels of the American Frontier*

SHORT STORY COLLECTIONS
*General Murders*
*The Best Western Stories of Loren D. Estleman* (edited by Bill Pronzini and Ed Gorman)
*People Who Kill*

# SINISTER HEIGHTS

# LOREN D. ESTLEMAN

Published by Warner Books

An AOL Time Warner Company

Copyright © 2002 by Loren D. Estleman
All rights reserved.

 Mysterious Press books are published by Warner Books, Inc., 1271 Avenue of the Americas, New York, NY 10020.

Visit our Web site at www.twbookmark.com

An AOL Time Warner Company

The Mysterious Press name and logo are registered trademarks of Warner Books, Inc.

Printed in the United States of America

First Printing: February 2002

10  9  8  7  6  5  4  3  2  1

Library of Congress Cataloging-in-Publication Data
    Estleman, Loren D.
        Sinister Heights / Loren D. Estleman.
            p. cm.
        ISBN 0-89296-738-2
        1. Walker, Amos (Fictitious character)—Fiction.   2. Private investigators—Michigan—Detroit—Fiction.   3. Detroit (Mich.)—Fiction.   I. Title.

PS3555.S84 S56 2002
813'.54—dc21                                                2001017797

*To Teamsters Local 299,*
*For Leauvett C. Estleman*
*(1910–1994)*

*Delenda est Carthago.*

—Cato

# SINISTER HEIGHTS

# CHAPTER

# ONE

AND NOW HERE I AM, stopped around the corner from the second oldest automobile factory in the world, sitting in a stolen pickup truck and smoking a Winston down to the filter. Here in the poured shadow is the only spot in the city where the throbbing glow of the hot steel can't be seen. Everywhere else it's like looking into the yellow eye of a killer. Two people are dead and the chances are better than even there will be more by morning.

The Ram's motor idles smoothly. Even the crickets are louder. A jet that is only a turquoise blue and an orange winking light is rushing to catch up with the muted surflike roar of its engines as it heads somewhere that is a hell of a long way from here. My eyes burn from lack of sleep. My ankle is hurting again and my neck never stopped.

Now the bitter scorched-rubber stench of the filter igniting stings my nose. I snap the stub out the window, check the load in the .38 one more time, and put the indicator in Drive. The dream ends when the pickup rolls and then it's then again. . . .

• • •

The driver's seat of the Viper gripped my thighs like a big hand in a soft glove. That didn't place on my list of priorities, but I liked the climate control, and the dials on the dash awakened something in me I thought had died with Buster Crabbe. I had no idea where they had put the cigarette lighter.

I cracked the window to expel the new-car odor, which made me woozy and came from an aerosol can anyway, and aced the tricky bracket-shaped turn from Larned onto West Congress going the other direction. I couldn't open up the monster V-10 downtown, thanks to pedestrians and the UPS truck that had been double-parked in front of the Penobscot Building since Disco. It was enough to feel its pulse in the soles of my feet. The car—Heineken green, low as an asp—turned heads at signals and got me the granite look from a tired-faced cop drumming his fingers on the wheel of his cruiser. An automobile designed to do 162 in sixth is going to break the law on general principles.

Connor Thorpe was standing on the corner of Washington and Congress waiting for the light. I spun into the curb and called his name. His long basset face took a moment to process the evidence. I popped the latch. He swung inside and we took off in third. They don't put that kind of torque on the street every day. You have to wait six weeks.

"Prowling in the bushes must pay," he said. "This model lists at sixty-six thousand."

"Seventy-five. It's got a CD player. We still meeting at the Caucus Club?"

"Just long enough to tell you they need me uptown. I wish to hell you'd get a cell phone."

"Maybe when I give up smoking."

"Don't tell me you believe that airborne cancer shit."

"I meant so I can afford the bills."

"This from a man driving my first divorce settlement. I lived on sardine sandwiches for a year."

"With me it was peanut butter and jelly."

"Not enough balance. This thing loaded?" He ran his blunt fingers over the pressure pads that operated the stereo system.

"It comes loaded from the factory. A.C. and color are the only options."

"You went with goose shit?"

"It's called Guadalcanal."

"Same thing. I was stationed there eight weeks. Just take me to the New Center area. I'll snag a ride back."

"Won't compare with this one."

"I guess you bought the right to pull down your pants and wave it around. I like my old Chevy. They offer me a new one every year, but I got better things to worry about than scratching the finish. What happened to the Cutlass?"

"I'll take it out when it rains. What's in the New Center area? Not GM anymore."

"I think they need help taking the letters off the building."

It was like Thorpe not to be specific, even about his destination. After Saigon fell old Leland Stutch had hired him out from under Naval Intelligence to direct security in his plants worldwide. These days he worked as a security consultant for all three major U.S. automakers, and not a single board member had raised the question of conflict of interest. The joke went that his left and right socks never shared the same drawer. In his first six months he discharged sixty-eight employees for theft, including a vice president of engineering and design and an executive assistant to a board chairman. Before his record became too consistent to attract special notice, he'd turned down an FBI directorship and a Reagan cabinet post. In twenty-five years he'd had the same job and four wives.

He got his suits from the same tailor who'd made his uniforms, using the measurements he'd taken in 1970. They were loose in the shoulders, tight across the middle, and made of some gray-green material that wore like chainmail. He divided his time between an office in the former National Bank of Detroit building downtown and a basement bunker in Stutch's old plant in Iroquois Heights. Where he slept was anybody's guess.

We took Cass up toward Grand. He watched an old man in ragged army surplus dragging a duffel along the sidewalk. "Are you free tomorrow? I want to hear your report."

"I'll give it to you now. I've got a line on Tindle."

"So have I. Every time I crunch the numbers he's stolen another ten thousand. My odds are better yanking the handle on a slot machine." He hated casinos. He'd even changed his route to work in order to avoid passing the gambling hell that had opened in the old Wonder Bread bakery.

"Marks, yen, guilders, or dollars? Whose idea was it to put him in Overseas Acquisitions, anyway?"

"Someone who is no longer employed by the automobile industry."

"That how you plan to handle Tindle?"

"Where he ends up working isn't my concern. It can be the rockpile or the prison library."

"The board decided to prosecute?"

"They will."

One of the advantages of three companies sharing one top cop was his salary didn't make a ding in the third-quarter profits. One of the disadvantages was he knew where all the bodies were buried; and the grave was only half full. They'd hired a hawk to end the sparrow problem and wound up stuck with the hawk.

"Shareholders will scream."

"They scream when the NASDAQ slips half a point. It's why I don't accept stock options. Clouds the judgment."

"What happened to preserving customer trust at any cost?"

"With luck, the same thing that happened to peace at any

price. I'm a vindictive old bastard, Walker. Steal from my boss, steal from me. But you better kill me first."

"Company man."

"A maligned race." He produced a worn leather case from an inside pocket and a thick black cigar from the case and lifted his sad brows at me, daring me to ask him not to smoke in the car. I told him go ahead and good luck finding the lighter.

"Never use 'em. They're always busted and when they aren't they smell like scorched feathers." He lit the stogie with a wooden match and flipped the burnt stump out the window. "Before I put Tindle's nuts in the cracker, I need to know what he's been doing with the money he embezzled. If he put it in Krugerrands, I want to run my fingers through the coins like Scrooge. If it's in Switzerland, I want the number of the account. If he bought porno, I want every sticky page on the table in the executive lounge. That's why I retained you. I know *where* he is. I know he buys colored condoms and rolls his toilet paper underhand. I had his place tossed before you came on board."

"Find anything?" We were passing Wayne State University on the old Corridor. The city was considering changing the name of that stretch of Cass to encourage business other than drugs and prostitution. Anyway, it was a plan.

"Oh, I didn't expect to see it piled up in sacks with dollar signs, but I thought we'd turn a passbook, brochures on Tahiti, a closing date on a beach house in Carmel—something to indicate he isn't counting on his forty grand a year and 401K. Which if I hadn't been suspicious to begin with would have made me. Who the hell lives within his means under the present tax system?"

"Judging by that cigar I'd say you."

"Cubans are for commies."

We drove for a while listening to nothing but ten cylinders firing. It was warm for April. Students were strolling about with their jackets tied around their waists and sunning themselves stretched out on last year's grass. No one in the Rust Belt complained about global warming.

"How clutched up are you right now?" Thorpe asked.

"It's my slow season. May through April."

"A friend's been after me for months to investigate something. I keep putting her off. If it doesn't have anything to do with the industry I'm boned, but I don't want *her* to know that. She's got it in her head I'm by Dick Tracy out of Miss Marple."

"You should set her straight before the wedding."

"It's Rayellen Stutch." He got interested in the one window in an apartment building on Antoinette whose shade was drawn. The nearly naked blonde co-ed reading *The Collector* on the front step might as well have been an inflatable doll.

"Related to old Leland?" I asked.

"Widow."

I ran the numbers. Leland Stutch had shot air rifles with the first Henry Ford and offered Teddy Roosevelt a spin in a car he'd built when he was twenty. A photograph of him shaking hands with the old Rough Rider had run with Stutch's obituary eighty-six years later. I'd met him once, when he was past the century mark and thinking about retirement. His life had bracketed the journey of the automobile from an Edwardian joke to a computer on wheels with a Garfield doll stuck to the rear window. He'd endowed two hospitals, the second on the site of the first after it fell down from age. As far as I knew, they were the only two times he'd ever been inside one. They'd found him sitting at his desk with the dictaphone running.

"She pass a hundred yet?" I asked.

"If you're interested in the job, you can ask her."

"What's the job?"

"You can ask her that too. I may be violating a confidence just by bringing it up."

"If it's that dicey, tell her to let it lie. You never know what's on the bottom side of a rock."

"Just the bottom side of the rock. I hope."

"Now I'm curious."

"I'll set it up."

"I said I was curious. I didn't say I was interested."

"Just drop me off on the corner. I'll walk the rest of the way."

I pulled into a slot in front of the Fisher Building. Across the street, atop the sprawling General Motors office complex, a crew was at work with cutting torches on the two-story-high neon letters, with a Tinker Toy arrangement of pulleys and winches waiting to lay them flat on the roof. Thorpe sat glowering at the operation.

"I don't know how they figure to gain by moving their head-quarters to the RenCen from the biggest office building in the world," he said.

"I think the Pentagon's bigger."

"It lacks charm."

"Times change."

"People don't. I wish just once it was the other way."

"Not me. It's the business I'm in."

"Get me something on Tindle I can use. Find out what he did with the money." He got out.

I climbed out my side. "Mr. Thorpe."

He'd started down the sidewalk. He swung around like an old gunfighter, nothing on his face but the stubble he'd missed that morning. I flipped the Viper's keys across the roof. He caught them one-handed.

I said, "Title and registration's in the glove compartment. He put them in his mother's name."

He looked up from the keys. "You stole it from his driveway?"

"Garage on Howard. I broke in. The trouble with most thieves is they think they cornered the market."

His smile made him look even sadder.

# CHAPTER

# TWO

THE NEW CENTURY was full of changes. In addition to GM moving into the Renaissance Center, evicting the handful of tenants who had managed to keep their shops afloat in the longest-sinking enterprise since the *Andrea Doria,* the City of Detroit was preparing to shift its own base of operations into the old GM headquarters from the City-County Building; which had just been rechristened the Coleman A. Young Municipal Center after the mayor who had stolen everything but its doorknobs. The Tigers had vacated their historic stadium for a splashy new park downtown with the biggest scoreboard in baseball, suitable for recording the most zeroes in both leagues. Casinos had begun fleecing customers in the old IRS building (big change) and the Wonder factory, the birthplace of sliced bread, and had already racked up their first casualty in the person of an Oak Park police officer who followed up a ten-thousand-dollar loss at blackjack with a bullet to his brain. Twenty-one more shots and a color guard saw him into the ground. J.L. Hudson's, the largest department store in the world, was gone, and with it a chunk of the People Mover commuter train, dynamite being notoriously nonspecific about what it blows to electrons. Even the Grand Prix was moving again, from Belle Isle to the Michigan State Fairgrounds. It seemed like everybody and everything was going somewhere but me.

I was still conducting business, although not the busy kind, from my little grass hut on the top floor of a three-story building that had occupied the same spot on Grand River Avenue since shortly after the bottom dropped out of the beaver market. The winds of change had found their way there as well, through spaces where the mortar had eaten away, but they'd whistled right past me. After the travel agent next door went bust, the office had stood empty six months, then was leased twice in four weeks, first to a stationer who'd been removed quietly by Treasury agents for running off reasonable facsimiles of old-style tens and twenties on his laser printer, then to a website designer who was always there in the mornings when I came to work and in the evenings when I left, bent monk-fashion over his mouse with his door open and oversize posters of busty female superheroes all over his walls. We'd spoken only once, in his doorway when he offered to set me up with my own web page if I agreed to introduce him to the redhead he'd seen leaving my reception room the day before.

"Why would I want my own web page?"

"Well, to advertise your services."

"I do that in the telephone book."

"A lot of people with computers never open the telephone book. What is it you do?"

"I look for missing persons."

"Anyone with a computer can do that."

"Then why would I want to advertise on a computer?"

"Have it your way. I could upgrade your system. What do you use?"

"Cigarettes and whiskey."

"I mean what kind of computer."

"No kind of computer. I don't own one."

He banged the door shut.

Just as well. The redhead, a local TV reporter, had hurled my stapler at my framed autographed picture of Joel McCrea when I declined her retainer to follow around a *Free Press* journalist for the purpose of identifying all his sources. I hadn't stapled anything in a month, but I liked the picture. I should have fixed her up with the web guy.

I was thinking of changing my specialty. The spread of the One-Eyed Wonder had made it possible for every adopted child, deserted wife, divided twin, and class reunion secretary to tap into every records bureau in the world and find that long-lost individual during a coffee break. The odd credit check, an old reliable fallback, had gone down the same fiberoptic follicle, and corporate theft had grown so high-tech it required a plugged-in type like my neighbor to scope it out. I'd had to put the arm on my friend Barry Stackpole and his supercharged PC to track down Jerry Tindle's shady Viper. The rest of the job had involved a pinchbar short enough to get me arrested for possession of a burglar tool and a stroll around three levels of the garage on Howard Street, pushing the button on the keychain I took from the attendant's booth until the car's horn blatted in response. That was a larcenous gap even Bill Gates hadn't gotten around to bridging.

The modem hasn't been designed that can slip a latch, boost a hard file, intimidate a suspect, or contuse and lacerate an uncooperative witness into changing his mind. It can't seduce a receptionist or blackmail an accomplice, and it lacks the character needed to process a quart of gin and keep its circuits intact while the other fellow is overloading his. If it somehow managed to do all that, it couldn't erase its hard drive fast enough to avoid a stretch in the Stone Motel. If I work it right I might be able to squeeze in a career before Windows 2050 makes me completely redundant.

FedEx knocked and the telephone rang at the same time. In

both cases Connor Thorpe was responsible. I shouldered the receiver and signed the electronic clipboard.

"You must be one of those guys who overtips and hangs around for the reaction." I slid his check out of the gaudy cardboard envelope. He'd added a bonus.

"I never overdid a thing in my life, if you don't count marriage." There was an echo on his end, as if he were speaking from the bottom of a steel-pouring vat; which wasn't far off the mark. He was in his basement office in the Stutch plant. "Rayellen Stutch is expecting you at four this afternoon. That's an appointment, not a social invitation. Don't arrive fashionably late. Your first impression may be your last."

I wrote down the address in Iroquois Heights, suppressing a sigh like a bad cough. It had to be *there*. "That was fast work." We'd parted company less than two hours earlier. I'd cabbed it back to Howard to pick up my Cutlass and stopped for lunch on the way to the office.

"The New Center meeting was a moron marathon. I made my calls from the conference table and the fucker at the head never stopped talking about his pie chart. One thing: Mrs. Stutch is old-fashioned. You'd better bring a gift."

The telephone went dead before I could ask what kind of gift. There was nothing wrong with the line; greetings and farewells were alien concepts to Thorpe.

I thought about it for a while, but my detective skills were unequal to the problem. I locked up and went across the street, where a doodad store had opened in the glazed-brick building that had housed a Shell station until the Arab oil crisis, then a colony of raccoons and Scientologists. A strip mall had built off one end, selling hearing aids, bladder-control pills, and devices to improve TV reception. Planet Hollywood is not going to move into the neighborhood anytime soon.

A bell tittered when I opened and closed the door of the gift shop. A fortyish blonde in a white sailor suit appeared behind a counter display of Hummel figurines and we went into a huddle. Five minutes later I walked out carrying a package wrapped in silver paper. I drove for twenty minutes with the window open before I stopped smelling potpourri.

I went out past the zoo and along four lanes of resurfaced highway, passing miles of greensward tended by convicts in striped suits like the Beagle Boys, to where a sign greeted me:

WELCOME TO IROQUOIS HEIGHTS
PROUD HOME OF THE WARRIORS
1995 DISTRICT CHAMPIONS
YOU ARE UNDER SURVEILLANCE

To underscore the point, a city prowler sat on the gravel apron with only the lower half of the driver's face visible beneath the tilted-down visor, chewing gum.

Beyond this was a string of placards belonging to the city's seven Christian churches and one synagogue, a MURIEL FOR MAYOR sign left over from the election, and a simple wooden cross marking the spot where the local police had run a carjacker into the side of a hatchback being driven by a mother of three. I passed the usual hell of drive-throughs and cheapjack superstores and hung a right before the half-empty buildings of the old business district, heading for the original neighborhoods laid out by auto money to escape the thud and jangle of the factories. Auto money went a lot farther in the Heights than it did in Detroit.

The house was a battleship-gray box built at the end of a street named NO OUTLET, with another sign in the driveway reading NO TURNAROUND and a NO SOLICITORS card stuck in a corner of the leaded-glass window in the front door. It was the one time of year, before the trees and hedges leafed out on the east side, when you could see that the place was three times as big as it appeared from the front. It went back and back to claim two large lots, each addition constructed of a slightly different grade of material according to what was available at the time, like an old English manor house with a new wing for every beheading in London. A yellow cat built like a medicine ball snored in a wallow of dead fur in a rocker on the porch.

A woman of indeterminate age, wearing a gray dress like a jail matron's uniform, asked me to wait in the foyer and took my card down a hallway that led past the stairs. I was alone with a bronze Ali Baba vase and a portrait of Leland Stutch, painted sometime around the collapse of the Ottoman Empire. He'd been middle-aged even then, with a scant widow's peak and skin beginning to wattle over the top of his detachable collar. The eyes were light-eating black holes, the mouth bent down at the corners like Somerset Maugham's. One hand rested on a world globe, with the long fingers encompassing the northern hemisphere from Prince Edward Island to the Gulf of Mexico. At an age when most men had been retired twenty years, he'd sold his interest in General Motors and invested in research to improve the efficiency of fossil fuels, where he'd made his fortune all over again. Today Stutch Petrochemicals had facilities on six continents and was rumored to hold the title on a country in Southeast Asia; ten years after his death, Antitrust was still following the paper trail.

"Mrs. Stutch will receive you now. She's having her physical therapy session." The woman had come up behind me noiselessly on rubber soles.

I said, "She sounds pretty lively."

Her face got a puzzled look. "Yes." She turned and went back down the hall. I followed.

"I had some business with Mr. Stutch about a dozen years ago. I didn't realize he'd remarried."

"Mrs. Stutch came later. The grandson was quite upset. He gave the Commodore his youth."

You never hear anyone called Commodore anymore. They'd buried the title with the old man. It had been honorary, earned during two years when he lent his engineers to the U.S. Navy. A minesweeper of their design occupied a panoramic photo on the hallway wall. It went like hell with the other decorations: costume sketches in metal frames of attenuated models in ruffles, pleats, and suits of armor, all bearing the same illegible signature in the lower right-hand corner. We passed open doors belonging to side rooms, including a sort of conservatory with a white baby grand piano on a polished wooden floor, and a studio setup complete with a drafting board and brushes growing like cactus out of tin cans and clay pots. Music, art, and the theater seemed to be what was filling the lonely days of widowhood.

The woman tapped on a quilted door at the end and opened it. I trailed her into a large room throbbing with Pink Floyd's "The Wall." A tilted skylight poured sun into a white interior with exercise equipment scattered about, treadmills and rowers and progressive-resistance machines in gleaming chrome. A square platform stood in the center with turnbuckles at the corners and ropes stretched all around, and in the center of that, two women in lace-up boots and headgear and not much else were bouncing about poking at each other with boxing gloves.

"Which one's Mrs. Stutch?" I shouted above the electric guitars.

"The one in the red trunks. I think she's ahead on points." The woman in gray touched a keypad on the wall. Silence slammed down.

Red Trunks got in one last shot, just above the earpiece, and caught her opponent under the arms just as her knees started to fold. She helped her over to a stool in the near corner and snatched off her own headgear, letting loose a fall of black hair to her shoulders. In that bright light, without makeup, she wasn't even close to forty.

"Are you all right? I'm sorry, Cassie. That was a sucker punch." She wedged a glove under her armpit, pulled out her hand, took off the other, and helped the seated woman out of her headgear. Cassie was a short-haired redhead with freckles and a mannish chin.

"I'm okay." Her voice was thick.

"Mrs. Stutch?"

The brunette looked at me and came over to my side, leaning on the top rope. "Mr. Walker. You look like you know your way around a ring. Would you care to spar?"

"Can I go home and get my brass knuckles?"

She had a girlish laugh. "I'm not as bad as all that. This is just my version of 'Sweatin' to the Oldies.'"

"What's Cassie think?"

"Cassie's my niece. I'm putting her through school."

"Hell, too. What's she studying, cranial surgery?"

"Now you think I'm a sadistic rich bitch."

"I know you're rich."

She leaned over the ropes. I could feel the heat off her skin. "What can I do to change your mind?"

"Not a thing. It's my job to make the first impression." I gave her the gift-wrapped box.

She straightened, examining it from all sides. Finally she tore off the silver paper, opened the flap, and laughed again as she lifted out a fat-cheeked shepherdess done in pink and yellow porcelain.

"I thought you were a hundred," I said. "Thorpe didn't tell me you were training to fight Muhammad Ali's daughter."

"Oh!" Redheaded Cassie got up from the stool and came over. "It's just the most beautiful thing. My landlady collects Hummel."

Rayellen Stutch smiled a question at me. I moved a shoulder. She held out the figurine to Cassie.

"Tell her you had to fight someone for it." She raised her chin toward the woman in gray. "Mrs. Campbell, please show Mr.

Walker to the music room while I slip into something a little less comfortable." As she spoke she crossed her arms in front of herself and peeled off her damp tank top, exposing an industrial-strength sports bra. Her navel was a deep dimple in a set of abs like a pineapple.

# THREE

"THE HOUSE IN GROSSE POINTE went to Hector, Leland's grandson," said Rayellen Stutch. "So did most of the estate. That's why you didn't read about me in the papers; there was no dispute. I got the portrait in the foyer and that minesweeper shot in the hall. Oh, and a tenth share in the petrochemicals company. That pays me thirteen million a year."

We were in the room with the white piano, sitting on a couple of leather slingback chairs with aluminum frames. The piano was the only thing you couldn't carry out under one arm; everything else, including the clear Lucite rack containing sheet music, had been selected not to interfere with the resonance of the keys. There were more costume sketches on the walls and three narrow floor-to-ceiling windows with the view of horizontal housing developments and the hill where the original Stutch Motors factory still stood, looking like a brick prison. Black smoke from its triple stacks clawed the sky. I asked her if she missed Grosse Pointe.

"Not for a minute. The house required a huge staff. I was never alone. I'm not completely comfortable with just Mrs. Campbell knowing most of my secrets, and I'd trust her ahead of anyone, even Connor. She'd worked for Leland for years before I came along. Have you ever noticed how only the rich talk about being private people? That's because they aren't."

"Life's a bitch."

She started to smile, but jerked it back. "Anyway I've felt more at home here than I have anywhere."

"You could feel the same way in West Bloomfield."

"Mrs. Campbell recommended Iroquois Heights. Her mother worked for Leland when he ran Chevrolet. She counted out the payroll up on the hill for forty years. I know what people say about this town, but you get a different picture when you live in it."

"Not if you're in jail." I drank water from a glass on a tall stem. It was city water, treated and passed through filters belonging to a private contractor who had bought the system from the council when the cash was needed to avoid default. In the past five years the local residents had paid more than three times the selling price to lease the service. Meanwhile the city attorney who brokered the deal had retired to Texas. It was good water, pure as a bishop.

Mrs. Stutch had showered and changed into a loose silk shirt and black stirrup pants. Her unpainted toes showed in a pair of woven leather sandals. She had nice feet, tanned and pumiced.

She laughed, as if the jail comment were a joke. Her black hair was still damp at the ends and her high cheekbones wore no powder. Her eyes were a very dark brown, almost black. I wondered if she was part American Indian. "I know what you're thinking," she said, "and you're right. I was twenty-six when Leland proposed. Why would I marry a centenarian, except for money? He knew it. He also knew I'd see he got better care than Hector would have. If I hadn't, and he cut me out, there was no way under heaven I'd break the will. We lived without illusions, which is more than you can say about most married couples. And I liked him. I miss him."

"He was pretty hard to miss when he was alive. They built a whole century around him. Do you play the piano?"

"Mrs. Campbell does. She used to be with the Detroit Symphony. I pay better. Shall I invite you the next time I have people over? She knows all of Ellington by heart."

"I like Chopin."

"Ouch." She sipped from her glass and set it down on a table with a clef-shaped base. "I went slumming there, didn't I? After I spoke with Connor I searched you out on the Net. You've made the papers a few times, not the Lively Arts sections. I figured you drank straight gin and listened to gutbucket. People have been jumping to conclusions about me for ten years. You'd think I'd know better. I'm truly sorry."

"Me too. I wouldn't know Chopin on a cracker." I tilted my glass toward the wall. "Those her doodles?"

"No, I did those. Before I was married I designed costumes for the stage. I met Leland at a party at the Fisher Theater. Someone talked him into backing the road company."

"Congratulations. Broadway angels usually wind up with actresses."

"The understudies alone were stacked six deep, with the boys from the chorus chirping around him like buffalo birds. I had to hack my way through." She crossed her legs. "I'm a hard-fired little chippie, Mr. Walker, you might as well know that up front. Do I sound like Brooklyn?"

"The one in Michigan, or the one on *The Honeymooners?*"

"The one that berls eggs and feeds boids. I try not to talk like that even in jest. It took me six years in speech training to shuck it and I'm still afraid I'll forget and slip back. That was in the daytime; at night I studied art, and in between I waited on tables. Was I a girl with a dream?"

"You tell me."

"Smart man. Art was just a vehicle. If I were seven feet tall and black, I'd have learned to dribble a basketball. You go with what God gives you. My father was in and out of the money all the time I was growing up. I preferred in. I never managed to sell Broadway, but even a third-rate road show needs costumes. If Leland hadn't come along, I suppose I'd have landed on the faculty in an art school somewhere. The pay wasn't any worse and I wouldn't have to prop a chair against my door to keep out the night manager. But I wasn't looking forward to it."

"You keep your hand in. I saw your studio."

"That's just a time-waster. It keeps me from becoming one of those rich widows pickled in alcohol. What about you?"

"I can't draw a straight line. I can sometimes walk one."

"I meant detective work. Is it your consuming passion or just a vehicle?"

"You go with what God gives you. Or in this case Rayellen Stutch." I set my glass on the floor and got out my notebook and pen.

She didn't need any more nudging. "Connor says you're a Detroit native. Do you remember hearing about Leland's paternity suit?"

"Only that there was one. It's mighty hard to be male and have money and not attract at least one. Also those old auto barons played as hard as they worked. How'd it come out?"

"First, can I offer you a real drink? Leland always said water's only good for making ice."

I looked outside. The sun was behind the old plant now, shining straight through the windows from the opposite side as through a paper shell. Most of the machinery had been scrapped or stripped for parts; only the steel-pouring paraphernalia remained, and the evolution of the all-plastic body had killed the midnight shift. GM was talking about knocking down the old hulk and building an engineering complex on the site. Briefcases instead of lunchboxes.

Mrs. Stutch caught me measuring daylight. "I'll tell Mrs. Campbell to take her time."

"She doesn't have to gather dust."

She got up. "Not gin?"

I asked for Scotch. She went to the door and called out into the hall. I'd tagged her for something and tonic, but it was vodka neat and a water chaser. In a little while the woman in gray brought in a pitcher and glasses and two bottles on a tray, set the works on the table next to her mistress, and left with our empty water tumblers. At the door she touched a switch and a couple of lamps came on. The sun had slipped a few more inches, and now the plant had grown more solid, its shadow swinging around like a scythe to darken the tract houses. Molten steel glowed white-orange in the windows: They were making monsters again up there on the hill.

I balanced my notebook on my knee and drank between scribbles. It was single malt, smoky with old heather.

"It's been fifty years," Mrs. Stutch said. "Weird to think about it. I mean, picture having a stepdaughter who's almost twenty years older than you are."

"It's definite?"

"I'll come to it. Leland was about sixty-five, still married to his first wife, with a grandson. The woman's name was Cecilia Willard, a telephone switchboard operator at the plant. In court he claimed they never met, but sometime or other they had to have spoken, even if she was just putting through a call. She said she was nineteen when they had their fling.

"She delivered in the old Woman's Hospital in Detroit. I'll give you a copy of the birth certificate. It was a daughter. She named her Carla, with a *C.* No father's name given. The child was three years old when Cecilia filed for paternity. That worked against her in court; the judge couldn't understand why she'd waited so long. *She* said she was proud and wanted to make it on her own, but when a recession set in and she lost her job the going got too hard. Also she resented Leland for chucking her out with the rest of the batch. They hadn't had any contact after their affair ended, when she was transferred to the switchboard at GM headquarters, probably because the first Mrs. Stutch got suspicious. That's an educated guess. By all accounts the old witch died of pure spite. Anyway, Cecilia's explanation didn't play, and the blood test was inconclusive. The case never went to the jury."

"Did she appeal?"

"No; and that's important." She knocked the top off her vodka, then followed it with a drink of water. It was that old shot-and-a-beer action on which Detroit holds the patent. Stutch had had his influence. "There are two newspaper clippings in the envelope with the birth certificate. One of them is Cecilia's obituary. She had an aneurysm seven years ago at the age of sixty-two. You didn't see the item? I'm not surprised. There were only a couple of lines about the paternity suit. It's a jaded old world when even sex scandals get stale. She kept the name Willard. Apparently she never married. The article listed two survivors: her daughter and a grandchild."

"Ah."

She folded her hands under her chin. Her fingers were unpainted as well, and on one of them she wore a blue diamond in a fussy old-fashioned setting. That would be her late husband's taste. Everything else about her was ceramic and sleek. *Hard-fired*, she'd said. "I think I resent that 'Ah.' You think I'm pursuing this because I may still be on the hook into a third generation."

"That's a lot to get out of one syllable."

"Never mind. Don't judge me until you've heard me out. When Leland died and his safe deposit box in the National Bank of Detroit was opened, it contained eighteen years' worth of canceled checks made out to Cecilia Willard against his personal account. He'd been sending her between one and five thousand dollars a month since just after her case was thrown out of court. In the light of that I don't think there's any reason to wonder why she didn't bother to appeal the decision."

I rolled Scotch around my mouth and let it evaporate up my nasal passages. "It wouldn't be looked on as any sort of admission once a good lawyer got through with it. He might just have felt sorry for her."

"My husband wasn't a philanthropist, Mr. Walker. He built two hospitals, but that was when he was getting old and he refused to trust his health to the existing facilities. If he helped Cecilia out, it was because he felt responsible. It's significant that he stopped writing checks after eighteen years. That's as long as the law would have required him to provide child support. He paid what he thought he owed, no more and no less."

"Then he shouldn't have contested the suit."

"Understand, he never said a word to me about the case, or anything else associated with his past life. He lived in the present. I think it's possible he never knew about the child until he was asked to submit to a blood test. She might as well have waved a red flag in his face as a sheet of legal stationery. Leland was one of only two people who held out against the courts in 1903, when they said all the auto manufacturers had to pay to use George Selden's patent. It took eight years of lawyers' fees and appeals to win a ruling in their favor. The other holdout was Henry Ford. Leland wouldn't eat lima beans if a judge ordered him to. And he loved lima beans."

I wrote down *lima beans* and underlined it. "He was probably only worth about a billion then. Twelve to sixty thousand a year was a bargain."

"He spent less raising his legitimate son. 'Lavish' is not a word you'd use to describe Leland. He only bought the place in Grosse Pointe for privacy. A cabin and an outhouse on some mountain would have suited him just as well."

"Uh-huh." I didn't write that down. I got up and splashed a little water from the pitcher into my glass. My head wasn't used to
good liquor. "What is it you want me to do, Mrs. Stutch?"

"Rayellen, please. And you're Amos, right? I mean, we've broken our fast together, so to speak."

"Uh-uh. Mrs. Campbell might get jealous."

She unfolded one of her hands in a flicking movement. "I want
you to find Cecilia's heirs. I want them to benefit from Leland's
will. They're entitled to half of what went to Hector and his family, but if that's contested I'll cut them in on mine. No one needs
thirteen million a year."

"Some chippie you are. You wouldn't even make the semi-
finals."

"Bullshit."

I grinned. She held up her glass and I leveled it off from the
Stoli bottle. "What's the real reason?" I asked.

"Good business. DNA testing is new since Leland. If the
daughter and granddaughter—it's a girl, I don't think I said that;
Constance is the name—if one or both of them decide to revive
the suit, they stand to prove their case and take the estate to the
cleaners. I don't need an income of thirteen million, but after ten
years one-point-three million would be an unnecessary hardship.
Call it a pre-emptive strike." She moved a shoulder and drank. "I
learned a lot from Leland."

I returned to my seat and warmed my hands around my glass.
"You mentioned two newspaper clippings. What's the second?"

This time she got up. She was one of the few wealthy people
I'd met who didn't seem to be hard-wired into the domestic help.
The piano had a bench with a hinged seat upholstered in white
satin. She lifted the seat, removed something from the recess beneath, and laid it in my lap.

It was a blue eight-by-ten envelope, fastened with a string tie.
I undid that and rummaged around inside. I ignored for the mo-

ment the photocopy of a Wayne County birth certificate, glanced briefly at Cecilia Willard's obituary on yellowed newsprint, and turned to the other clipping. This one, larger, included a photograph of a smiling couple, a pretty assembly-line blonde and a young roughneck in a plaid sportcoat with an arm around the girl's waist. The article reported the impending nuptials of Constance Witowski, daughter of Carla Willard Witowski of Melvindale and Fred Witowski of Grass Lake, and David Glendowning, parents deceased, of Toledo, Ohio.

I squinted at the date penciled faintly in the margin. Mrs. Stutch helped me out.

"I clipped it from the *Free Press* five years ago. Assuming the wedding came off and the marriage worked out and there were no medical problems or objections against children, the odds are my slice of the pie is already smaller. Naturally I'd like to get this worked out before another century is heard from."

# CHAPTER

# FOUR

Mrs. Campbell brought a checkbook bound in red leather and a gold fountain pen and cleared away the tray. Since this one didn't promise to go longer than a day I told Rayellen Stutch to make the check out for five hundred. She did that, blew on the ink, and handed it to me. I held it while it finished drying.

"I'll start with Carla," I said. "It looks like she's separated from this Witowski, and since she's living in Melvindale, she doesn't have a pile. She'll know this isn't about pin money. You'll want to move fast, before she decides she needs her own private island."

"Just tell me when you've made contact. Then find Constance. I'll deal with both of them together or not at all. This isn't an auction."

I was still holding the check. The ink was dry by now, but I made no move to put it away. "Why wasn't I on this job ten years ago, when you opened the safe deposit box and found the canceled checks? Or someone else if not me?"

"Another heir might have kicked the will into probate for five years. As it was, I wasn't sure Hector wouldn't contest the will. It wouldn't be *his* slice that disappeared when it all got untangled. When I read about Cecilia's death three years later I thought about it, but I held my breath hoping I wouldn't hear from the daughter, and I didn't. The granddaughter's engagement, though, made up my mind. You know that joke about the minister who died when his church flooded because he trusted in God instead of the men who came to rescue him in a Jeep, a boat, and then a helicopter? God said, 'What more did you want? I sent a Jeep, a boat, and a helicopter.' If I let three warnings go by without acting, I deserved whatever was going to happen to me."

"And five years later here I am."

"You'll have to ask Connor Thorpe about that. That's how long I've been after him to look into it. At first I thought he was putting me off because he was busy."

"He is busy."

"No argument. But I doubt he ever took five years getting around to doing anything Leland asked him to do. You wouldn't be here if I hadn't made myself unpleasant company of late in re-gard to this Willard business."

"Why would he drag his feet?"

"I wish I hadn't a clue. When you're a woman dealing with men who deal generally with men, you have to subtract that dy-namic and see if it makes sense." She refolded her hands beneath her chin. "When you need doors opened, call Connor. When you have anything to report, come straight to me."

I nodded, but kept my seat. "Have you tried the telephone book? You could save the five hundred."

"I wouldn't know how to break the ice. You impress me as a man who can bring himself to be charming when charm is in order. You handled that thing with the Hummel quite neatly."

"So did you. Bringing a gift was Thorpe's idea. He said you were old-fashioned."

"Really. He has a lot to answer for."

"Except getting him to do it would run you a lot more than five hundred." I thanked her for the drink, folded my check, and stole away. When I drew the door shut behind me she'd picked up the gold pen and was tapping it against her bottom teeth, looking at nothing that I could see.

It was almost dark out now, with only the silhouette of the old plant showing on the hill, a shade blacker than the sky, and now and then the angry glow of the hot steel throbbing in the windows. I fired up the Cutlass and headed for the state highway. I didn't get ten blocks before I picked up a cop.

Red and blue lights pulsed in my rear window, a siren growled. I pulled onto the apron, killing the motor, and the prowl car drifted in behind and slammed on its spot. The thousand-candlepower shaft whited out shadows and blazed off my mirrors, bright enough to fry both retinas. The Wall of Light, they call it. Cops have a nickname for everything and it always sounds like an oak stick bouncing off bone.

Some time went by, quite a lot of it, before the doors opened on the marked car, showing the Iroquois Heights seal decaled on them and the slogan "To Serve and Protect" broken in half, and two uniforms climbed out. The one on the passenger's side paused behind my car and I heard and felt a couple of thumps before he straightened and moved on, sliding his two-foot skullbuster into its loop on his gun belt. The one who had been driving waited behind the window post on my side until he caught up. Then the driver stuck a big blur of face into my open window and shone a Malice Green flashlight around the inside of the car, making sure to finish up on my face and leave it there. His partner stood on the other side resting his thumb on the hammer of his sidearm. There was a shiny white spot on the back of his hand where an old tattoo had been burned off.

"License and registration," said the cop with the light. He had one of those shallow, callow voices that never seem to age, like a pro ballplayer's. He'd been chewing Dentyne.

I got my license out of my wallet and the registration out of the glove compartment and handed them over. I kept out the wallet. He moved the flashlight then and I chased purple spots while he read the information. "You've got a defective license plate light, sir. Were you aware of that?"

"Was it defective before your partner banged on it?"

This was not the right answer and there was a little silence before the partner spoke up. His voice was deep, with an oddly gentle Delta underlay, but filtered through a couple of generations of gritty urban black. Any high, hard ones that got past the ballplayer would stop with him. "You got a loose connection. It came back on when I tapped it."

"Thanks, Officer. What do I owe you?"

"Step out of the car, please, sir." Now the ballplayer was thumbing his sidearm.

I laid my wallet on the passenger's seat and put both hands on the wheel. "Sorry about the crack. I missed supper."

"Just step out of the car."

"Why the roust? You ran my plate."

He drew the weapon and rolled back the hammer. It was an army-issue .45 automatic, not a regulation piece in most police departments. In Iroquois Heights, crossbows were not frowned upon unless they spoiled the line of the uniform.

There was no sound from the other side of the car, but without looking I knew I was sitting between stereo muzzles. I reached down and opened the door and stepped out.

The rest was routine, fast, and only a little harder than it might have been in Detroit if I'd exposed myself to the chief's daughter. The hood ornament scratched my cheek when my face struck the metal and an old shoulder dislocation I'd forgotten about yelped when the ballplayer yanked my arms behind me and hooked on the cuffs. A hand tore loose my inside breast pocket looking for weapons.

"My wallet's on the seat." My breath fogged the hood's finish.

"Bribery, Russell, pipe that," said the ballplayer. "The bar just keeps going up." He was panting. He'd reported late for spring training.

I said, "There's a check inside. You might want to look."

"We don't take checks. So sorry."

But the passenger door opened. Paper crackled. "So there's a check, and it's for five hundred bucks. What's that make you, Ross Perot?" This was Russell.

"Read the signature. If you can't make out the handwriting, read what's printed in the upper left-hand corner."

A foot hooked my ankle and jerked. I slipped, banged a knee against the bumper, and got a burn on my face from friction on the hood.

"Jay, it's Rayellen Stutch."

"Old Man Stutch's widow?" It was almost a whine.

"It don't say on the check. But then I don't guess it has to."

"What's Old Man Stutch's widow into you for?"

I said, "I'm her dance instructor."

I felt a foot hook my ankle again. I braced myself.

"He's a private cop, Jay. Here's his license."

"What's that to us?" But he retrieved the foot.

"Better take off the bracelets," Russell said.

"He resisted arrest."

"He didn't resist nothing."

Crickets sang. "That's how it is, is it?"

"Hell, Jay. Depends what your definition of *is* is." There was a grin in the deep voice. I couldn't tell if it was a wary grin or just a grin.

"Shit." Keys tinkled.

Thirty seconds later the cuffs were off and I was standing upright, rubbing my wrists. In the light from the spot, Jay was sandy and freckled and beginning to go to fat beneath his chin. Russell was a pair of eyes that shone like wet stones in a face as black and shining as his patent-leather visor. They were neither of them young, but still on the hazard side of a pension. Their guns were in their holsters.

"Sorry we bounced you so hard." Russell gave me back my wallet. "Fella stuck up a party store by the interstate a half hour ago. Your car didn't exactly not match the description."

I made sure the check was inside and counted the bills. I felt the cops stiffen at that, but I finished counting and put the wallet back in my hip pocket. "Bullshit."

Russell said, "What."

"I'm quoting Rayellen Stutch. The car's got some dings, and they don't go with this neighborhood, so you fell in behind. Then you ran the plate and got a Detroit address. In this town that's PC. Probable cause, not political correctness. Not that you'd know the term."

Jay said, "You're not out of the woods yet, asshole. We can pop you for obstruction."

"See if you can get me Cell Eleven. It's got a good mattress."

"Keep talking, asshole."

"Not that I'll get the chance to sleep on it."

"That's it." He fumbled the handcuffs off his belt.

"You never know when Mrs. Stutch will decide she needs a rhumba lesson."

"Son of a bitch." He lunged for my wrist. I swiveled out of his way, his fist closed on air, and he had to do a quickstep to avoid sprawling over the fender of the Cutlass.

"Better give him back his license and rej," Russell said. "Don't you think."

This gave Jay something to get his claws into. "Who the hell's side you on?"

The black cop took in some air and let it out. This was no new discussion. "The president's. How's he going to look come November if you and I fuck up full employment?"

Jay called him something they don't teach in sensitivity training, banged my license and registration down on the hood hard enough to dent it, and crunched back over the gravel apron to the prowler, where he sat down behind the wheel and cranked up the scanner loud enough to make the speakers buzz.

"I won't apologize for Jay," Russell said. "We're married and that's that."

"Don't invite me to the anniversary." I put the papers back in my wallet.

"How's Mrs. Stutch to work for?"

"Forget it. She's already got security."

He exchanged some more air. "That's cold, mister." He crunched away. He walked with a slight hitch in his right leg. There was an old injury there, and probably a story to go with it.

To hell with him. When you start feeling sorry for a cop it's time to move to the beach.

I drove home through three jurisdictions without obstructing any of them and let myself in through the side door from the garage. The telephone was ringing in the living room. I let it ring while I fetched a carton of milk and half a can of tuna from the refrigerator, but it wouldn't wear down. I folded a slice of bread to make a sandwich, picked up the receiver, and spoke my name through a mouthful. I remembered I wasn't at the office and tacked a "Hello" on the end of it.

"How'd it go with Mrs. Stutch?"

It was Connor Thorpe. I swallowed. "What, you got someone watching my place?"

"I've been calling all night. You take her out to the show or what?"

"I could've got her in for half price. Why'd you tell me she's old-fashioned?"

"You had your mind made up she loaded Washington's musket at Valley Forge. You'd have been disappointed otherwise."

"Are you sure you didn't just want her to fire me before I was hired?"

"What, did she say something?" The question came quickly.

I juggled the sandwich into the hand holding the receiver and swigged milk from the carton. There was no reason not to tell him I knew she'd been after him for five years to find the daughter and granddaughter, except it was none of his business. "You did. You told me you hoped all I found was the bottom side of the rock."

"I meant it. Dead dogs ought to stay dead." But he sounded relieved. I wondered why.

"I'm turning over the rock. It's okay if you're not okay with that. I just need to know before I have another run-in with what's pinned to a badge in Iroquois Heights."

"Why, what happened?"

I gave him the short form. He said "Sons of bitches" twice, then asked me for their names.

"I'm a big boy, Mr. Thorpe. I fight my own fights. Just so I don't have to keep fighting the same one, though, I'll take a letter from you on GM stationery saying I'm working on a confidential matter for the board of directors. If I go on showing Mrs. Stutch's check, her signature will get rubbed off and they won't cash it at my bank."

"I'll have it on your desk tomorrow."

"The day after will be soon enough. I try not to visit the Heights two days in a row. It voids my insurance." We talked around in a circle for another minute and rang off. I finished my supper in front of a giant parade of TV commercials without ever finding out what show was playing, then read for a while and went to bed. I had a big day tomorrow, starting when the bank opened.

# FIVE

MY BANK, a 150-year-old Detroit concern, had recently taken down its sign and replaced it with one bearing a name more suited to its new conglomonational status; whether it had merged with, been bought by, or had bought a chain of similar institutions stretching from Key West to Point Barrow was a Chinese puzzler for its shareholders to figure out; its immediate concern to me was that all of its services had dried up like the ink in its ballpoint pens. A snazzy pamphlet had come my way by mail, announcing the name change and informing me that three withdrawals of my own money in a single month would be considered excessive activity and cost me a buck and a half. I'd made up my mind to cash out my balance as soon as I had one and look for another mattress to stick it in, but that would have to wait until I had a handle on the heirs of Leland Stutch and Cecilia Willard.

The blonde in the teller's cage took Mrs. Stutch's check, gave me a flimsy printout that told me how much I'd just deposited, no extraneous information such as how much I now had in the account, and gave me back the two hundred I was holding out for cigarettes and bribery. The remitter's signature didn't get so much as a flicker from her. She'd been born since fuel injection; she would pronounce *Renault* without the *t*.

Back at the office I spent a little on Information in Grass Lake and called the number the operator gave me for Fred Witowski, husband or ex-husband of Cecilia's daughter Carla and father of Constance. I got a gruff outgoing announcement on a warped tape and hung up without leaving a message. I only wanted him for Carla's address in Melvindale, and waiting by the telephone was not a good use of Rayellen Stutch's money. I dipped into my bag of special detective tools and opened the telephone book.

Witowski is not an uncommon name in a metropolitan area built on the strong backs of Poles who had fled the Czar to grade and lay track for the Michigan Central Railroad, and later to forge engine blocks at old Dodge Main. There were several Witowskis listed in Melvindale, but only three C. Witowskis, and no Freds; not that many divorced or separated women were still listing themselves under the names of their exes. Fewer yet in this age of stalkers and demographers cared to advertise their single sisterhood by using their Christian names, so there weren't any Carlas either. I called the first one on the list and got a recording giving just the number. I hit the plunger before it finished and tried the next.

"Hello?" A female voice, age indeterminate.

"Is this Carla Witowski?" I asked.

"That depends on who wants her."

"I'm with UPS. I've got a package for a Carla Witowski in Melvindale, but I can't make out the number or street."

"What's in the package?"

"I wouldn't know, ma'am. I left my fluoroscope in my other pants."

"And what have you got in this pair?" She was purring now.

"Nothing for you, Cornelia." I reached for the plunger.

"It's Cynthia, smartass. Now, who—"

I cut her off and tried the third number. No one answered. Sometimes you have to let your feet do the walking. I was starting to do just that when the telephone rang.

"A. Walker Investigations."

"Gotcha, smartass. You ever hear of star sixty-nine?" She'd lost the purr. Its place had been taken by a rusty alcoholic edge. "Who says you can insult a woman in her own home?"

"Thomas Jefferson. Bye-bye, Clothilde."

The bell had started ringing again when I went out the door.

On the way downriver I pulled into an oil shop and dropped a little more client money on an overdue lube and a change. When the junior mechanic lifted the hood to replace the air filter he said, "Holy shit."

"So size does matter." I blew smoke and pushed myself away from the pillar I was leaning against.

"Outside it's a heap. What do you do, run dope?"

"I'm a dance instructor."

He slitted his eyes at me. He was a clean-cut black kid who had knocked the top off every knuckle he had. "That don't make no sense."

"That's what the cops in Iroquois Heights said."

"That place." He spat and rubbed the spittle into the concrete floor with the toe of his shoe. "They ought to take it down brick by brick and throw salt on the dirt."

"You and Cato."

"Cato, my ass. I'd do it myself if I could afford the salt. They got a funny curfew there. It only works if you forget to be white."

When he handed me my keys I said, "I'm on my way to Melvindale. I'll bring you back some salt."

"Do what?"

"You know. From the mine."

He shook his head. He was too young, a condition that was becoming epidemic. I tipped him two bucks and pulled out of the bay, gunning the big 455 as a gift. He probably didn't know who Cato was either.

Underneath Detroit is another city, inconceivably old and made entirely of salt. It's a thousand feet underground and extends more than two miles between the cities of River Rouge and Melvindale, in a vein that stretches from Wyandotte to Port Huron, an area roughly the size of Costa Rica. For a hundred years the International Salt Company excavated thousands of tons of chalk-white deposits from an ancient ocean, first to cure meat for pilgrims traveling west, then to mix with cinders and spread on roads and highways throughout the northeastern states during the winter, to melt snow and ice and incidentally christen the entire region America's Rust Belt. Operations on the American side have been shut down twenty years for unexplained reasons, obliging the various road commissions to purchase their salt from Canada. Meanwhile the original equipment, more than a century old and preserved by the dryest air outside the Presbyterian Church, sits undisturbed among caverns blasted from pure salt, with salt roofs supported by salt pillars anchored to salt floors. Melvindale, which holds title to the only remaining unsealed entrance, scratches up some money from time to time conducting guided tours; otherwise there's no reason to go there unless Melvindale is where you live. Detroit has three times as many satellites as Jupiter, and most of them are just as difficult to tell apart without a glass.

The address listed for C. Witowski in the telephone book belonged to one of the newer houses in a snarl of serpentine streets and cul-de-sacs off Oakwood, which did not mean that it was at all new; the housing sprawl that had begun nine months after V-E Day and ended with the Edsel had left its droppings all over Wayne and Oakland counties. The inspirational touch here was that the contractor had reversed the blueprints from time to time so that the *faux* stone facing to the right of the front door on one house was to the left on the next; or maybe the straw boss had dropped the plans and spread them out any old way when he picked them up. Some of the roofs had been replaced over the years by the individual homeowners, eroding further the uniform scheme, and here and there a hawthorn hedge or a low redwood fence had boldly supplanted the architect's junipers, but except for that and the occasional Toyota truck in a neighborhood of Fords, Chevies, and Chryslers, the homes were as alike as barracks on a military base. If one of them sold for sixty thousand, the property values would spike up fifteen percent.

I parked on the street and walked up a composition driveway past a nine-year-old Cavalier hatchback with an S.O.S. sticker on the rear bumper and a fat asterisk next to the legend SAVE OUR SCHOOLS. On the other corner was an older one, scuffed and peeling, on which faded letters spelled out TEACHER OF THE YEAR 1991.

The doorbell imitated a set of chimes. Someone had a coughing fit inside and a set of off-white curtains in the window next to the door parted, revealing a black nose on the end of a shaggy tan muzzle. That was the source of the coughing noise. It was like a bark with a silencer.

"Yes?"

The woman who opened the door was about fifty, with blondined hair waved back from a handsome sort of face that wore a little more makeup than Rayellen Stutch, but little enough still to annoy Revlon. She was tall and stood unnaturally stiff, as if she had a bad back. She had on a dark brown scoop-necked top with sleeves that came to her elbows, beige pleated slacks, and brown leather loafers, scuffed just enough to have character. She wore no rings or jewelry of any kind except for pearl buttons in her ears to keep the holes from closing. She had steady eyes and a strong jaw, but I'd been fooled by those before.

"Mrs. Witowski?" I asked.

"Yes?"

"Mrs. Carla Witowski?"

"Yes." Now her brows were separated by a vertical line. She hadn't many.

I pressed my luck. "Carla Willard Witowski?"

The line smoothed out. Her eyes were dark and deep-set, like those in the portrait of Leland Stutch in the foyer of the house in Iroquois Heights. I didn't see the fiercely glowing centers I'd observed in person, but she had another fifty years in which to acquire those; if they were his eyes, and if she'd inherited them.

"What is it you want?" she asked.

"To confirm you're Carla Willard Witowski, for a start. Would you mind telling me your mother's Christian name?"

"If I did that, I'd have given you four names. You haven't given me even one."

"You teach math, don't you?" I grinned, but she didn't do anything with it. I gave her a card.

"Amos Walker," she read. "Is that your real name?"

"It's the one I use most of the time."

She read the rest of the card. "It says here you're a private detective."

"It does not. It says 'Investigations.'"

"What's the difference?"

"There isn't any. The state police don't like anyone who is not a policeman printing up cards calling himself a detective. I humor them, in return for which they let me keep my license."

"My mother's name was Cecilia. I taught English, not math. I retired last year."

"Not many teachers can afford to retire before fifty-five."

"I'm not one of them. I'm shopping around. I'd rather try to live on my savings than draw a paycheck from a school system with a dropout rate of seventy percent."

"That's what convinced you to quit?"

"Persuaded," she corrected. "You convince someone of an idea; you persuade him to an act. Did you attend school in Detroit?"

"Yeah, but don't blame the principal. In my work I don't get to diagram many sentences. Is it all right if we take this inside? I'm getting a sunburn."

"I can see."

I touched my skinned cheek. "No, I got that last night. A cop bit me."

Her dark eyes considered, but she let it loose. "I still don't know what this is about."

"It's about your inheritance. I'm working for Leland Stutch's widow."

Now came the fierce glow, but only for a second. She got out of the way and I stepped over the threshold.

A brown and tan miniature chow about the size of a lunchbox braced itself against a square of linoleum and coughed at me. Its ears were perfect triangles and its shaggy tail curled up over its back like a scorpion's. It sounded like a lawn mower that wouldn't start.

"Moo-goo, don't!" Carla Witowski snapped. The dog ignored her. "He's very protective. I don't get many visitors."

"What's wrong with his bark?"

"I had his vocal cords surgically altered. The neighbors kept complaining."

"You should've had theirs altered."

"Are you a dog lover, Mr. Walker?"

"My father gave me a lab when I was ten. He's on a farm somewhere, my mother told me. The lab got run over."

She leaned down carefully and scratched the pooch behind the thick ruff at the base of its neck. It stopped coughing and waggled its curly tail. "I don't talk for Moo-goo, or dress him up like Santa at Christmastime. I didn't even name him Moo-goo; he came with that. I'd probably have opted for something ridiculous, like Spot. When you're alone it's just good to know there's another heart beating in the house."

"You have a daughter."

"I have a daughter." It was a confirmation, not a concession. "I think you'll find the armchair more comfortable than the sofa. Men generally do. Would you like something to drink? I'm afraid all I have is juice."

"Thanks, I'm full of coffee."

The living room was small but cheerily lit through a window with spread curtains in front of which stood a cherrywood half-table with a bowl of flowers on a scarf. It had a sculptured carpet—brown and tan to match the dog, a practical choice—a seventeen-inch TV on a rolling stand, a straight-backed chair upholstered in stiff-looking fabric, and a skirted sofa and easy chair covered with nubby brown cloth with gold threads glittering in it, a set. There was a fake cuckoo clock on the wall opposite the window, family pictures in different-sized frames on a decorative shelf, and a dog bed in the corner shaped like Moses' reed basket. There were more dog hairs in a hollow on the sofa's center cushion than there were in the bed. It was a tasteful room; a little dowdy, but pleasant to spend time in.

I took the easy chair while she lowered herself into the one with the straight back. Years of standing in front of blackboards are murder on the lumbar. The dog scampered over and tried to climb up onto her lap, but she brushed it away. It sneezed indignantly, swung its rear end on her, and pattered over to the sofa, where it braced itself to leap. Its mistress snapped her fingers—the crack was worthy of a .22 pistol—and the dog thought better of the plan and went over and hopped into the basket-bed and curled up without the circling that usually precedes that business. In Mrs. Witowski's classroom, iron discipline had been served up between the first and second predicates.

"I wasn't aware Stutch left a widow," she said.

"It wasn't a secret," I said. "Just quiet. I gather the ceremony was civil and probably out of town. Also he had more money to spend on keeping his name out of the news than most movie stars spend getting theirs in. And no one squawked when the will was read."

"I wasn't invited to that." A nerve jumped in her cheek. It might have been a back spasm.

"Mrs. Stutch is aware of that. She realizes the extent of the injury that was done to your mother and you, long before she met and married Mr. Stutch. It's too late for your mother, but she wants to make it up to you and Constance. Constance, that's your daughter's name, right? Constance Glendowning?"

She let that branch wave in the air. "My mother died alone in her house in Redford. When the pain in her head got so bad she couldn't stand it, she called me instead of 911, because she didn't think she could afford the ambulance. I made the call, but she was gone before it got there. I arrived five minutes later. The paramedics said they couldn't have saved her even if they'd been on the spot when the artery exploded. They're supposed to say that. It might have comforted me if I'd heard it in a waiting room at Detroit General instead of my mother's kitchen. Can Mrs. Stutch make up for that?"

Her voice didn't rise or shake or give any other indication that she was doing anything but reciting the *i* before *e* rule. She sat with her chin lifted and her back pressed tight against the back of the chair, her hands resting on her thighs.

"Here's a thought." I leaned forward. "They cremated Stutch and buried his ashes in Centerline, where he started out way back when they burned cowflop for fuel. I'll dig him up for you and you can spit in the urn. Then you and Mrs. Stutch can talk."

"I know it's not her fault. Do you know that man sent my mother money until I was eighteen, which is as long as the court would have required if she'd won her case? Sometimes I feel I'd think better of him if he'd never sent a dime. Since he didn't have to anyway, why did he stop when the law would have told him he could?"

"I don't try to think like rich people, Mrs. Witowski. I might spend the money I've been saving for braces."

"The question was rhetorical. He used the money as a cold compress on his conscience, what there was of it; then as soon as he felt better he took it away. Meanwhile in the eyes of the world my mother was a gold-digging slut."

I couldn't do anything with that, so I hung one knee over the other and channeled Father O'Malley. The dog was asleep on its bed, snoring louder than it barked. It had heard all this before.

Carla Willard Witowski shut her eyes for a moment. When she opened them, Leland Stutch looked out at me. If her mother had just taken her to court and let her look at the judge, the case would have gone to the jury. "Do you realize, Mr. Walker, that if I'd been born forty years earlier—about the time my father turned twenty-five—I would not have been permitted to teach school in the state of Michigan? My bastardy might have polluted the entire seventh grade."

I made a note on my brain to look up *bastardy* when I got home. I'd never heard it used before, but being an English teacher and a bastard both she seemed to have the provenance. I said, "So hooray for the twenty-first century. You don't need a crank to start a new automobile built in the Stutch plant either. When can you meet with Mrs. Stutch?"

She worked her hands on her thighs. It wasn't quite a rubbing motion. "Exactly how much money are we discussing, Mr. Walker?"

"That's what the meeting's about. Is Thursday good?" I didn't know if Thursday was good for Rayellen Stutch. If it wasn't they could work it out. I wanted to be somewhere else than in that pleasant room with those eyes, down on the docks where all you had to stare down were belly guns and rats the size of chimpanzees.

"Who else will be there? Her lawyers?"

"Not if you don't want them. You may want a lawyer there

yourself. A witness anyhow. People sometimes forget things they said without someone to remind them, preferably with a writ. Your daughter's invited too, of course. Mrs. Stutch wants to take care of all the heirs. I'm looking for her, too, to deliver the same message. Do you have her current address? I couldn't find a listing."

She lifted her right hand to stroke her left upper arm, as if it tingled. I wondered if she had a weak heart. The leg of her slacks where she'd been gripping her thigh was a crush of wrinkles.

"I'm not sure." She stopped the stroking, but left the hand on her arm. "We haven't had contact in more than a year. The last I knew she was living in Toledo. She may still be, if that animal she married hasn't killed her. My daughter made an unhappy match, Mr. Walker, just like her mother. Perhaps your client's late husband acted in my mother's best interest after all, when he refused to make an honest woman of her."

# CHAPTER

# SIX

I LOOKED AT THE DOG asleep on its bed, for no other reason than the thought that staring too long into Carla Witowski's eyes might give me cataracts. The dog's legs twitched and now and then a little whimper made its whiskers ripple. Somewhere it was chasing rabbits and barking in a deep *basso profundo*.

"I liked David Glendowning when Constance introduced him to me," Mrs. Witowski said. "He was a rough cob, but I've been around those most of my life. You don't have to dig back more than a generation in this town to find a blue collar in every family. He drove a truck for a cartage firm in Toledo, a solid occupation and decent pay. He was running for shop steward then. Wanted to make the union his career, so he had ambition, and he watched his manners around me. They seemed to be in love. I didn't see any reason to meddle beyond that.

"The wedding took place in Toledo, a small affair in a Methodist chapel. My ex-husband and I were on our best behavior, which means he didn't try to feel up the maid of honor and I didn't throw any crystal at him at the reception. We even posed for pictures. If you knew what our marriage came to be, which you won't because it isn't any of your business, you'd know what a minor miracle that was."

None of this was any of my business, but I didn't stop her. You never know what might come out of an open window.

"You're still a young man, Mr. Walker, but you look as if you've taken your share of dings. I'll tell you a number of things that happened once the Glendownings began married life, and you can tell me what you think they mean. They spent their honeymoon in a resort on Lake Erie. She called me twice during that week. When they got back home she called me every day, at first, then once every few days. By the end of the first month I was hearing from her once a week. The calls got shorter, then farther apart. By their six-week anniversary I was calling her. These calls usually ended in quarrels about unimportant things. Sometimes she'd complain about David's behavior—he'd taken to leaving her alone most evenings while he drank with his trucker friends in some bar or at their houses, and it got so he wouldn't spend even an hour with her after coming back from a week on the road before he went out drinking again—but when I agreed he was treating her atrociously, she'd turn square around and defend him, accuse me of interfering. That was when we spoke. Often the phone would ring and ring and nobody would pick up. One time David answered, said Constance wasn't home, and hung up before I could ask when he expected her back. I'm sure as I am of anything that she was home. Where would she go? All her friends were here, and I'd hear from them now and then asking how Constance was, because they couldn't get through to her, they said.

"The next time I got hold of her I asked her about it. There was a pause before she said David had told her about the call, but she'd been preoccupied and forgot to return it. She said she'd gone out to get a few things. I may not be Mother of anyone's Year, Mr. Walker, but I know when my child is lying to me. She knew nothing about that call until I told her. Does this pattern suggest any-thing to you?"

"There's always the possibility he forgot to tell her. Husbands do that."

"If it were as innocent as that, she wouldn't have felt the need to lie. I asked you a question."

"It sounds like the M.O. of the textbook wife abuser: Isolate her from friends and family, turn her against them, make her de-pendent on him, and treat her like pocket lint until there's noth-ing left of her self-respect. *Dear Abby* runs a checklist twice a year, like the *Cosmo* quiz. If you score high, you lose."

She colored a little when I mentioned *Dear Abby.* "I eventually fell back on the hackneyed device of clipping out that very column and sending it to her anonymously. I might as well have included my return address. The last time we spoke, she threw it in my face and said I was trying to drive a wedge between her and her hus-band. I thought it was interesting that she could charge me with David's crime, but I didn't get the chance to say so. She said that until I felt like apologizing to her and David for my hatefulness, she didn't want to hear from me. As I said, that was more than a year ago. I haven't felt like apologizing in the meantime.

"The worst part is I haven't seen my grandson since he was an infant. They were always too busy to come up and visit, or little Matthew was sick. They used variations on the same excuses when I suggested visiting them. Matthew would be three now. Quite a little man." She lifted her chin, daring me to find any moisture in those dark eyes. The tear ducts might have dried up and blown away.

I got out my notebook and added the name *Matthew Glen-downing* to the list of Leland Stutch's heirs. It was getting to be a cottage industry.

I said, "If you'll give me Constance's most recent address and telephone number, I'll get out of your hair."

She gave them to me without getting up to consult anything. "Thank you," she added.

"For?"

"For not saying you're sorry. That would be just a little more than I could take."

"You were wrong about me before, Mrs. Witowski. I'm not still a young man. I've got ten years left to call myself middle-aged and I don't plan to spend them feeling sorry for relative strangers. For what it's worth, I hope you and your daughter work things out. I don't guess it's worth much." I put away the Stutch family tree and rose. "Thanks for seeing me. Mrs. Stutch will be calling you."

"Please tell Constance her mother's in good health. If you see Matthew"—she shook her head and returned her hand to her thigh—"I'm not in a position to ask favors."

"I'll let you know how he's doing."

She murmured something I didn't catch, a first in that conversation. Her speech in general was as clear as a seventh-grade English teacher explaining diphthongs. I told her I'd missed it.

Her chin went up another click to accommodate my manly height. "It's worth something," she said. "I said it's worth something."

I just made it outside without disturbing the dog. It started coughing again when the doorlatch snicked home behind me.

I'd earned half my fee and it was still morning. I grabbed an early lunch at a cafeteria on the Dix Highway and belched onions at the wall by the telephone waiting for someone to pick up in the house in Iroquois Heights. I got Mrs. Campbell. "Mrs. Stutch is out on her bicycle, Mr. Walker. May I take a message?"

"Just tell her I'm halfway home and I'll call her from Toledo if I don't snag a run in my hose."

"You've found the daughter? That was fast work." Her voice

was warm. "I should tell you Mrs. Stutch and I have few secrets. Has she agreed to a meeting?"

"I have plenty of secrets, and I mean to keep them. Please give her the message."

"I will. Thank you for calling." The receiver plopped on her end. Her tone had gone to an early frost.

I tried the number Carla Witowski had given me for her daughter in Toledo, got a busy signal, smoked part of a cigarette and tried again. Same thing. Well, it was a nice day to drive.

They were tearing up I-75 again, looking for pirate gold or maybe just for the hell of it, because it didn't seem as if anything could have gone wrong with it since the last dig, and so I slalomed among orange barrels and got the fantods from stern signs saying FINES DOUBLED IN WORK ZONES all the way to Ohio. At one point I followed a complicated series of detour signs and actually went back in time. My right cheek felt as if it were drawing up, but when I looked at it in the rearview the burn was just a healthy blush. The Red Badge of Stupidity. It didn't pay to backtalk an Iroquois Heights cop without knowing what they were serving that week at County.

When I left the lane shifts behind and entered the wide boulevards on the outer edge of Toledo, I cranked into a Total station and used the telephone. The Glendownings' line was still busy. I bought a city map and charted a route along the southwest shore of Lake Erie. Following it I glimpsed afternoon sunlight sparking off blue water, a couple of sailboats playing midweek hooky out beyond the dirty foam where the lake had no choice but to make contact with the State of Ohio, and far out on the clean horizon the profile of an ore carrier shaped like an overturned telephone receiver, deadheading back to Superior for a fresh load of iron. My skin prickled for no good reason, as it always does when I've crossed the Michigan line going the wrong way into Buckeye territory; one hundred sixty years ago, Andrew Jackson deeded the

City of Toledo to Ohio, throwing Michigan the Upper Peninsula as consolation for the loss of a key port. The decision was based on the fact that Ohio had more electoral pull, and even though the booby prize was later found to contain the richest copper and iron deposits in the world, nothing runs deeper than an old animus.

The house was a brick split-level on a street that had come up several notches from its beginnings in the dead center of the American middle class. Some of the original ranch-styles remained with their simple shotgun lines, but a handful of stately Tudors had sprung up where others had been demolished, and a framing crew was at work on a real monster covering two adjoining lots on the corner.

The driveway of the split-level canted down steeply from the street to an attached garage. I parked in front of the garage and climbed flagstone steps to an exposed front door in a redwood half-wall, above which the 1960s yellow brick had been painted white. The Glendownings, or whoever had owned the place before them, had caught the upwardly mobile bug, but it hadn't quite taken; the grass needed cutting and hornets had built a nest inside the plate glass of a carriage lamp mounted above the door. The little man sawing wood on a wind-driven lawn ornament didn't seem to be half trying.

I pushed the button and listened, but couldn't hear a bell. When nothing happened I tried the miniature brass-plated knocker. It made a die-cast clink. I tried again with bare knuckles. At the end of thirty seconds, floorboards shifted on the other side and the door opened just wide enough for a face to plug the gap. It was an ordinary sort of male face with pale blue eyes, glinting blonde stubble, and one of those spiky Briggs & Stratton haircuts that a couple of years ago were an ensign of rebellion, but have since spread throughout a generation that isn't mine. The blue eyes were swimming in blood. I smelled a familiar combination of stagnant male and beer. There were too many layers of the latter to have come from one six-pack.

I said, "Mr. Glendowning?"

"That's the name on the mailbox." This reply wasn't nearly clever enough for the length of the pause that had preceded it.

I showed him my license in its little window. A sheriff's star, a loaner from Wayne County, was pinned to the bottom half of the folder and I held it so he could see that too.

He pretended to read the information. It would have taken him twice as long to read both the images he was seeing. "What's the deal?"

"I'm a state-licensed private investigator." For once I left off the "Michigan"; I didn't have the time required for him to come up with a Wolverine insult. "I tried calling earlier. Your phone is off the hook."

"I must have wanted it that way. What's the deal?" he said again.

"No deal. I'm here to see Mrs. Glendowning about her inheritance."

"No shit. The old lady kicked off?" He looked interested for the first time.

"If you mean Mrs. Witowski, she's in excellent health, not counting a bad back. Is your wife at home?"

"Who wants to know?"

"We had this conversation. If we're going to have it again I'd prefer Mrs. Glendowning be present so I won't have to say it a third time."

"She's out. Give me the message and she'll get back to you."

"Do you know when she'll be home?"

"I guess you don't hear so good. Now, what's this about an inheritance?" He burped in the middle of "inheritance" and had to start it again.

"I'll come back later." I pocketed the folder and turned away.

"Just a second." He reached a hand through the gap and closed it on my shoulder. He had a brute of a grip. I remembered he drove a truck; most of the power in a big rig's power steering is supplied by the operator. I pulled back, not sharply enough to break the grip. It pulled his center of gravity forward and I spun to face him and took hold of the front of his shirt and pulled him the rest of the way through the opening. He stuck his hands out in front of him to avoid landing on his face and I pivoted and planted a foot between his shoulder blades, pinning him to the concrete stoop. I'd learned the first move from the army. The second was made in Detroit.

"Son of a bitch." He was talking to the concrete, but I felt the resonance all the way to my knee.

"Rewind," I said. "Where's your wife?"

"Let me up."

I tried to think of a good reason why I should let him up. I don't like standing on many complete strangers and damn few friends. I couldn't think of one.

Then he gave me one. "I got blood pressure issues."

I took my foot off his back and stood clear while he pulled himself hand over hand up the doorframe. When he was upright I watched him set his feet with his back to me, watched with clinical interest. I moved my head out of the way when he swung his fist, then stepped in and clipped his chin in a short straight uppercut. His mouth shut with a clop and light evaporated from his eyes. I caught him under the arms when he sagged and we went inside.

# CHAPTER

# SEVEN

W<small>E WENT DOWN A STEP</small> into a sunken living room that smelled as if it had gone down with the Armada. It was carpeted in deep pile from which Glendowning's heels dragged up dust and strips of cellophane from cigarette packages past as I hauled him backward toward the nearest chair. This was a fat gray recliner that went into its act when I dumped him into it, stretching its spine and swinging up its footrest. My host had on a blue twill shirt, faded jeans, and white athletic socks with dirty black soles, no shoes. From the smell he had had them all on for days, or had put on the same ensemble every day for a week. If there was an ashtray under the bent cigarette butts on the end table by the chair, or for that matter an end table under the squat brown beer bottles, I would have needed a shovel to find them. There were more bottles on a glass coffee table, atop a bookcase filled with Time-Life books in sets and on the TV cabinet a Curtis Mathes in dark walnut. When I started to walk across the room, I kicked a bottle that rolled in a half-circle and came to rest with its neck pointed at me. I didn't feel like kissing anyone. The room was too close for that, or anything else except Greco-Roman wrestling. I found the switch to the ceiling fan and tipped it up. The blades came around in a lazy swoop, stirring the socks and dead tobacco and beer into a kind of gay collage: *Jersey City Locker Room, 1933.*

Glendowning was snoring, the grackles and plooeys drowning out the hum of the fan. The TV was on with the sound turned down. I watched a white golf ball arch against a blue Augusta sky and plop onto a green that looked as if it had been dipped in the dye they used for the Irish flag. The spectators in the gallery applauded in silence. There were brown smears of grime on the corners of the glass screen. Everything in the room was dusty except the beer bottles. My reflection was dusty in the glass of a framed poster from the Toledo Art Museum above a gas fireplace, and a dustbunny the size of a Chihuahua, coaxed from hiding by the fan, scudded across my shoe and caught in the skirt of a sofa upholstered in Sunday sports sections. It left a mark on my toe that made me think of a snail. Instinctively I scrubbed my toe against the carpet. That only made it worse. I was beginning to get the idea. Mrs. Glendowning wasn't at home.

The man of the house was out of the inning. I went through an arch into a kitchen with crumbs and crusty spills on every horizontal surface. The dishwasher was jammed with dirty plates and cups and knives with their wicked tips pointing up. The double sink was a graveyard of pots and pans. It didn't take a geologist to identify the stratum where the utensils had run out and the take-out had come in; a trail of ants as straight as a plumbline led from a baseboard across the linoleum and up the steel leg of the kitchen table to a forest of open cardboard containers. I opened the refrigerator, then closed it quickly against the stench. There ought to have been a Sell By date on the door.

I opened the door next to the pantry and descended gridded metal steps to the rubber-smelling garage. I switched on the overhead bulbs and looked at a new Dodge Ram parked on the near side, spotless white and nearly seven feet tall on high-rider tires. An oil stain marked the concrete on the other side where there was room for another vehicle. The fact that he was still parking to one side meant nothing. Some habits are hard to break, and hope springs eternal, if you read the poets and believe what they wrote. I put out the light and went back upstairs.

A small den off the opposite side of the living room contained a half-size pressboard rolltop desk for paying bills, no interesting bills in its pigeonholes or drawers, and nothing entertaining in the register of a checkbook belonging to a joint account in the names of David and Constance Glendowning. On the writing surface was a Packard Bell computer and printer with the monitor switched off. I didn't turn it on. What I didn't know about computers hadn't made Bill Gates any less rich. The room was neat and clean except for some dust and had that stale smell of a room that hadn't been used in a while except as a repository for third notices in unopened envelopes. The half-bathroom next door was just as sterile, but only in the way of enlightenment. It needed cleaning and the toilet seat stood at attention. A soaked cigarette butt lay on the surface of the water in the bowl.

A brief flight of carpeted steps took me to another level. A small bedroom had posters on the walls—the latest action-figure tie-ins from Japan—and a chest with clowns painted on it, half filled with toys; the rounded, soft kind approved for toddlers. I remembered there was a three-year-old boy named Matthew. There were drawers under the midget bed for storage. They didn't seem to contain nearly enough clothes for a normal kid who liked candy bars and mud puddles, but I hadn't any of my own and the world had heaved itself around the sun a tired number of times since I wore corduroy overalls. Boys might have changed. However, the place had the same disused smell as the den, no peanut-butter sandwiches or iodine for scraped knees.

The master bedroom was decorated tastefully in rose and gray.

Men's clothes were flung everywhere and the queen-size bed was a snarl of sheets with two pillows stacked one atop the other and in the top one a slightly soiled hollow made by a single head. I couldn't tell if anything was missing from among the bottles and lipsticks on the little vanity table, but there were not as many women's clothes behind the sliding doors of the closet as there should have been. That's one thing that hadn't changed.

A drawer in one of the nightstands held a nine-millimeter Beretta on a .45 Colt frame, a nice weapon that would have almost no kick at all, sweet for shooting targets and men alike. The permit was there too, up to date and in David Glendowning's name. It allowed him to own the pistol but not lug it around. I flicked out the magazine, put it back in, and checked the slide. Fully loaded. They aren't much good any other way, although the Million Mothers might have had something to say about live rounds and curious children sharing the same floor. I sniffed the muzzle. It hadn't had anything hot through it recently.

The bathroom was my last stop. The toilet seat was standing and the mold on the shower curtain was coming along splendidly. No loofa sponge or feminine moisturizers by the tub, no Lady Schicks in the cabinet above the sink. By then I wasn't really looking for such things. I didn't expect to find them.

What I was looking for I found in a plastic bottle in the cabinet: small round pills coated brown so you wouldn't mix them up with aspirins. Caffeine tablets. No self-respecting trucker would be caught dead on the interstate at 3:00 A.M. without them. I shook three into my hand, started to put the bottle back, then uncapped it and milked out two more. I went back down to the living room, where Glendowning was still making the John Deere mating call, crossed into the kitchen, and filled a debatably clean glass with water from the tap. Back in the living room I shoved over a bottle to make room for the glass on the end table, straightened, and took aim with the first of the pills. Glendowning's head was tipped all the way back with his eyeteeth showing, the better to increase the decibel level. I flipped the pill square into the hole and picked up the next from my other palm. I scored five for five. One of them caught sideways in his throat, choking him in mid-snore. When he shot forward, coughing, I was there with the water. I pounded him on the back and pressed the glass into his hand.

He must have thought it was a beer, because he closed both paws around it and dumped the contents down his throat. That brought on a new fit. His face turned red and he sprayed snot. One of the pills shot out of his mouth and landed on the arm of the sofa. I'd expected at least one to go wild, which was why I'd fed him five.

This time I didn't do anything to help. I stood back with my hands in my pockets and watched him excavate his lungs for oxygen. He found a good wheeze, then another, and very slowly his color went from magenta back to red and finally the grayish pink of the serious drunk. "Jesus Christ." His voice was a raspy bass, like a Muppet monster's. He glared down at the clear liquid in his glass, then as if he'd seen my reflection his eyes climbed out of it and shook themselves off and focused on my face. "What the fuck you looking at?"

"I'm not sure. It might not be classified yet."

"What's that supposed to mean? And who the fuck are you?"

"Walker's the name. I told you I was an investigator. I still am. You weren't out that long. But man, you were out."

A sluggish tongue found its way around his teeth, tasting caffeine. Just then he seemed to understand what I was saying. A hand went to his chin. "Jesus. What'd you hit me with? And how many of you did it take to lift it?"

"You helped. You were moving forward. And it wouldn't have put you down so deep if you didn't have half of Milwaukee swimming through your veins. How's the head?"

He reached up both hands to knuckle his temples. The glass

was still in one and he spilled water on his shirt, but he didn't seem to notice. "I might of went on forgetting about it if you didn't ask. Jesus."

"The caffeine should help. It opens up the arteries."

He tasted again. "I thought that's what it was. Any left in the bottle?"

"Plenty, but forget it. As things stand, when the alcohol burns off you'll jump like a flea. Give them a few minutes to work."

"Jesus. I'll be dead in a few minutes."

I went back into the kitchen, took a deep breath and held it, and opened the refrigerator again. There were two unopened bottles of beer left in the cardboard six-pack inside, an omen. I took them both out and twisted off the caps and returned to the living room and stuck one under his nose. He couldn't get rid of the water fast enough. What was left in the glass slopped onto his jeans as he set it down and grabbed for the bottle. He tipped it straight up and left it there like a quart of oil. It gurgled four times before he brought it back down. That left less than half.

The slug I took was dainty by comparison. I flicked away the fugitive pill and sat on the arm of the sofa. The part with the cushions looked like a maneater and I wasn't sure he'd smoldered out. There was always the chance he'd flare up again without warning. I stayed in starting position.

"That's better," he said, sounding dreamy enough. "Jesus."

"I don't think He's in to you. God knows you paged Him enough."

He ran fingers through his spiky hair without visible effect, scowled, and studied the lay between his chair and the sofa. It must have looked like the center span of the Mackinac Bridge, because he settled back with a heavy sigh. He was as hard to read as a stop sign.

"So your name's Walker and you're a private eye."

"That's right," I snarled. "A dick. A sleuth. A peeper. A lone star, a plastic badge, heat on a stick. Alternative law." I stopped, not because I'd run out of euphemisms, but because I thought he might have the idea by now. I looked at my watch. I don't know why, except it seemed a long time since I'd been outside. They might have finished I-75 and started planting trees.

"You working for Constance's lawyer?"

"Why would Constance have a lawyer?" When he didn't react I said, "So you've split up. Mind telling me where she went?"

"If I knew that, I'd go there and bring her back."

"She take the boy?"

He looked at me with what he thought was pity. His eyes might have been a pair of ice cubes melting in tomato soup. "Well now, what do you think? She's a good mother. If she left little Matt with me he'd be picking pockets by now. That's how she'd see it anyway." He took a swig from the bottle and blasted a belch they heard in Kentucky.

"When did she fly the coop?"

"May fifth. *Cinco de Mayo.* I know that because I stopped at a Mex place to celebrate on my way home. Happy Hour all day, that's what I was celebrating. I don't know what the Mexes were. Their green cards maybe."

"We had a fight when I got in around eleven," he said. "I missed the end of it. I went to sleep in this chair. She and Matt were gone when I woke up. No note. I thought they'd be back when she cooled off. I guess she ain't cooled off yet."

"She didn't go to her mother's. I just came from there. What about a friend?"

"She don't have any friends."

His fault, if Carla Witowski hadn't just been blowing bubbles. I didn't point it out. If this was going to work without breaking up the furniture, we had to be pals. I can make a Cape buffalo curl up in my lap when I have to. It's on the license application.

I was getting the drift of what had gone on in that house, but it was something I would have to sneak up on.

While I was thinking about it he rubbed his free hand over his face. The caffeine was kicking in. The cobwebs came away with the hand. "You said something about an inheritance. What's the deal?"

"Family thing. We need her signature. I hear you're a union rep."

The zoo air in the room was getting to me. I should have opened a window. But the ham-handed attempt at a change of subject worked. He got lively.

"I'm just a shop steward, but I'm a good one. Guess you wouldn't know it to look at me at the moment. I don't drink behind the wheel and you don't have to be careful about lighting a match around me when I'm shut up with management. The boys want me to run for president of the local."

"Uphill climb. These days they like college diplomas."

"OSU offers a night-school course on contract law. I guess I can pick up enough Latin to pass. Anyway the college crowd is what got us in the ditch we're in, so I figure the pendulum's swinging my way. You boys got representation?"

I shook my head. "You wouldn't want to try it on, either. All the ops that can swing the dues work out of air-conditioned offices with a modem and a key to the executive washroom. It'd be like negotiating for the enemy." I took a pull from the bottle, for effect. For effect it tasted pretty good. "My old man was a Teamster twenty years. Worked his way up from a pedal truck to a diesel rig back when people ran outside to watch one go by."

He grinned for the first time. It made him look younger. He was just past thirty. "They didn't have power steering in them days. I bet he had an arm on him."

"You couldn't tell by me. He never used it on anyone who couldn't hit back."

It was more or less a blind cast; I was still pondering my approach and didn't even know I'd made it until I got a strike. The grin went out like a smashed bulb. He leaned forward to fumble his bottle onto the endtable, knocking off one of the empties in the process. He stayed leaning forward with his feet on the floor, straddling the footrest, and covered his face with both hands. "Oh, God," he said. "Oh, Jesus God." His shoulders shook. He was sobbing.

## CHAPTER

# EIGHT

I FINISHED MY BEER while he was crying. He wasn't through by then so I lit a Winston. I got up and went over and pried up the sash of a window that looked out on the street. It was a quiet street: no backyard hot-rodders or chainsaw maniacs, just houses and trees and a solitary roller-blader padded up to the gills racing his shadow along the opposite sidewalk, making no more noise than a handful of marbles rolling downhill. My street had been like that once and might be yet again, if the reform crowd downtown managed to resist graft for another term or two. It was a lot to hope for.

The fresh air and new tobacco improved the atmosphere in the room. I drummed a Winston partway out of the pack, nudged Glendowning's shoulder with the back of my hand, and held the pack out. He took his face out of his hands to look at it. After a moment he snuffled, dragged his twill sleeve across his eyes, and took the cigarette. His hand shook a little as he pushed the tobacco end into the flame of the match I held for him. When he had it burning he nodded and sat back. He sniffed, composing himself.

His eyes were redder than they had been, but apart from that he might have been anyone else coming off a bender.

I cleared space on the sofa and sat down. My back was nearly as stiff as Carla Witowski's after the drive down and the workout on the porch, and I didn't think there was going to be a rematch right away. I picked up my empty beer bottle and tapped ash into it. A little on the rug wouldn't have hurt the room in the condition it was already in, but there is a protocol.

"Which one did you hit, your wife or your son?" I asked. "Or both?"

"Who says I hit anyone?" He flicked his cigarette toward the heaped ashtray. He didn't even come close.

"There are shelters for that kind of thing. She could have checked into a motel, but she'd go to her mother's before she did that. The only time a shelter's better than family is when there's a question of safety. That means beating. Also there are the tears. We're all of us very sensitive today, very New Wave. I don't think. A trucker needs a reason to cry. More so a champion of labor."

"I never hit little Matt."

I smoked and said nothing.

"I never meant to hit Connie. I mean I never planned it. She has a way of getting to me. Well, shit, that makes it sound like it's her fault. It isn't. I never laid a hand on her sober. I'm a mean drunk. I guess you know that."

"I've seen meaner. But I'm not your wife."

"I never beat her up neither, just smacked her a couple of times. Okay, more than a couple. I might of busted her nose once. Put a bump in it anyway. She had two black eyes for a week and didn't go out. That wasn't my idea, I mean the not going out; she didn't want people to ask questions because the answers would get me in trouble. She loves me all right. Or she did." He sucked hard on the filter, got mad at it and tore it off. The butts in the tray were unfiltered Pall Malls. He took in a double lungful of full leaded, tried to blow it out his nose, and coughed. He was still sniffling. "I'm a rotten son of a bitch."

"You hit her the last time?"

He nodded. Then he laughed, a short bark full of self-hate. "The joke is it wasn't all that hard. Not nearly hard enough to raise a welt. I guess it was just one feather more than the pile'd hold. I'd give up drinking if she'd come back. I miss her even more than I miss Matt. Is that bad? I love that kid more than I love me. When I loved me."

"You're bargaining in the wrong direction. She might come back if you give up drinking, or maybe she wouldn't. I never met her, she might be smarter than I'm giving her credit for. It still wouldn't be enough. You'd have to start talking to someone."

"You mean a shrink? I thought of that. I can't afford it and I wouldn't go to the one that works with the union. It's like using a toilet on a plane. Everyone knows where you're going."

"There are good ones that will work with you on their fee. I know a few around Detroit. I could give you some names."

"Maybe everyone'd be better off if I just blew my brains out."

"It's a way out," I agreed. "You've certainly got the firepower upstairs."

He looked at me the way he had just before he took his swing at me. Then he took a drag and let it out with the smoke. "You're a detective, all right. You find the magazines in the back of the closet?"

"They wouldn't interest me unless they told me where your wife went. Just for argument, though, you should lock up the piece. It might be a start."

"Connie was always after me to get rid of it. I only bought it when I got involved in the union. You meet some types that just knowing you own one makes you feel better, even if you don't keep it with you. I don't guess it matters what I do with it now."

I poked my stub into my empty and let it fall. It spat when it hit the dregs. "That's the trouble with you pity bugs. You never follow one line of thought to the end. First you're going to reform, then you're going to clock yourself, then you're right back where you started. Why don't you buy another case and drown yourself in it?"

"Why don't I punch you through the back of that fucking sofa?"

"I think you found out that's not as much fun as you thought."

He gave that some consideration. Then he nodded, laid his stub on top of the heap, and drank the rest of his beer. He made a face, as if the beer was flat, but it was just another crying jag. When it was over he wiped his nose on his sleeve and said, "I'm a piece of work. What makes me think I'm worth some cop digging a bullet out of my skull? Did you mean that about giving me the name of a shrink?"

"It's not like getting fitted for glasses. You'd have to keep going back. And you have to want what he has to peddle. The good ones don't like just drawing their pay."

"I'd do it for Connie and Matt."

"Forget it then. If it's not for you it won't take."

We sat saying nothing for a while. Cars began to go by outside. People were coming home from work, leaving the job at the office or the plant, looking forward to dinner and the tube, or not looking forward to a band concert at the kid's high school, or let's face it, a third straight night of the cold shoulder because someone smiled the wrong way at the wrong spouse at the company picnic; pick your scenario, whatever it was it was going on under someone's roof other than David Glendowning's. It looked like Walton's Mountain to me.

I got out one of my cards, wrote a name and telephone number on the back of it, and made room on the coffee table to set it down. "Try not to lose this under a bottle. He doesn't have a Viennese accent and he won't make you lie on a couch. If he doesn't hang up when you tell him who recommended him, he may be the man for you." I stood.

"Thanks." It's a simple word, but there are ten thousand ways to say it. This sounded like one of the right ways, but I'd been there too long.

"I don't expect it to do a damn bit of good," I said. "I think you're a cracked block. A lost cause. But you can return the empty gesture by telling me what kind of car your wife drives."

"Gray ninety-six Chrysler LeBaron, Ohio license GBX-121. It's leaking fluid. Damned if I been able to find out from where. I don't suppose them shelters let them stand out in the street."

"You never know. They're like any other place with too many secrets and not enough closet space." I put away my notebook with Constance's LeBaron in it. "Anyway I know most of the shelters between Battle Creek and Cincinnati. They can use the practice throwing me down the front steps all over again."

He lifted his bottle. Then he returned it to his knee. "I don't guess I could hire you to report back when you find her."

"It'd be my license if I did, and if it wouldn't I still wouldn't do it. Your wife's a pretty woman, Glendowning. I've seen her picture. In the morgue she'd be just another puffy face with broken bones under it. The next time you might raise more than a welt."

"I'll call your guy," he said after a moment. "You think I won't, but I will." He started to raise the bottle again. He looked at it and his face turned the color it had turned when he'd been choking on an unexpected slug of water. He leaned forward, kicking the footrest back under the chair, and set the bottle down on the carpet with a thump.

I said, "You can drop-kick it through the window if you like. It won't stop you from buying another six-pack."

"I'll call your guy." He sounded petulant.

I knew a curtain line when I heard one, but I was too soft a slab of ham to let him have it. "When I see her I'll tell her what went on here," I said at the door. "What she does with it is her business."

He screwed up his face to bawl again. I stepped outside and shut the door fast.

# NINE

On my way out of town I stopped at the same Total station for a fill and a telephone call. This time Rayellen Stutch took it. She sounded out of breath.

"I didn't think people who employed housekeepers had to run to catch the phone," I said.

"I just got through pedaling around the city limits. Or don't rich people get to sweat in the world you live in?"

"In the world I live in they don't stay long enough to work one up. I thought that bit about you being on your bicycle was just a clever euphemism."

"Nope. I figure if Leland could make a hundred and six on straight whiskey and T-bone steaks, I ought to have a shot at two hundred. Are you in Toledo?"

"Wholly. But not for long. I just had a talk with your grand-daughter's husband."

"She's Leland's granddaughter, not mine. I'm not two hundred yet. You didn't see Constance?"

I backed up and brought her up to the post, beginning with

Carla Witowski and finishing with Glendowning, editing for length; especially the brief round on his doorstep. The fights you lose make better listening.

"He sounds horrendous. The little one is named Matthew? Well, he'll go to college. Oxford, maybe, if he minds his grades. Are you checking out the shelters next?"

"Not personally. Not here. I was stretching the blanket when I told Glendowning I knew them all. I used to know a couple around Detroit, but I've been off the wandering-wife beat for years now." I rapped on the laminated wood of a Slim Jim display; I didn't want to go back. "I'll have to farm it out. It might take a few days."

"Sounds more like a month." She was stating a belief, not haggling over my day rate.

"I doubt it. She's from Michigan, and I have it on her mother's authority and Glendowning's she didn't have any ties down here. She'd run to cover somewhere north. I know someone here who specializes in this kind of case. We'll split my fee. It won't cost you anything more than his expenses."

"I'll cut you another check. How's two thousand to start?"

"I don't need anything right now. The last I knew my credit was still good with the party I have in mind."

"Would I know the party's name?"

"Not unless you lied on that résumé you gave me yesterday. It's not a nice party. But it works hard and it's as good as its word."

"All that was true of Ted Bundy."

"Not quite. Bundy didn't blow his nose in his napkin."

The pause on her end was just long enough for a woman who had lived in Grosse Pointe, but not too long for a girl from Broadway. But she didn't change subjects any more smoothly than I did. "What's Carla like?"

"Like every schoolteacher I ever had who cared if I knew 'all right' was one word or two. She's bitter, though. It won't be cheap."

"In my bracket nothing is." She said good luck and we were through talking.

I found Jerry Zangara where almost no one else would, behind a battleship gray desk of booming steel in the airless little security office at the end of an outlet mall off I-75, square on the state line. He couldn't walk the thirty yards to the pay office to pick up his check without paying income tax in two states. I tugged open a steel fire door with a NO ADMITTANCE sign on it in white and red enamel and had to walk around it to use the metal chair on the customer's side. There were two metal file cabinets, gray like the desk and chair, and a set of gray bolted utility shelves holding printed regulations or typewritten reports or something held together with brads, or maybe they were old student dissertations rescued from a dumpster on the Ohio State campus and placed there for effect. The walls were gray too, and they had been painted recently; the sheen was still on them and the smell of turpentine was the first thing you noticed when the door drifted shut.

The only decoration in the place was a large poster on one wall itemizing the legal rights of suspected shoplifters, with check marks in blue ballpoint beside all but a few. I couldn't tell if someone had started to keep track and lost interest or had checked off the ones he'd decided he could do without. It was that kind of office.

Jerry was a little fat guy with a nice head of wavy black hair, white teeth in a small shy smile bracketed by his apple cheeks, and shiny black eyes with no more expression in them than nailheads in Sheetrock. He had on a black-and-white cowboy shirt with pearl snaps and a bolo tie with the turquoise slide drawn up just under his double chin. When he recognized me he lifted himself an inch off his seat and stuck out his hand. It was like shaking hands with a boneless chicken breast.

"Amos. How's my favorite Michigander?" He knew I hated the term.

"I'm okay, Jerry. I see your grammar is coming along. The wind must be blowing from the north."

"That'll be enough of that. I strip-searched a three-hundred-pounder not fifteen minutes ago. I had to keep chalking my place. A thing like that can put you off your game. What's on your plate you can't finish?"

"I'm looking for a batter job. She took her kid and slipped the knot about three weeks ago in Toledo. I'm banking on her going to a shelter."

When he wrinkled his nose he looked like a big fat baby. "You're too late, old son. I don't moonlight no more. I ain't had my nuts kicked in over a year. You ought to give it a whirl."

"I don't think so. I'm out of chalk. What'd you do, give up on the sports book?"

"Naw. I got married. She's a senior clerk in a credit union. Double-Income household, No Kids. You know what them initials spell?" He tried to leer, but his cheeks wouldn't budge.

"Everyone knows what they spell, Jerry. There's cash in it. Client's strictly blue chip." I smoothed out the bill on the desk. It was one of the new hundreds. Franklin's face looked more bloated than usual.

Jerry Zangara's little black eyes glittered, but he kept his hands on his side of the desk. "You don't keep up. Blue chip went out with the Macarena. These days it's e-trade or nothing."

"You get another one when you turn a lead. More if you have to cover ground and you can prove mileage. Printed gas receipts, Jerry, from chain stations. I know all about those blank receipt books in your bottom drawer."

"That's cold. I'm a reformed character since I wandered into the snare." He lifted an old-fashioned postage meter off the corner nearest him and set it down on top of the bill. "Details, please."

I gave him as much as he needed to start looking, including the license number of Constance Glendowning's gray Chrysler. He didn't have to know the name of the client or that an inheritance was involved. I trusted him up to three figures, that was all. But it was farther than I trusted most presidents.

He took it all down in his big moronic hand on the back of an invoice, putting in the last period with a bang that made the desk reverberate. "Got it. You want me to make contact?"

"No, and don't let her see you. Just give me a ring when she surfaces. That's her on the right." I skidded the engagement picture Mrs. Stutch had clipped from the newspaper across the top of the desk, minus the article identifying Constance's parents. I'd torn that off and put it in my pocket. Jerry was just the kind of elephant that might remember the name Willard.

"Pretty," he said, committing the face to memory. "Not special. This the husband?"

"That's him."

"A puke. You see mugs like this whenever the Nazis march or the cops bust a gang of Goths using skulls for skillets. She should of consulted me first. Okay." He gave back the picture. He'd know her in a short wig or a Zorro mask now. "I thought you got out of divorce work."

"Gas is going to two bucks a gallon. You snapped up the last senior clerk." I put the newspaper shot in my wallet. "This one's a snowbird. Draw a circle around everything within thirty minutes of Toledo and concentrate on that for now. I'll cover Detroit. You know where to reach me day or night." I stood.

"It won't be night. Nights I lay my head in the lap of do-mes-ticity. You still divorced?"

"The statute of limitations ran out on that after twenty years. Now I'm just single."

"Ring-a-ding-ding." This time he managed a leer. He looked like a woodchuck with a porno collection.

I shook my head. "Sinatra checked out. You ought to get out of this changing booth once in a while."

"Naw. I just got it fixed up the way I like it."

I shook his hand again and didn't wipe mine on my coat until I left the office. I made room for a uniformed security guard duck-walking a teenager down the short hall by the back of his neck. The teenager had on black baggy clothes and lips to match and smelled emphatically of nightshade. At least he didn't weigh three hundred pounds.

A No. 10 envelope with General Motors in the return address was waiting for me under the slot when I swung into the office the next morning. The letter was brief, signed in Connor Thorpe's no-bullshit hand, and advised all these present to know that Amos Walker was engaged upon corporation business and that cooperation would be appreciated and noted. An assistant had run it off on a computer from his dictation and had probably put it through a couple of times more to restore Thorpe's pet phrases. He went through secretaries like tailgunners. I re-folded the letter and stuck it in my breast pocket next to the county star where they could have a power party while I unlocked a drawer in one of my file cabinets, never mind which drawer or which cabinet.

In a manila folder that is otherwise empty I keep a little fat blue notebook that I have had long enough for the cardboard corners to have poked through the vinyl like the bones of a compound fracture. Some of the names and telephone numbers and addresses are now obsolete by reason of relocation or death, or in the case of some cement company executives and certain members of the old mayor's staff, in jail. None of the rest is listed anywhere the public has access. The book would buy me a comfortable retirement if word of the book's existence got out among the muckraking press and I gave out the key to the code. It would be a short retirement followed by services, if my carcass turned up. Just having it out in the open air makes me nervous, and so I scribbled down the half-dozen numbers I needed on my telephone pad without identifying them and locked it back up. The safe is just a dodge to draw lightning. No one rifles the files of a PI in my unfashionable district.

The shelters that take in battered women and children, when they are listed in the public directory, don't include their addresses. The telephones are answered by experienced personnel, some of them former battered women themselves, who know what questions to ask and hang up when the answers don't fit. The information in my book contained addresses and the numbers of private lines belonging to the offices of the directors. Those who didn't know me knew my references. All others could go climb up their own legs. Husbands and their representatives, and those who are suspected of being one or the other, are about as welcome as a roast pig at a bar mitzvah.

I got my swivel chair squeaking and began dialing. Two of the numbers bought me an irritating three-note squeal and a recording informing me they were out of service. I drew lines through them on the pad and continued through the list. One of the numbers had been reassigned to a twenty-four-hour doughnut shop. I wrote "doughnuts" next to it, not knowing when I might crave a cruller at 4:00 A.M. Next I spoke to a director who knew me, who assured me that no one of Constance Glendowning's name or description had been checked in since April 1, or going back sometime before that date. At another number I reached someone who was new since my original contact, who wrote down my references and called me back after ten minutes to tell me I had a clean bill of health and sorry but nothing there either. A tough female voice dripping with Twelfth Street answered at the last number, listened to what I had to say, provided me with a thorough and not entirely inaccurate account of my lineage, and gave me an earache on the disconnect.

I cradled the receiver, entered a question mark next to that line on the pad, and checked my wristwatch to see how long I would have to wait before the air had cleared enough to try again. For that I needed a calendar.

At home and in the trunk of my car I had a set of ingenious disguises for dealing with similar situations, including an assortment of utility-company coveralls with barely adequate credentials clipped to the breast pockets. I'd selected them with relaxed-fit crotches to accommodate an athletic cup in case I got found out, which was fairly often. I didn't want to put them on, but I didn't want to count too heavily on Jerry Zangara either; he was on his third cup last I knew. So I didn't think about it at all. I typed up a report on the case thus far, ran a credit check I'd been putting off for a client who ought to have had a credit check run on him, answered a few messages waiting for me at my telephone service, went out for a long lunch and a short beer, and took the rest of the day off to scout some junkyards downriver for a hubcap to replace one I'd lost off the Cutlass. I got home at dark with a dashboard compass instead, opened a can of supper, and went to sleep in front of a three-dollar rental movie I'd managed to avoid in the theaters for seven-fifty.

Sometime later I turned off the fuzz on the TV screen and stumbled to bed. I wasn't in it five minutes when Jerry Zangara called, direct from the lap of domesticity. He'd found Constance Glendowning, he thought.

"**Y**OU *THINK*?" I could just make out the time on the living room clock in the light from the bedroom. It was too late for hunches.

"What's that margin the pollsters use, six percent?" Jerry asked. "I'm inside that. I got a woman at the door, a real diesel job: straight hair, glasses, no makeup, gray sweats. I'm betting you could lose a shoe in the hair under her armpits. She wouldn't even take my card."

"They never do. A husband's lawyer could use it to prove they know where the wife is. If that's all you've got, to hell with you and good night."

"You know me better than that, and to hell with you too." He said it as if he were wishing me good health. "I poked around outside with a penlight. It's a big old house with a garage in back. Driveway needs asphalting. There's a patch where a car sat for a while leaking fluid; trans, I think. Anyway it smelled like it when I got down on all fours and took a sniff. You said Constance's Chrysler has a leak."

"Get into the garage?"

"Naw, I don't do that no more. Also there was a bright son of a bitch of a security light right in front. Did I tell you this was in Monroe? I got to be careful about bending the law in Michigan. Matter of an outstanding warrant."

"I didn't know there were any shelters in Monroe."

"I did. That's what makes me worth the two hundred. Anyway this patch might be two–three weeks old, but I ain't Kit Carson. I networked the neighborhood until I found an old crotch that lives next to his window, there's always one. I had a friend in Shipping at the mall print me out a picture from his computer of a ninety-six LeBaron. I showed it to the old bastard along with a couple of other models. He picked it out quick."

I grunted and found a cigarette. Jerry was a storyteller; his reports read like pulp fiction. There was no use asking him to skip to the last page. He'd just go back to the first and start over.

He said, "I thought the same as you, probably: Nobody's memory is that good, I'm just a time-killer between his Malt-O-Meal and Ted Koppel. Then he springs the license number on me."

"You're kidding."

"Straight money. I says what are you, some kind of fucking Rain Man, you want to hop the redeye with me to Vegas, bust the blackjack bank at the Sahara? He says no and shows me the spot on the windowsill where he scratched the number with a safety pin. He seen the car swing into the driveway and a woman pile out with a little kid that looks like his. The old man's lost some sawdust out of his head since the Kaiser surrendered; if he's got a kid he's older than I am or dead. Either way he probably don't visit. The old man's smart enough to take down the number so he can put the cops on the case, but he's fuzzy enough to forget all about it until I come along and remind him. He don't even know what day he scratched it in the sill."

Jerry's tone was ripe with being impressed with himself. Pure dumb luck has done that to better men than he. I snuffed out my butt in the ashtray next to the telephone. "Who runs the shelter?"

"Broad named Mrs. Emory Chapin owns it, that's public record. She might run it or not. I could find out, but it'd cost you a lot more than two hundred. The fucking CIA should be so quiet."

"What's the address?"

He gave it to me. I didn't have a pencil or even a safety pin, so I repeated it aloud, committing it to memory. There was a pause on his end then, and I knew the story had a kicker. I waited him out.

"I got Mrs. Chapin's address too," he said. "Also her phone number."

I told him to hang on and went into the kitchen. I fetched a magnetic pad off the refrigerator and a pen and returned to the living room. "Okay, Jerry, I'm impressed. I'll lay twenty on OSU next time they're in Ann Arbor."

"Lay it on me instead. I let a vice president at Ameritech pay for a Rolex I fished out of his kid's skivvies last year. He's good for an unlisted number every couple of months. You got a kid, Walker?"

"Not yet. Probably not ever."

"Good. They're a fucking Achilles heel." He gave me the information.

I wrote it down. "I'll send you a check."

"Send cash."

"It might get stolen."

"It won't. I told you, I don't moonlight no more. Come back down to God's country anytime you can't stand the mosquitoes in Michigan."

He hung up. I didn't hear of him again until a minister's wife got frisked at the outlet mall for a pair of pantyhose she didn't have on her and she sued for half a million. The mall let him go. I don't know what his credit union clerk did to him, but a couple of months later the minister's wife got nailed wheeling a display model gas grill out the door of a Montgomery Ward's in Cleveland, and this time the charge stuck.

It was too late to call Mrs. Emory Chapin. I went back to bed, woke up when the alarm clock clicked just before seven, drank two cups of coffee, and sat around reading the *Free Press* until eight. There was a long piece about neighborhood improvements in the Mexican community on Detroit's west side; another ethnic group heard from, adding salsa to the baklava and cannolis and kielbasa and barbecued ribs aboard the groaning local table. It made me hungry, so I got up and made French toast.

Before making the call I used the bathroom and set out a fresh pack of cigarettes and a book of matches. There was no telling how long I'd be charming Mrs. Chapin over the telephone before my shovel rang against metal.

I got a putative female voice with a strand of barbed wire running through it. I pictured Jerry's diesel job. She was only mildly abusive, but it was early yet and she hadn't caught her stride. She knew nothing about shelters or any party named Constance Glendowning. I asked if I happened to be addressing Mrs. Chapin. She knew nothing about anyone who went by that name. She knew nothing about pretty much everything and made it plenty clear it was my fault for assuming otherwise. Just for the novelty of it I told the truth, that the Glendowning party was in line for an inheritance and if she preferred to be the one who did the calling she could reach me at that number or the office later. I left the usual references—police, lawyers, a couple of state legislators not yet under indictment—and threw in the name of a social services caseworker from a child-abandonment job, to knock the sharp corners off the testosterone; but she stepped all over the names, insisting someone had given me the wrong number, said good-bye, and went away with the connection.

I got out of the robe and into the shower, scraped off the Cro-Magnon growth of the night, put on a suit fresh from the cleaners, and drove to the office, where I sat around making a good impression on the walls until the telephone rang at ten.

"Amos?"

That Jamaican lilt sent me way back. I felt the outer layers of shell dropping off like something I didn't need anymore, or hadn't yet needed then; or maybe I was just coming down from a hot flash.

"Iris?"

"Only to you. I'm Mrs. Emory Chapin to everyone else. You need to work on your people skills. You didn't make a hit with Ms. Stainback."

"If she'd let me get as far as knowing her name was Ms. Stainback I'd have sent flowers."

"That's what I mean. She isn't the type that appreciates them."

"To hell with her, then. You got married, I heard. The name wasn't Chapin. And it was Kingston town, not Monroe."

"Kingston. Roger Whittaker's the only one who calls it Kingston town. Charles died; leukemia. I won't discuss Emory. I only wear the name because if he heard what it's connected with now he'd have a stroke. And how are you? Still single and mean as a sewer cat?"

I didn't deny either assumption. I'd known Iris when she worked the streets for a needleful of Mexican brown; any secrets we had were new since then. "How long have you been running a shelter?"

"Two years. Five years before that running errands and observing while I waited out accreditation. I saw things I never saw in a crackhouse. I thought I was a tough little street rat before I got this gig. I can't blame Ms. Stainback for being the way she is. I'd have got that way myself if I didn't know there was more to the world than this. What do you want with Constance Glendowning?"

That was Iris: business up front, no sitting around chewing over old times and Ferris wheels. I told her what I'd told the other woman. "It isn't a cover," I added. "There's serious money involved."

"Money's always serious. I'm giving a deposition in Detroit today, and I'm late. Where would you like to take me to dinner?"

"Ms. Stainback might not approve."

"To hell with her, to quote a wise old sage. Make it some place that serves steak without a pile of underdone Brussels sprouts on the side. I gave up vegetarianism when I gave up Mr. Chapin."

"Smoking or no?"

"No. The son of a bitch may drive up my cholesterol, but he won't give me cancer. I've had my fill of hospitals after Charles."

I said there was a place I hadn't tried down the street from the MGM Grand. "It should be quiet. People who lost the rent don't whoop it up. We can meet there."

She got the name of the restaurant and the location and said six-thirty. "If you get there early, go down the street and put down fifty for me on seven."

"Red or black?"

"What you think?" She could still put on the Twelfth Street twang when she wanted to. "Don't bring flowers."

"How about a Hummel?"

"What's a Hummel?"

"A kewpie doll with a pedigree. Bum joke. Will I know you?"

"You're still a detective, right?"

When we were through talking I sat thinking for a little while, about a Detroit with an annual homicide rate approaching four figures and a man in the mayor's office that had cost the city a million dollars to redecorate to his taste. There'd been plenty of work in those days, with cops moonlighting as contract killers and jealous wives looking for their husbands with magnums in their handbags. When I'd had enough nostalgia I called to reserve a table for two in nonsmoking and did a little investigative work not related to the Stutch case until noon. Then I went out looking for a place that served underdone Brussels sprouts for lunch. I had a hankering.

When I came out picking my teeth a caramel-colored Chevy was parked behind my Cutlass on the street with someone smoking a cigarette on the passenger's side. The visor was down and I couldn't see his face. It was only worth noticing because I sometimes do that when I'm watching for someone and I want the idly curious passersby to think I'm waiting for the driver to come back from an errand.

A few blocks later I spotted a caramel-colored Chevy in my rearview mirror, three lengths behind and a lane over. There was no passenger and the driver's face was just a blank oval in front of the headrest.

It didn't mean anything. It's a popular color and there are more American-made cars in the city than anything else except one-way streets and liquor stores. Just because I was brought up on Steve McQueen movies I took several shortcuts and a couple of long ones, nicked a yellow light on Michigan, and looked for the car. It wasn't there.

# CHAPTER

# ELEVEN

As it happened I didn't get the chance to bet on the black seven or any other number. A squirt in a ballcap was waiting in my reception room to deliver a summons on behalf of a deadbeat dad I'd flushed out of a woodpile six months before, and I was on the telephone with a lawyer all afternoon getting out of it. His fee ate up what I'd earned on the job. No one sues you over the cases you can't close. It's hell on incentive.

I got to the restaurant ten minutes late, but still ahead of Iris. That much about her hadn't changed. An aristocratic hostess seated me out of the main traffic path and a chirpy young waitress wearing a necktie with Yosemite Sam on it brought me a double Scotch. I was stirring the ice when Iris drifted in.

The clientele was mostly the MTV generation, black-dyed hair and clothes from the Morticia Addams line, so she didn't turn as many heads as she would have among the general population, but she didn't slip in under the radar either. She wore a cherry-red blazer with suede pumps to match, an ivory silk skirt, and a turban that might have been made from the same bolt of cloth, at one time available only to members of the Egyptian royal family. She didn't wear a blouse. The dusting of freckles slightly lighter than her medium-brown skin spilled like gold dust into the shadow where the blazer's lapels met. I knew where it ended, but that had been a long time ago, when there were still canals on Mars. She looked like Cleopatra after a makeover.

I rose and she made a little purring growl deep in her throat and hugged me tight. She wore no scent, which didn't mean she had none. She smelled as clean as Kilimanjaro.

Keeping her hands on my upper arms, she pushed back for an objective view. "You haven't aged a minute. What's your secret?"

"Choosing liars for friends. You look like a new car."

"Today I feel like an '83 Pacer. My past came up in the deposition. It was like drowning and seeing my life flash in front of my eyes. It got an X rating."

"I think it's NC-17 now."

"Who gives a shit? I spent most of it in sweaty little rooms filled with smoke. I ought to look like a Virginia ham."

"I just came off four hours with a lawyer. That makes me an all-day sucker. What are you drinking?"

"Whatever's open. In a bowl."

I caught the waitress' eye while Iris was seating herself and ordered another double Scotch. When we were alone, Iris placed a red handbag on the corner of the table. It made a thump.

"That sounds heavier than a twenty-five," I said.

"Thirty-two. I traded up after Mr. Chapin. I've got CCW permits in Michigan and Ohio. My life's been threatened so many times I just tell the cops to use the same report and plug in new names. When I bother to call them at all."

"Husbands?"

"Wives, too. I don't counsel battered men but I refer them to people who do. Then there are the women who start remembering all the sweet little things once they've healed up. To hear them tell it I've broken up more happy homes than I did when I hooked. I don't keep a cat anymore. They nailed one to a tree in the yard and wrung the other's neck and threw it through my bedroom window."

"Why do you stick?"

"Why do you? That's not a razor scratch on your cheek. Looks like someone's class ring."

"Hood ornament. I got lost and wandered into Iroquois Heights."

She shuddered, without affectation. "Aunt Beryl used to tell us horror stories about that place, just to keep us on John R. I hoped when Detroit started sweeping the ordnance off the streets they'd pick there to blow it up."

"It would take at least that. The dirty cops need somewhere to go, and the Heights is as far as their beer bellies will take them." I swirled my cubes around the glass. "How is old Beryl? Is there an alumni newsletter?"

"I heard she's in a nursing home in Lansing. Probably organizing the geriatric talent and smuggling in Viagra to keep up the demand, among other things. Word gets around. It's a small community and getting smaller. AIDS scared off all the customers with anything to lose. What's left is barely human and not quite animal. I got out under the wire."

Young Lady Yosemite brought Iris her drink and waited while she read the menu. Iris had developed fine lines around her eyes and a crease at one corner of her mouth that I might have mistaken for a dimple if I hadn't known her when she didn't have it. Apart from that she could have passed for ten years younger than she was. It had been nothing but gale-force winds for her since bloomers, and all they'd managed to do was wear her smooth, like a ship's figurehead carved from amber.

"I'll have the rib-eye," she said. "Blood rare, with a baked potato."

"What dressing would you like on your salad?"

"Iceberg lettuce?"

"Romaine." The waitress sounded offended.

"No salad then. If I get the craving I'll munch on a dandelion in the parking lot." She handed back the menu.

I ordered fettuccini and another Scotch. When the waitress left I said, "Tough day in court?"

"No serious complaints. When they're suing me they're not throwing their wives and sweethearts through glass doors." She smiled. "You'll make it up to her. You've always been generous to working girls."

"You haven't seen me when I'm going my own expenses."

That made it business. She sipped her drink, set it down, and folded her hands on the table. She wore no rings or other jewelry except a tiny gold heart on a chain around her neck, an old trinket I remembered well. "I'm not sure I can give you Constance Glendowning. Two weeks ago she couldn't face anything in pants. Last week she started to thaw toward the son of a bitch that put her in the shelter to begin with."

"It happens."

"It shouldn't. Not since Betty Friedan. She's got an education, computer skills. They need updating, but she isn't one of those Depression wives who can't balance a bloody checkbook without running back to Andy Capp. What do you think of this?" She touched a finger to the crease at the corner of her mouth.

"It makes you look a little like Drew Barrymore."

"Thirty-six months ago I looked like Freddy Krueger. Mr. Chapin threw an ice-crusher at me. Three thousand bucks' worth of oral surgery. He's still paying it off; that was part of the settlement. When he pays. I'll go back to him, too, someday. With a chainsaw."

"I didn't know they still made ice-crushers."

"Back then I didn't know they still made Chapins. Now I

know it's a growth industry. Anyway, a few days ago, Constance finally started to get angry—partly for what Glendowning did to
her, partly because of what he might have started doing to her son
if she didn't get out when she did. I'd like that to continue. Your
taking her to see someone about an inheritance might set her
back."

"He's Glendowning's son too."

"Well, you know what the man said when his neighbor tried
to stop him from shooting his ducks: 'They're my ducks.'"

"Glendowning isn't in this."

"Not the point. She's living in the present finally, thinking
about the future. You're talking about taking her back to the past.
Now that I've said that I'm sure I can't give her to you."

"This accreditation you've got," I said. "That make you her
legal guardian?"

"It doesn't have to, Amos. The house is built to last. And I've
got friends on the local Domestic Violence Unit. Those cops are
like dogs: One year there is like seven anywhere else on the force."

We were still looking at each other when the waitress came
with bread. She set down the basket noiselessly and retreated without a word.

I said, "The inheritance is from Leland Stutch."

The ice-crusher had killed a nerve or something; that corner of
her mouth remained motionless while a twitch shot through the
rest. She raised her glass and took another sip. The effort of moving slowly would have been less plain to someone who didn't know
her.

"Those lawyers take their time when it comes to making someone else rich," she said finally. "How long's he been in the ground?"

"It isn't even the lawyers' idea to include Constance in the circle. Stutch's widow hired me to find her and her mother. It seems
the old pirate had a late-life fling and sprouted a whole new limb
on the family tree."

She made that same cockeyed twitch. "That's the problem with having too much money for too many years. You get to thinking you're outside the reach of the laws of nature. How much are we talking about?"

"How many zeroes does it take to make it all right with you?"

"Go to hell. If it's just four it means a whole new life for Constance and Matthew, separate from Glendowning's. Money buys everything."

"It will be more than four. If she wants to get a blood-and-tissue test and take it to a jury, it could be seven, but Matthew will be out of college when it's finished, by which time all the lawyers will be up to their briefs in Porsches. It might be seven anyway. Stutch made most of his principal when the IRS was still a gleam in Woodrow Wilson's eye."

Our meals came. Iris made a test cut on her steak to make sure the blood was running and shot the waitress a smile from the hip, which sent her away on a pink cloud. She'd forgotten my drink and didn't give me the chance to remind her. There was a lesson in that, but I'd hang on to it the same way I remembered my high school French. Anyway the fettuccini was good.

"I'll talk to her," Iris said between bites. "I'll call you. If she agrees to a meeting I want to be there. Leland Stutch. I'll be damned. If that creep husband tries to come in for any part of it, I'll put Mr. Chapin farther back in the line for that chainsaw."

"How long's the line?"

"Amos, you can't see the end." She buttered her baked potato. "Did you get a chance to play that number at the Grand?"

"I got hung up, sorry."

"Just as well. I'm lucky at roulette; it makes up a little for the rest of my life. If I hit it big I might retire. Where would the women go then?"

"To you."

"I wouldn't count on it. There's no telling how long this humanitarian streak will last. Prostitution didn't take. I crapped out on paradise, and you know what happened when I went for the white picket fence and two-point-five kids. Who was it said you can only go so far in one direction?"

"I think it was Columbus."

"Yes, and look at all the trouble he caused. What about you? When you put in for your license, did you think you'd still be doing the same thing all these years later?"

"I didn't think about it. It beat where I was when I got the idea."

"I'll bite. Where?"

"In a hole, avoiding a flame-thrower." I twirled my fork in a pile of pasta. "Maybe when Constance's ship comes in she'll make you a donation."

"No, they only remember me when they go back to their men and wind up in the hospital. It's my fault for making the sons of bitches mad." She lifted her glass. "Self-pity. Who else if not us?"

I lifted my glass. It was empty.

When the check came she asked if I was going home.

"Probably. I'm not as lucky as you at roulette."

"Can I go with you?"

I hesitated, then continued counting out bills. "How do you feel about dust? The maid didn't show up this year."

"Just as long as the sheets are clean."

I overtipped the waitress in spite of the dry spell. On the way home with Iris close beside me, defying the seatbelt law, I checked the mirror for caramel-colored Chevies. She was right. I'd been going in one direction too long.

# TWELVE

"I KNOW WHAT I *SAID*, Mrs. Stainback. Listen to what I'm saying now. Well, ask her to come to the phone." Iris looked up at me. "I never let calls go through to residents. It's a decision I defend in court three or four times a year."

"Bill of Rights," I said. "What a bother."

"I'm peddling survival, not liberty." She bent her head to the receiver. "Hello, dear. How are you? Yes, I really want to know. I wouldn't have asked if I didn't."

She was sitting in the easy chair in the living room, wearing one of my shirts and nothing else. The tails came to mid-thigh. With her legs crossed, the long muscle in her right thigh stood out like insulated cable; all those trips up and down courthouse steps made owning a Stairmaster redundant. Her naked feet were long and slim, with high arches and clear polish on the nails.

She smiled thanks when I set a saucer of buttered toast and a mug of black coffee on the table beside the telephone, but she wasn't there. She was in the shelter in Monroe, telling Constance Glendowning about the Stutch inheritance, telling the story in detail as I'd told it to her and as if Constance hadn't heard it from her mother all the time she was growing up. All those depositions had trained her to park the emotions around the corner; she might have been discussing the previous fiscal year with her accountant.

I sat on the end of the old sofa that retained most of its stuffing, drinking coffee and admiring the view. She was wearing her hair short again, nearly as short as it had been when we'd met. It made her look younger than she'd looked in the turban. She'd grown leaner in the years since I'd last taken inventory, but not thin; last night had been like wrestling a mountain cat, only without as much bloodshed. The scratches would heal.

The receiver went into its cradle. "You heard?"

"I don't listen in on other people's telephone conversations."

"Balls. You were staring at my ass."

"I offered you a robe."

"Saying no to one thing is not saying yes to another."

"Objection," I said.

"On what grounds?"

I swallowed coffee and grinned.

"I had a good time too." She smiled back. "She wants the day to prepare little Matthew, who's been through a lot of changes lately for a three-year-old. Meet us at the shelter at six-thirty." She gave me the address. "Don't ring at the front door. There's a screened porch out back where residents receive visitors. Go around there."

I picked up a pen and wrote the address on the cover of *TV Guide*. "No Y chromosomes allowed inside the house, I guess."

"Only the nonthreatening kind. You know, sensitive and caring and probably not anatomically correct. Obviously, you don't qualify. Don't take that as a compliment. Big, good-looking brutes are the reason most of my residents are residents. A substitute mailman is enough to put them back several squares." She munched toast. "Decision's hers whether she'll come back to Detroit and with who. Whom? Fuck it. That's the deal, Amos. The money's important, but it's just paper if getting it undoes the progress she's made. If she doesn't want to go, that's the end."

"I hired on to find her, that's all. I'm fresh out of gunny sacks." I swirled my coffee to no good purpose. "She can go to her mother's first, if it'll help. Mrs. Stutch wants to see them both at once or not at all."

"They should have a lawyer."

"Come along. At this point you could pass the bar. They don't have to answer her offer right away. If Rayellen brings a lawyer, or asks them to sign a piece of paper, we'll each grab one of Constance's arms and haul her out of there."

She lifted her brows over her mug. "So it's Rayellen, is it?"

"I'm not trolling for millions, Iris. She's only had the other name a little while. Old Man Stutch had it all stretched out of shape a half-century before she was born."

"She's better-looking than I thought. You don't usually go on the defense so fast."

"I didn't get in my eight hours last night."

"Yes, you did." She started and glanced at her wrist. It was bare. "What time is it?"

I looked at the shelf clock that was older than the house. "Ten to eight."

"Damn it. I'm meeting the secretary of the county planning commission at nine. They want to rezone me out of business." She stood and brushed the crumbs off the shirt. Now the tails fell about her knees. Barefoot, she was a lot smaller than she was. "I parked at the MGM Grand. Do you think they've towed me?"

"They probably think you're still inside."

"Wish I had time to play that number. I feel lucky."

"I'll play it for you after I drop you off."

She came into my arms, warm and clean-smelling. "Would you? I'll split the take."

"What if we lose?"

"Too bad for you. It would be your Walker luck snagging up my kind."

We kissed. She tasted of coffee and tart strawberries. I hadn't served any strawberries.

We were moving onto another level when she planted her palms against my chest and pushed loose. "Uh-uh. Ten minutes of that and they'll put up a Speedway on my lot." She ran off to dress.

When she came out, makeup on, tucking a tendril of hair up under the turban, she looked fresh from the box. I drove her downtown and into the flashily lit parking deck at the Grand, where a black attendant in a red jacket with a gold crest took her claim ticket.

"Steel-gray Volvo, brother," Iris said. "Ten bucks if I'm behind the wheel in one minute. You got ten?" she asked me, as the attendant sprinted off.

I found a bill and held it out. "What if I didn't?"

"I'd dock him ten seconds. That's just an advance on what you owe me, sugar. Your gender, I mean." The West Indies was back in her speech; it had always been good for a fifty-dollar tip back on John R.

When she left, in just under a minute, I went into the jangling casino, past banks of senior citizens in pastel sweats working the slots with nothing on their faces but doom, and waited my turn at the roulette wheel. A floor man gave me the fisheye; in January an off-duty cop had shot himself in the Motor City Casino after a bad run of cards, and I must have looked like sad heat. I stepped up and put down the last of what I'd drawn on Rayellen Stutch's check on the black seven at roulette. It was gone faster than Iris.

Mrs. Campbell answered the telephone in Iroquois Heights. I had a mind's-eye glimpse of a map of the United States crisscrossed by red wires, describing a network made up of husbandless matrons running interference for their female employers. While I was waiting for my client to come on I dealt myself a Winston and contemplated the three bank calendars hanging on the wall opposite my desk, representing the months of March, April, and May. Free calendars were becoming rare. Before long it would cost me a little more to know where I'd been, where I was, and where I was going.

"Mr. Walker." She was panting.

"What is it this time?" I asked. "Running with the bulls or heavy dusting?"

"Nautilus. The wealthier you are, the more you pay to sweat. Do I take this call to mean you've rounded up all the relatives?"

"I caught a break. The woman who runs the shelter where Constance is staying is an old acquaintance. I'm meeting with them both tonight. If I don't scare her off, you'll see her tomorrow. Maybe as early as tonight, but I haven't checked in yet with Carla Witowski."

"Call me as soon as you know. I'm hosting a fundraiser at the civic center for a new library at eight. I'll need time to call and cancel."

"I didn't know anyone in the Heights read books."

"Don't be a snob. Connor Thorpe roped me into it. He's invested a lot in the city. GM is counting on tax breaks for its new industrial center."

"What's a security man got to do with investments?"

"For years he was the man you had to see first if you wanted to run something past Leland. He has a lot of friends here. I guess someone on the board thought it wouldn't make sense to send in a Baby Buster business grad instead. I don't pretend to understand all the politics. All I need to do is look good in a low-cut evening gown. That's why the Nautilus and everything else."

"I didn't know being rich was such a tough job."

"Staying rich is. Will you call?"

I said I'd call. "This a family affair, or are you bringing the troops?"

"If you mean my attorneys, that comes later. Talking takes twice as long when people won't let you. I want it to be a pleasant experience. Mrs. Campbell will serve refreshments. In addition to her piano playing, she's a world-class chef."

"She isn't an ice sculptor, by any chance?"

"I don't know. I can ask. Why?"

"A life-sized study of your late husband might be a good thing for Carla to go at with an ice pick. That would guarantee a pleasant experience for one of you."

"I'll ask."

I cut the connection and dialed another number.

"Witowski residence." It was Carla's low tone. Her dog was coughing in the background.

I identified myself and said I was meeting with her daughter that night. She took in her breath, then snapped at Moo-goo to shut up. The coughing stopped. "Is she all right? That creature she's married to—"

"I haven't spoken to her yet, but she's in good hands. You can ask her yourself when you see her. Mrs. Stutch wants to meet with you both at the same time."

"I want—I'd like to see her before I walk into that room." She stopped short of making it a request.

"I'll put it on the list. It's up to her. You were right about her husband; she's taken her boy and left him. Being right can be a hard thing to be forgiven for."

"It's never worth the cost, Mr. Walker. I don't know why it's so important to so many people when all it does is cause pain."

There wasn't a thing in that I could use, so I let it lie. I told her the meeting with Mrs. Stutch could take place that evening or more likely tomorrow. "If it's tomorrow, Constance will need a place to stay overnight. If I leave her in the shelter she may change her mind."

"I'll have her old room ready."

"The boy may be with her. In fact, he probably will be. At this point you probably couldn't pry them apart."

"It's a queen-size bed. There's a rollaway in the basement I can bring up in case Matthew's such the little man he won't share a mattress with his mother."

I grinned at the calendars. "You sounded like a real granny there."

"I hope so, Mr. Walker. I need the running start."

"Let's not lose sight of the main objective," I said. "This means a fresh start anywhere in the world if you both play it right."

"It would be a fresh start anyway. Oh, my." She sobbed out the last.

I said I'd call when I knew the plan and we exchanged good-byes.

I closed out a small flock of cases whose clients didn't care much when they were resolved or even if, without moving any far-ther from the telephone than my boarding-house reach to the file cabinet. That took me up to the lunch hour. When I got back, there were no Hindu pashas waiting in the reception room, no sea captains cackling over precious bundles, no exotic women or deaf hunchbacks or flashy gangsters or tragic clowns. There were just the same aging magazines and a little pile of plaster dust on the rug from a hole in the ceiling, chewed by a squirrel under the impres-sion we could both make a living from what was inside.

I let myself into the war room and sat down behind the desk and smoked a cigarette and waited for the telephone to ring. I smoked another, checked to see if the telephone was working, and waited some more. I was beginning to miss the squirt with the summons. I locked up finally and went home, where it was sup-posed to be quiet. Iris's empty coffee mug and the saucer containing the ruins of her breakfast were still on the table next to the easy chair. I carried them into the kitchen with no expression on my face and rinsed them off in the sink.

There was nothing on television at that hour except a couple of shrill talk shows and a children's program featuring an animated tugboat. I watched the tugboat. It made me feel like I was having a sick day, so I switched it off after ten minutes. I shuffled through the books stacked on the coffee table, selected one I'd been nibbling at for the better part of a month, and sat down to finish it. It was the true-life account of an intrepid band of adventurers who decided to climb a mountain in Tibet, only the mountain didn't feel like being climbed that day, so it knocked them all down and climbed them instead. Most of the corpses were still up there on the north face, brittle as Pixie Stix. It gave me a chill, so I took a hot shower and shaved for the second time that day and put on fresh clothes; I almost pulled on a heavy turtleneck, then remembered it was April and reached for a long-sleeved polo in brushed cotton.

I called for the correct time, reset the clock on the shelf and wound it, but that didn't make it go any faster. I walked around, touching furniture. I needed another hobby. There didn't seem to be much point in that one. Mountain climbing, maybe.

I made an early supper out of a can of chili and a couple of knuckle bones, washed it down with cold beer, and did the dishes, including those from that morning. After Everest they were just dirty dishes. When I finished it was five o'clock—rush hour everywhere else, meditation time on the freeways serving Detroit, under perpetual construction, like Penelope's shawl or a hepatic liver. I had an hour and a half, just time enough to make the thirty-minute drive south. I got the car out of the garage and pointed it toward Monroe, Iris, and Constance Glendowning. I didn't even feel the wind pick up and change directions. My mind was on the top of the mountain.

# CHAPTER

# THIRTEEN

DUSK WAS GATHERING as I entered the city of Monroe, but the streets weren't glowing, a positive sign. A near-meltdown at Enrico Fermi, the world's first nuclear energy plant, at nearby Lagoona Beach came within atoms of wiping out Southeastern Michigan in 1966, along with part of Ohio and the entire fishing industry on Lake Erie. The plant closed soon after, but cloned itself into Fermi II, and a generation of Monrovians had come to their majority uncertain about how much time they had before the next—and last—incident. Pedestrians walk the small-town streets with a cringing gait, the way West Berliners used to when they entered the shadow of the Wall.

The house was big and solid and old, just as Jerry Zangara had described it, and as ugly as they knew how to build them when function capped the list of priorities. Yellowish tile like discolored dentures covered the frame and a double row of narrow guillotine windows marched across the porchless front, their blinds drawn irregularly, as if stifling yawns. An arched roof, contributed at a later time, sheltered whoever rang the doorbell, while any companions he might have brought with him stood out in the rain and snow. Fortunately it wasn't raining or snowing, and anyway the front door wasn't for me.

The driveway was paved, but a dozen winters of frost and thaw had sunk holes in the earth beneath, scooping out bowl-shaped depressions in the asphalt, which had then crumbled. Weeds had spiked up through the cracks, and patches of sand and gravel showed like naked skin through ripped seams. A faint stain was still visible where automobile fluid had soaked into the dirt. This was what had aroused Jerry's suspicion: evidence that Constance Glendowning's incontinent Chrysler had parked there before someone whisked it into the garage out back and out of sight. The grass was cut but untreated, with bare patches and fistfuls of quackgrass growing more healthily than the seeded turf, the way it always seemed to do. The place had been someone's private home about the time of the invention of the electric iron, but now it had the stale frayed anonymous look of an institution.

Iris's steel-gray Volvo, five years old but dingless and detailed recently, was parked in front of the garage. That put some warmth into the location. I laid my hand on the hood on my way past. The metal felt cool. She'd been there awhile, arguing the case, probably.

The back porch was an add-on with freshly painted wood siding and a roof that had been reshingled sometime in the last year. It was open on three sides and screened in black nylon. I could see shapes moving around inside, but that was all. I was pretty sure the shapes could see me a lot more clearly.

I climbed two wooden steps and raised my knuckles to rap on the screen door frame. A hook squeaked out of an eye and I retreated to the bottom step to keep the screen from hitting me in the face. A small woman in a gray sweatsuit and running shoes with soles as thick as snow tires hung on to the door handle. She had on rimless glasses and straight gray hair chopped off just short of her shoulders like Montezuma's. The eyes behind the weak lenses were white all around the irises, like a convict's caught in the shaft of a searchlight mounted atop a tower.

"It's all right, Ms. Stainback." This was Iris's voice. "He's the man I told you about."

Ms. Stainback swiveled out of the way, like a second door. I stepped up and inside. A moth slid in around the edge of the door before she could get it closed and threw itself against a bare bulb burning overhead, hitting it with a tink. It went into a flat spin, made a six-point landing on the floorboards, and lay there without twitching a feeler until one of Ms. Stainback's thick rubber soles came down on it with a crunch.

Iris went up on her toes to wind her arms about me and kiss my cheek. The only time she did that in company was when she was putting on a show. As she came back down, one hand brushed my back where the curved butt of my .38 Chief's Special stuck up above the belt holster under my Windbreaker. Her nod was almost nonexistent. She'd changed into a white blouse, loose pleated slacks, and stout loafers. You never know what attention you might attract when you remove a resident from a shelter for battered women, or whether you'll have to run away from it or shoot at it.

"Amos Walker, Constance Glendowning. You met Ms. Stainback over the phone."

The back porch was the homiest thing about the place. An old rug the color of burlap, its pattern trod into the background, had lain on the floor long enough to assume the shape of the boards beneath. There were a couple of wicker chairs painted white, with coarse faded cushions, and a four-passenger swing suspended by chains from the roof. The thin blonde woman sitting on the edge of one of the chairs looked older than her engagement picture, and older than she was. The smile she cranked on for my benefit was largely mechanics. Her eyes were cloudy, as from drugs or too many bad memories brought back all at once, or maybe they were just naturally cloudy; you can't analyze a person you just met without some kind of gauge. She wore a denim work shirt, old jeans, and black combat boots, the kind teenagers wear. The outfit looked borrowed.

"It's a pleasure." I let her lay her hand in my paw. She withdrew it almost before contact.

"Yes," she said.

"And this young man is Matthew," said Iris. "Matthew, say hello to Mr. Walker. He's an old friend."

"Hello." Matthew stopped swinging to look up at me with David Glendowning's eyes. He had the swing to himself, sitting in the middle with his short legs sticking straight out ending in tennis shoes too big for his feet. His hair was in straight black bangs and he looked skinny and undernourished in corduroy pants worn shiny in the knees and a T-shirt with a creature on it I recognized from the posters in his room in Toledo. They always look like they're not getting enough to eat when they're going through a growth spurt. His expression was grave but not at all frightened. The art of dissembling had come to him more quickly than most.

"Hi, Matthew. Or do you prefer Matt?"

"My daddy calls me Matt," he said with contempt, and resumed swinging. It's tough not to try too hard with a kid. That's why I don't take family-service cases.

"Ms. Stainback, would you put on a fresh pot of coffee?" Iris asked.

The woman in sweats removed a tray containing two stained cups from a low rattan table and went through a second screen door into the house, circling wide around me. She eased the door shut to keep the spring from slamming it.

"Sit down, Amos."

"Where will you sit?"

"With my boyfriend, if he'll let me." Iris smiled down at Matthew, who scooched himself over without hesitation. She sat close against him and put an arm around his thin shoulders. He struggled, but when she let go he stayed put. Men of all ages were just Legos to Iris.

I settled into the other chair and crossed my legs. I felt like smoking but I didn't; David Glendowning smoked. I let Iris start.

"Constance is afraid this is some trick by her husband to flush her out. I told her you can be trusted, but he can be sneaky. He's a real charmer when he isn't drinking, she says."

"You couldn't prove it by me," I said. "Maybe this will help." I got Connor Thorpe's letter of authorization from my wallet and held it out. Constance hesitated, then took it and unfolded it. The paper rattled as she turned it toward the light.

"I don't know who this is." She gave it back.

I said, "He handles security for the Big Three. Leland Stutch gave him his start. He's the one who put me on to Rayellen Stutch. If you think he'd run interference for a union man, you don't know much about Detroit history. I can put in a call, have you talk to Mrs. Stutch yourself, but she couldn't prove who she is over the telephone. If you won't trust me—and there's no reason you should, unless you trust Iris—you're better off staying where you are."

"I'm only thinking about Matthew," Constance said. "David's crazy about him. He's a good father, I've always known that. I'm afraid he'll try to take my son from me. I guess that makes me pretty selfish." She lifted her chin. When she did that, the resemblance to Carla Willard Witowski was undeniable. She was Leland's granddaughter.

Iris crossed her legs and spent some time smoothing the crease on her slacks. She had a whole new approach to clothing since she'd stopped working naked. "A mother doesn't get to be called selfish until her children are grown. Mr. Walker and I go back almost to before you were born. Neither one of us trusts anyone, that's why we trust each other. I won't lay a guilt trip on you; if nothing in you says you should do this, you're right not to do it."

"I don't know." Constance's voice was barely audible.

Ms. Stainback returned with fresh cups on the tray and a steaming glass carafe filled with coffee as black as printers' ink. There were packages of sugar and Sweet 'n' Low and a black-and-white creamer shaped like a Guernsey. I waited until everyone had his cup the way he wanted it, then I took a sip. I could have floated my keys in mine. Iris liked everything strong.

"There's a point we haven't discussed," I said. "Mrs. Stutch's part of the inheritance pays her thirteen million a year. We're not talking about toothpick money. It means food and clothing and a house—at least one house—and Harvard for Matthew, if he doesn't flunk algebra; Princeton if he does and they need a new library. It means independence. Neither one of you has to see his father ever again unless you feel like asking your lawyers to offer him visitation rights."

"I wouldn't want to keep them apart," Constance said. "A boy needs his father. I realize that's not politically correct, but I happen to believe it. And David needs his son. If I denied him that, I wouldn't be any better than he is when he's been drinking. Iris said you saw him. Is he all right?" She turned her cloudy eyes on me.

Matthew was watching me too. I drank again.

"He isn't in good shape. He's just starting to realize how badly he screwed up. I'm supposed to know something about people. I don't think he was acting, but I didn't marry him."

"He wants the money."

Everyone on the porch looked up at Ms. Stainback, except Matthew; he was admiring his shoes. The woman stood with her back to the door leading into the house, ready to repel invaders, of which she would acknowledge only one likely candidate among those present. She was glaring at me as if I were David Glendowning.

"He doesn't know about the money," I said. "Not Stutch money. I told him her signature was needed in the matter of an inheritance. He may put it together once he sobers up. You told him the family story?" I looked at Constance.

"It started a fight once. He told me if I couldn't get it to shut the hell up about it." She was stroking her right arm with her left, as if she were cold. I remembered her mother doing the same thing.

"Mommy said hell." Matthew was alert.

"I'm sorry, darling. Mommy was bad."

"Mommy's bad."

"Men only want two things," Ms. Stainback said. "Money's one."

"I dealt in both. If that's all there was to them, I'd have finished up in a dumpster with a needle in my arm." Iris watched her coolly. "If you can't stick to subjects you know, go back in and make the beds."

Ms. Stainback stood still, as if someone had struck her across the face with something that stung and she was afraid if she moved it would happen again. Then, very slowly, her face fell apart. She turned quickly, tore open the screen door, and went through it, not bothering this time to keep it from shutting behind her with a bang. Presently from the other end of the house there came a low hooting, the sound of a swamp bird in distress.

I got out a cigarette then, just to be doing something with my fingers. "I miss her already. As long as she was here I knew where I couldn't turn my back."

"I'll apologize to her later," Iris said. "I get tired of her sometimes. She got a raw deal from men starting with her father, and she gets to acting like she was the only one. But then it's all she has."

Matthew said, "She smells funny."

Iris nudged him. "That's because she's afraid. You'd smell that way too."

"I ain't 'fraid."

Constance began laughing. A high shrill note ran through the laughter like a violin string stretched to the snapping point. Iris jerked her head around, startled. But it was just the tension of the last few minutes. Constance was laughing for real.

"I'm glad, Matthew," she said, when the peak was past. "Mommy's glad you're not afraid."

Matthew laughed too, bouncing his feet up and down. Iris hugged him to her with both arms and grinned at me with her chin on top of his head. "Matthew, how would you like to go for a ride in a very old car?"

# FOURTEEN

CONSTANCE WASN'T UP for a meeting with Rayellen Stutch that night. When I said her mother was offering her old room, she rubbed her arms for a moment, then: "Why not? If she promises not to run down David in front of Matthew."

I said I'd pass the message along. While mother and child were getting ready upstairs, Iris checked out the living room for residents, then let me in to use the telephone. The place had a community-room look: worn upholstery and picked-over magazines. Above the old-fashioned radiator hung a print made from a painting of stylized bodies dancing against a background of tropical colors, lifting the gloom a little. That would be Iris's contribution.

I kept the calls brief. Carla Witowski was breathless with anticipation. Mrs. Stutch was just out of breath; she'd done three miles on the treadmill before dressing for the fundraiser downtown. We made the appointment for tomorrow at noon. "Mrs. Campbell will serve lunch," she said.

Constance had put on a sweater and gotten Matthew into a

light cotton jacket and an Indians cap with Chief Wahoo on the front. He was dragging an overnight bag nearly as big as he was.

"He insisted on carrying it," his mother said. "He'd pull his arms out of their sockets before he'd admit it was too heavy. I guess I'll never understand men."

I looked at her. With her hair tied back out of the way and a flush on her cheeks, she looked younger than she had on the porch, her eyes less clouded. I said, "You look like your parole came through."

She glanced around. Iris had gone into the kitchen to make her peace with Ms. Stainback. Constance leaned in and lowered her voice. "Iris has been wonderful, but this place is depressing. The residents are so angry. I think it's that woman."

"Shell shock," I said. "You got out in time. Not everybody does."

Matthew said, "I want to see the old car."

"Pipe down and I'll let you turn the crank."

Iris came out, putting on a long-tailed shirt that reminded me of that morning. "Well, she won't quit tonight. I offered her minimum wage."

We went outside. It was a mild night and there was an early firefly or two winking turquoise out beyond the reach of the street-light. I struck the bottom of my awesome well of experience when it came to putting a three-year-old boy in the Cutlass. I test-tugged the safety belts in the rear seat, which hadn't been used since before the Kent State Massacre, and when they didn't come apart in my hands I left the business of anchoring Matthew in his booster seat to his mother. He sniffed the cigarettes in the air and said the car smelled like Daddy. When Constance slid in next to him I looked at Iris. "A shotgun would make me feel a little less like the family chauffeur."

"Thought you'd never ask," she said. "I've always wanted to see how the other half lives. Did you know three quarters of this country's wealth is in the hands of the rich?"

"Sure. If it were in the hands of the poor it wouldn't make any sense."

She shook a finger in my face. "You're a Republican."

"No, ma'am. I'm Episcopalian."

As I rumbled the engine to life, Matthew asked his mother, "Are they married?"

"I don't think so, honey. They just like to fight."

We headed up I-75. Matthew approved of the acceleration; he made a noise of pure joy as I slid into the pocket between a tanker and an RV hauling an inboard on a trailer, then swung out to pass the RV. I figured he'd been conceived in Detroit. Iris found a retro country station Constance liked on the radio, and we listened to Jerry Reid for four miles.

Traffic was light. The evening rush had been over for an hour, it was the middle of the week, and with the Tigers in the cellar nobody was in a hurry to get to the ballpark, especially the new one. I let the speed freaks take out their payment frustrations on the fast lane and tooled along at a safe ten miles over the limit.

Approaching Downriver a pickup got on my tail and stuck there like a decal. Its square headlamps were set just high enough to blind me bouncing off the rearview mirror. I flipped it to nightside and slowed down to let the truck pass. It crept a little closer, then slowed too.

I turned off the radio. Iris picked up on it. "What we got?"

"Could be nothing. They give out driver's licenses to the first hundred callers." I fed the 455 some gas. The pickup fell behind a length, then closed the gap. I could hear its engine winding up. He'd had some work done on it after it left the factory.

"It's David!" Constance's voice was almost a shriek.

The truck was pale in the reflection from my taillights, with rounded retro fenders, riding high on big tires. It could have been a white Ram. I'd seen one parked in Glendowning's garage.

Something bit into my right thigh just behind the knee; Iris's fingernails.

"Cheer up." I pushed down the pedal.

All four barrels dumped open and the big block pounced ahead. After a microsecond the rest of the car caught up, a stretching action, like the coaches falling in behind a locomotive. The bubbling acceleration vibrated in the soles of my feet. The truck slipped back. Then it began to come on all over again.

I nearly climbed up the trunk of a Ford Fiesta with dirty taillights, invisible until my headlamps threw its shadow forty feet ahead. Iris's nails drew blood, but I cranked the wheel and skinned past it in the passing lane, my chrome literally tickling its left rear fender. This brought me bumper-to-bumper with a U-Haul van, but instead of braking I cranked right and cut in front of the Ford, the Cutlass rocking on its suspension as I straightened out. The complaining bleat of the Ford's horn reached me with the remote impersonality of a gong struck underwater; there was already a quarter-mile separating us. I glanced at the speedometer, just for entertainment. We were coming up on a hundred—whoops, nope, we were past it.

In the mirror, square headlamps separated themselves from those of the U-Haul, like a cell dividing, and slid in front of the little Ford. For most of a mile, the Ram maintained the distance between us, neither closing nor falling back. Then it began to creep closer. From that point on the gap narrowed steadily. I looked at the speedometer again, on the hunch I'd blown the radiator hose or thrown a rod and was losing speed, but the needle was edging past 102. Glendowning had to have eliminated the anti-pollution equipment, added ballast to the pickup's box, struck a deal with Satan for immunity to the laws of physics. It had been thoughtful of whoever had customized the truck to remember to leave room for a driver in that rolling power plant.

"Amos," Iris said. It sounded like the opening of a prayer.

"There's a state police post in Trenton. Highway eighty-five. Keep an eye out for the sign. I don't know the exit number." I raised my voice for Constance. "Hang on tight to Matthew. I don't trust that belt."

"Maybe we should pull over." Her voice was thin and tight.

"No." Iris.

"We're just making him madder."

Iris twisted in her seat. "Listen. That's not David. It's a two-ton bullet, and it's already been fired. You don't stop to talk things over with a bullet. Do what the man says and we'll be out of this in a minute."

A sign flashed in my headlamps: TRENTON ONE MILE EXIT 28. The diamond-shaped state highway emblem showed and vanished. I eased up on the accelerator. I remembered it was a short exit ramp.

Glendowning read my mind. The black pavement between us shrank. The front of the heavy truck, with its curving lines and open grille, looked medieval, like a battering-piece with a crude face carved into it.

"Don't slow down! Speed up!" Iris was shouting.

"I won't make the exit."

"Screw the exit! Pour it on!"

I pushed the pedal the rest of the way. The needle climbed past 105, 108, 110. I'd never had it up that high. A thirty-year-old engine was prone to overheating at unaccustomed tachs.

In the back seat, Constance was making soothing shooshing noises, as much for herself as for Matthew. Hell, for me, too; I nearly lost it when a billowing plastic bag bounded across the lane and I thought it was a small deer. My tires screeched on the swerve and I only kept the rear end from fishtailing by main might on the steering wheel.

112, 115, 118, 120. And the Ram was gaining. The curly-horned emblem on the front of the hood was square in the middle of the rearview mirror.

"*Amos!*"

The second syllable was a scream. Iris's nails tore through the fabric covering my thigh. The benign front end of a Geo Prizm came up level with the windshield, with another stacked atop it. I hadn't seen the Christmas-tree lights of the haulaway trailer until I was almost aboard it.

I couldn't see if there was anything in the left lane. I tore the wheel right. I think my left front fender clipped one of the trailer's taillights, perched on a stalk on the corner of its bumper. Iris screamed again. Constance and Matthew screamed too. I joined them. I read the sign in a flash just before the post buckled the hood of the Cutlass and fissured the windshield:

TRENTON EXIT
MICHIGAN STATE POLICE POST 51

I didn't have time to appreciate the irony. Wrestling with a locked wheel, I heard gravel crunching, then grass swishing. Then the world stopped with a crush and blackness fell across me like a telephone pole.

# FIFTEEN

During the next few minutes—or hours, or days—my car entertained more visitors than it had anytime since it was in the showroom. David Glendowning showed up and poked around; so did Rayellen Stutch and Connor Thorpe and Ralph Nader, clucking about how unsafe my machine was. Some of the drop-ins had animals' heads on human bodies, and there was an assortment of griffins, sphinxes, and pesky fairies flitting about to vary the mix, along with the Taco Bell Chihuahua and Mr. Auerbach, my high school shop teacher, smelling as always of linseed oil and peppermint Schnapps.

"Walker," he said, "you're never going to make a first-class mechanic as long as you keep trying to put on a timing belt any old way. You want to be a grease monkey your whole life?"

Of course, I might have dreamt some of it.

The last time I woke up I got sore. Alternating strobes of red and blue light refracted through the fissures in the windshield, and a collision of distorted voices racketing out of someone's two-way radio stuck an icepick through my ear and stirred it around inside my skull.

I said, "I can't hear you with the bandsaw going, Mr. Auerbach. Anyway, you're dead. You passed out smoking a cigarette in 1969 and they buried you in a closed coffin."

"Don't move, fella. Wait for EMS. We don't know what's busted inside."

This wasn't Auerbach's voice; the German accent was missing, as well as the Schnapps. I blinked at a deep black face with regular features and kind tired eyes, movie-star handsome, under a flat felt brim and a shield bearing the Michigan State seal. He was leaning through the open door on the driver's side with his flashlight beam slanting away from my eyes.

I remembered the exit sign. The icepick in my skull poked out through the back of my neck when I turned my head. Iris was sitting calmly in the passenger's seat, still strapped in, a reassuring sight. A shaft of white, thrown by a search beam, lay across her left shoulder. Only it wasn't made entirely of light. The light shone flatly off a slab of dull steel with a pitted surface. The end of a guardrail had punched through the windshield and across the top of the seat, impaling the car like a giant harpoon. And I knew then why I hadn't noticed the pattern on Iris's shirt when she'd put it on for the trip. It looked purple when the blue light took its turn.

I lurched in my seat. My belt was still fastened, and when it resisted, the icepick stabbed my neck again and I fell back with blackness filling my head.

"Easy, I said. We don't want no more fatalities on this run."

The state cop kept his hand on me until I settled down, then withdrew his flash. Heavy feet slithered through tall grass going away. I let a minute go by—it might have been longer, I might have blacked out again—then groped for the release button on the belt. I made a careful inspection: arms, legs, ribs, collarbone, head. I had a knot on my forehead. I felt along the rim of the steering wheel and found the place where I'd caved it in. I'd been right not to trust the tension in my old seatbelts. Little cartoon lightning bolts shot out of my neck when I turned my head or tipped it back. Common whiplash. There was a whole chapter about it in Sam Spade's manual of home remedies for private eyes, right after the one on concussions.

There was nothing in it about decapitation.

I touched the back of Iris's hand where it rested between the seats. It felt cold. That was just shock, my shock. It takes hours for the body heat to drain, and I was pretty sure it hadn't been hours. I could still feel the pressure of her nails on my thigh. I squeezed the hand and withdrew mine. I had a hole through me as big as the Windsor Tunnel.

She'd accused me of being a Republican. Matthew had asked his mother if we were married.

Matthew.

Constance.

Pieces of memory were coming back, like lights clicking on in separate rooms. I'd had other passengers.

I couldn't twist my head around without pain, and behind it the lights clicking off; every time I lost consciousness, someone died. Moving slowly—I felt as if I'd gone over the falls in a barrel full of rocks—I drew up one leg, then the other, grasped the back of my seat, and pulled myself up onto my knees to peer into the back. Constance lay sprawled across the seat, her body covering Matthew's booster. I reached out and touched her arm. It felt warm through the open weave of her thin sweater. I grasped her upper arm and shook her gently. A noise came from her throat. She stirred and rolled half over. A claw-mark pattern of blood had dried down the right side of her face from a gash in the temple. The end of the guardrail that had killed Iris had grazed her.

The booster seat was empty. The two ends of the seatbelt lay loose inside. They weren't torn. The buckle had come open, or someone had opened it. I looked at the floor between the seats. It was in deep shadow. I groped through the darkness to the carpet. I didn't want to search too thoroughly. The guardrail had not gone through the back window. That meant the rest of Iris was still in the car.

I forced myself. On the floor my hand brushed something that was not Matthew. Blackness welled up. I hit the door handle hard and threw myself out.

My ankle turned. Pain swept up me like a sheet of flame. I raised the leg, crane fashion, and grasping the roof of the car worked my way toward the trunk. I was searching the ground to see if the boy had fallen out.

A hand grasped my shoulder. "I told you don't move. I seen folks walk around after a crash and laying dead an hour later."

It was the state cop. "There's a child," I said. "That's his mother in the back seat."

"She's unconscious, is all. Well, it may not be all. She took a hit in the head and I don't know what else. Let's go and sit down."

He laced an arm across my back and I leaned against him. His cruiser was parked broadside to the Cutlass with its doors open. He half-carried me there—me at one eighty-five stripped and one leg not doing anything to help—and lowered me onto the edge of the seat. The left side of the Cutlass was visible in his headlamps and spotlight. The frame was unbent and the engine probably hadn't been touched. Its lights were still on. It was skewered on the guardrail like a hog on a spit.

"I ain't seen one of these in years," the cop said. "These days they bury the ends of them rails in the ground, or bend them back so the cars just kind of scrape along the edge. They moved the ramp about fifteen years ago. I guess they just didn't get around to taking out the rail. I'm real sorry about your lady." He sounded real sorry. "It don't help much now, but it will later, so I'll say it: She never felt a thing."

I looked up at him. "How would you know?"

He nudged his hat back with a knuckle. He was six and a half feet and close to three hundred in a neatly pressed uniform and starting to get a paunch. It would be as hard as the rest of him. "Well, that's a point. I guess all the people who could tell you for sure couldn't tell you. But, mister, I seen more of these things than a human man should be able to stomach. I heard folks yelling, you know to look at them they ought to be dead and will be soon. Yelling and cussing so you want to draw down and put them out of it right there. I can't help but think this is better.

"I didn't see no boy. I saw the car seat, so I went looking. The doors weren't open when I got here and the windows was up, so he wasn't thrown out. He might of let himself out and went wandering. I called it in. I ain't been here but five minutes. You want to tell me what happened while we wait?"

I heard a siren far off, and then the insistent airhorn, activated for the benefit of the slow-to-react.

"I was run off the road. Late-model Dodge Ram pickup, white. One of those cute retro jobs. I had it up to a hundred and twenty, trying to shake him, when I lost it."

"I don't guess you got the license number."

"You guess right."

True so far; I hadn't looked at the plate when I was in Glendowning's garage.

"Get a look at the driver?"

I saw Glendowning's face, but it had been tangled up with others, including a number of mythical beasts and one advertising gimmick. "Too dark."

"The white pickup squares with the call we got. That's the upside of all these cell phones. Makes up a little for all the soccer moms we mop up with the things stuck in their fists." He seemed to realize what he was saying. "I'm real sorry about that. I'm spending too much time alone these days, been pulling double shifts ever since my wife died."

"Sorry." I didn't give a damn about his wife. I fished the pack out of my shirt pocket. It was full of crushed paper and loose tobacco. I'd been wondering why my chest hurt. I must have hit the steering column at the same time I struck my head.

"That your wife in the front seat?" he asked.

"A friend."

"Good friend?"

"They're all good when you don't have many." I rattled the pack between my hands. "You're the second person tonight to ask if we were married."

"Yeah? Well, race differences don't mean nothing these days. There's some say they do, but I didn't see none of them in the crowd when I heard Dr. King speak in Cobo Hall. It's all in how people look at you." He inspected his big flashlight, flicked the switch on and off. "You a police officer? I ask on account of the gun."

I'd forgotten I had it, as uncomfortable a thing as it was to wear. That was a sign I'd been wearing it too often lately. It hadn't meant anything against two tons of Detroit steel. "Private. I've got a carry in my wallet, if you want to look at it."

"We can do that later. I figured it was something like that. You got too big a plant in that car for a civilian, and if you was a cop, the taxpayers'd be standing the bills. You need body work."

"You think?"

"That's just sheet-metal damage and glass. Anyway, it's not what I'm talking about. That right front fender's been banged up since Nixon."

"Private cop doesn't mean I went to private school. I get five hundred a day and bottle deposits. I worked sixty days last year."

"It ain't the expense. It's some kind of a cover. You look to me like a man that likes an edge."

"It's gotten me where I am." It came out nastier than intended; or maybe not so much more.

"You working tonight?"

He wasn't playing with the flashlight now. He wasn't a man to use the same piece of business twice. But he overdid the casual tone.

I read the surgeon general's warning on the pack. Smoking was endangering my fetus. "No. Just giving some friends a ride."

"Okay." The light show from the ambulance reflected off the shining black planes of his face. He raised his voice above the siren. "In a couple of minutes it won't be my business. When the first team gets it, they'll be all coffeed up and fresh as milk. You'll need a better story. I hope you ain't forgetting that little boy."

"A boy's best friend is his father."

"What?" He leaned in and cupped his ear. He had a hearing problem the way he needed a ladder to change a lightbulb in an eight-foot ceiling.

I shook my head. It hadn't been meant for him to hear.

He strode off to talk to the paramedics, who had parked on the apron and got out to unfold the stretcher from the back. An unmarked Plymouth, white as justice, cut its engine and coasted to a stop behind the big square van. The first team was checking in.

# SIXTEEN

"**H**OW'S THAT? Too tight?"

I waggled my foot around. It was wound with ten yards of athletic tape and didn't waggle much. "A little."

"Good. You said you wanted to be able to move around; that will keep the circulation going. If you're going to take your weight off it for any length of time, you'll want to remove the tape. Gangrene's not nearly as much fun as it sounds." The paramedic, a kid with freckles and an impressive red handlebar moustache that made him look like an actor in a school play, returned the roll of tape and stainless steel scissors to his metal case, arranging them just right in their proper niches. He and his partner had strapped Constance Glendowning to a board, placed the board on a stretcher, and slid it into the ambulance. He didn't think she was in any danger, but you never knew with a concussion. I asked him when he thought she'd come around.

"Five minutes or five days. The human brain's got more heart than the heart; it knows when its owner's in for a world of pain, and shuts down until the timing's better. I understand her boy's missing. That's a biggie."

"I hope to get him back before she wakes up." I lowered my foot to the ground and tested it, supporting most of my weight with my hand on the door of the cruiser. The pain was there but muffled, like a toothache under a wad of cotton. It was just a sprain after all. I'd been afraid the foot was hanging by a thread. I pulled my sock on over it and stuck my shoe in a slash pocket of the Windbreaker. I knew without trying it wouldn't go on over an ankle the size of a bucket.

"I wouldn't worry too much about it. There's a little white pill that'll make her think he's in Mother Goose's daycare. It's no bigger than a Tic Tac. Street price of a bottle of sixty would put you in retirement. If you didn't mind spending it in Cell Block A," he added, when he realized the two plainclothes cops were approaching.

"What about—the other woman?" I asked. It was time to stop thinking of her as Iris.

He shook his head. "Nothing we could do. I'm sorry. If it helps—"

"She didn't feel a thing. I know. I was talking about the remains."

"Wayne County Morgue, until someone claims her. You next of kin?"

It was my turn to shake my head. I was getting tired of the question. "Both her parents are dead, and she was divorced. I never heard her mention any brothers or sisters. There's a woman in Monroe, but she was just an employee."

"Well, I hope she had a friend close enough to go to her funeral. Otherwise she might wind up on a dissecting table."

"Somehow I don't think she'd care."

The look I got surprised me. I hadn't thought it was possible to shock someone who paid his rent scooping up human entrails. "I can see you're not the friend I was referring to," he said.

I looked at the boy's face behind the man's moustache. I'd grown one once to look older, but that was someone else, like the woman in the car. I was too tired to deal with any of them. "Thanks for the bandage. It's the best job I've seen, and I've seen more than my share, most of them on me. You know your work. What kind of friend I am to the lady without a head is something you don't know a goddamn thing about."

He looked down and got busy latching shut his case. His face went as red as his handlebars.

"Hello, Eddie. Through with this boy?"

"All yours, Sergeant." He stood, opened his mouth, then used it to tell me I ought to get a brace for my neck. "I don't think there are any fractures, but a whiplash injury can take months to heal without support." He nodded at the other plainclothes detective and carried his case up the slope.

"I heard some of what you said. I think you hurt Eddie's feelings." The detective with the words was a woman about fifty, and fifty pounds overweight. She wore a dark gray jacket with bolero lapels buttoned too tight over a light gray skirt. The arrangement pyramided her figure unflatteringly. Her hair was dyed beige and bobbed just above her big shoulders. Her lipstick was too red, but it matched the satchel she had slung over one shoulder and her shoes, low-heeled pumps size 10EEEEE. Her companion was male and younger, possibly as young as Eddie; the prematurely bald head added ten years. He had on a black three-button sharkskin and a necktie he'd found floating in a bowl of soup.

"To hell with Eddie and his feelings," I said. "He's still got a head under his hat."

"We want to talk about that, also about a boy you say is missing." She fished a leather folder out of the satchel and showed me a badge plated in enamel and gold. "I'm Sergeant Loggins. This is

Officer Wilding. We're with the state police, Juvenile Division. How's the ankle?"

"Hurts like hell. So does my neck and chest and everything else except the little finger of my left hand, and I'm getting a hangnail. All of which makes me the winner here, if you use the bell curve. And how are you?"

"Not feeling sorry for myself. How's that for starters?" Her red lips were pressed together in a smile like a cut throat. "Tell us about the little boy."

I caught a ride home in the white Plymouth. Wilding drove, without having said a word since we'd met. In the driveway, Loggins hung an elbow over the back of her seat and smiled at me. "We'll be back to plug the holes in your story, after we head out to the wine country to pick up the corks. Don't plan any big trips."

"I don't have wheels." I put my good foot out onto the pavement. "Thanks for the lift."

"Thank Wilding. He talked me out of dropping you off at the corner and letting you hobble the rest of the way."

"What'd he use, smoke signals?"

"We've outlasted all our marriages; we communicate. He wants to jail you as a material witness to a possible child abduction, but you'd just occupy yourself worrying about getting out. I want you to spend the time thinking about all the things that can happen to a three-year-old kid in this world. If you're uninformed I'll send pamphlets."

"I was just helping out some friends."

"I heard it. I wrote it all down so I can read it back to you when it counts. Walker!"

I had shut the door and started across the grass, favoring my unsprained ankle. The little lightning bolts shot out of my neck when I looked back.

"Nothing. I just wanted to make you turn your head." She laughed, a short harsh bark, and ran up her window.

In the kitchen I wanted a drink, but couldn't reach the bottle in the cupboard standing on one foot. I filled a glass from the tap instead, drank it down, filled it again, and drank half of that. I took the rest with me into the living room, sat down in the arm-chair, and rested my foot on the ottoman while I dialed Connor Thorpe's number at the old Stutch plant. He spent most of his evenings at the office. Home was just a place to sleep and change horses. He never slept.

The line was busy. I drank off what was in the glass and called Carla Witowski. She made a few noises while I was talking, but didn't ask any questions until I was finished. I told her Constance was in Henry Ford Hospital. I said I'd call as soon as I knew any-thing about Matthew. I didn't tell her she knew more than I'd told the cops at this point, but she didn't ask about the cops, so she might have guessed.

She lowered her voice, as if to avoid being overheard. More likely she didn't want to wake the dog. "You won't do anything to David until you know Matthew is safe?"

"I'll do just enough."

The pause on her end was brief. "I suppose the police will want to talk to me. What should I tell them?"

"The truth. They'll work it out themselves anyway, and I've had more experience in their doghouse. I'm just buying a few hours. I want to talk to Glendowning before they do."

"If I'm not here, have me paged at the hospital." She hung up. Tough teacher.

Thorpe's line was still in use. I called Rayellen Stutch and spoke to Mrs. Campbell. The lady of the house was still out rais-ing funds. I just said there was a glitch and lunch would have to be postponed. Mrs. Campbell didn't press me for details. She wasn't the kind who got burned twice.

"Thorpe." He sounded as if he were talking through a rubber hose. The telephone lines at the plant hadn't been replaced since Ma Bell came out.

"Walker. I need a car."

"You should've hung on to the Viper."

I told him what had happened. I might have been reading an obituary off the AP wire.

"What do the cops know?" he asked.

"I was taking a friend and her son to see her mother. Iris was along for the ride."

"You're lucky they didn't run you in on general principles."

"Yeah, I'm a regular rabbit's foot. The boy's not in danger if he's with his father—I've got past procedure in favor of that, cops don't treat parental abductions the way they do straight kidnapping— and if he isn't, if he really wandered off or someone else has him, they couldn't do any more than what they're doing: getting the word out to all the posts and precincts and TV stations and digging up a picture to stick on milk cartons. That gives me a head start. When I brace Glendowning I don't want bars separating us."

Air stirred around his basement office, like someone blowing gently into a clay jug. "It's not my place to tell you how to run your business. When I have a security breach I plug it. It isn't a vendetta."

"You're right. It's not your place." I twisted the telephone cord around my right hand, tight enough to shut off circulation. "What about those wheels?"

"I can't get you anything tonight. All the lots are locked up."

"Kick somebody out of bed. The cops will be at Glendowning's house in the morning. The rental places are closed and I don't plan to waste what I've got for Glendowning on some hack driver giving me grief about driving all the way to Toledo. It doesn't have to be a Cadillac," I added. "A Yugo with its gas tank wired on is fine as long as it runs."

"I'll see what I can do."

"Don't see. Do."

"I'll call you back."

"You're goddamn right." I was talking to a dial tone.

I'd been off the ankle too long. My foot had gone to sleep. Before it could wake up I limped into the kitchen and cranked down the bottle from the cupboard above the sink and filled the water glass I'd used earlier. I leaned back against the sink with my ankles crossed and drank it down the same way I'd drunk down the water.

It was cheap Scotch, the kind that kills the nerves in the tongue on contact, like licking a twelve-volt battery. If you drank enough it did the same thing to your brain. I wanted to drink enough; wanted it the way I wanted an easy retirement and a cabin on the lake and all my dead friends to be alive. Instead I put the cap back on the bottle and pushed it to the back of the drainboard. I had a long way to go and a short time to get there. Jerry Reid. Carl Sandburg in boots and a cowboy hat.

I caught the telephone on the third ring, even though I had to hobble in from the kitchen and my foot was wide awake and letting me know how it felt about it. "Thorpe?"

"Yeah. I called in a favor. It isn't a Cadillac. It isn't even a Yugo, but it'll be at your place in twenty minutes. How's your midlife crisis?"

"I don't even remember midlife."

"Too bad, it'd help."

At the end of eighteen minutes something rumbled into my driveway. I went to the front door, snapped on the light over the garage, and looked out.

"Holy Christ," I said.

# CHAPTER

# SEVENTEEN

THE YOUNG MAN aboard the motorcycle hadn't been born the last time that model thundered off the line. He was in his tender twenties, slender and tattooed, in factory-faded jeans and a black T-shirt with a white legend reading RUNS WITH SCISSORS. He had a Kerouac goatee and when he swung down the kickstand and climbed off the machine and removed his helmet, his hair lay flat and sleek to his skull like a beaver's. He looked up at me on the front step, shielding his eyes against the bright bulb above the garage.

"You're Walker? Thorpe called me."

I said I was Walker. "Where's Peter Fonda?"

"Don't know him. The name's Dollier. I work security at the GM Tech Center in Warren. Thorpe said you need to borrow my bike. You ride?"

"It doesn't look that much more complicated than my old Schwinn." I stepped down and walked around it. It was a hike. It was a chopper on a six-foot wheelbase with red-and-black fenders and full chrome on the engine and pipes, a mirror finish, and *Indian* written in silver script on both sides of the fuel tank. The black leather banana seat had fringe hanging off it, a nice frontier touch. I'd heard about the 2000 Chief, the first reissue in almost fifty years of the legendary V twin, but I'd also heard of Sasquatch and the alien autopsy and I hadn't gotten any closer to them than the tabloid rack at Wal-Mart. It smelled of rubber and leather and hot shiny metal, a new-toy smell.

"C'mon, mister. Thorpe's Thorpe and I owe him my job, but I was only six months looking for this one. I was on a waiting list for the Chief four years."

"Mind if I try it out?"

He frowned at a scuff mark on the white helmet. "Sure. Why not? Hell, I mean I got out of bed."

I swung a slippered foot over the seat, felt a stab of pain when I rocked the weight onto my bad ankle to release the stand, and turned the key. I was grateful for the electric ignition. The motor started with a pleasant virile bubbling bass like hailstones on a kettle drum and I felt the vibration in my crotch. I twisted the throttle a couple of times, clearing its throat, then found the foot shift and took off. I wobbled a little at first, found my balance by the end of the driveway, and swung into the street.

I had the pavement all to myself at that hour, and I opened up around the corner, lighting up windows in my wake; the neighborhood was mostly retirees who called to complain whenever someone played Jerry Vale too loud on the stereo. The damp night air misted my face, gnats and tiny moths patted my cheeks and forehead and staggered away to sleep it off on a nice quiet burdock leaf. The rippling beat of the big 1442 between my knees blatted back at me from the brick and clapboard facings on both sides of the street. In my wild young days before the service, I'd torn about the countryside aboard a 350 Suzuki, blowing raspberries at God and man from a pipe I'd reamed out with a broomstick to eliminate the baffles; the two machines had as much in common as Hot

Wheels and a Bentley. The Indian weighed better than six hundred pounds and hugged the turns like a tank.

I circled the block, then as I approached my house I hunkered over the handlebars and twisted the throttle all the way forward. The curb slanted at a thirty-degree angle where it was cut down for my driveway. I hit it, went airborne for a giddy half-second, and turned the wheel as I landed on the grass, braking and pegging down my good foot as a pivot. I skidded in a circle and cut the motor. There was a little lagoon of silence, then the first brave cricket scratched its legs, followed by an ovation.

Dollier came sprinting across the lawn. "It's not a mountain bike. You want to lay it down?"

"Just shaking out the ticks. I'll stand you to a cab home. When do you need it back?"

"I need not to let it out of my sight. Tell me where you're going. I'll ride you over."

"No good. I'm moving fast." And dodging pickups; but I didn't say that. "You talked to Thorpe."

"You don't talk to Thorpe. He talks to you, and he doesn't say anything you can use. But it looks like you can handle it okay. Don't get cute and park it between two cars. It needs its own spot." He caressed the fuel tank. "I'll still be making payments when the Democrats get back in."

"What's it burn, regular or premium?"

That brightened him a little. "Regular's fine. Don't let it spill over. It's hell on the paint. You'll need this." He held out the helmet.

"Looks small. What's your hat size?"

"Six and three quarters."

"I'm seven and a half." I took out my wallet and stuck out two fifties. "Get it decaled."

He took them, nodding. They didn't make a dent in what he

owed on the bike. They were just a symbol, like the feathered chief on the fender.

Dollier was still there, using a handkerchief on a smudge on the chrome, when I came out of the house in my Windbreaker and a pair of elastic-sided boots I'd dug out of the closet, supporting the ankle without pinching it. The Windbreaker was leather, with a flannel lining. I felt like Brando; the ex-Wild One who had lost a daughter to suicide and a son to prison.

"You want to look out for the law," Dollier said, straightening. "They'll bust you without a helmet."

"They'll have to catch me first." I swung a leg over the seat.

"Where you headed?"

"Toledo." Fear flew up in his eyes like a spark. I smiled. "Don't worry, they only shoot during football season."

I started the motor. He shouted that he had to be at work at eight. I said I'd try to be back at the house by seven. I didn't say that if I didn't make it, it meant I was in jail or clogging up the treads in David Glendowning's oversize tires. My last glimpse of Dollier, standing in my driveway with his helmet dangling by its strap from one hand, belonged to an astronaut left behind on the pad.

The remains of red flares guttered near the Trenton exit over on the northbound side. They'd hauled away the Cutlass and a couple of troopers with flashlights were measuring the skid marks with a wheel the size of a barrel hoop. One of them was the big good-looking cop who had heard Martin Luther King speak at Cobo Hall. I wondered where he went when his second shift ended.

South of Woodhaven I buzzed past another trooper parked in a crossover, right under a stadium lamp. His lights flared in one corner of my left-hand mirror, then died. Reflex action. He'd decided saving one more idiot from splashing his brains on the asphalt wasn't worth the trouble of a possible cross-country chase. The best time to commit a misdemeanor is near the end of a tour.

I had a couple of close calls. The driver of a minivan nearly batted me off the interstate when he changed lanes without checking his blind spot, and a Lexus with a Mudhens pennant flapping from its radio antenna made a right turn directly in front of me as I swung off the exit ramp in Toledo, forcing me to gun it and heel around him. I nearly laid it down, and again on the other side when I overcompensated. A motorcycle is a good idea on paper, but it only works in a vacuum.

I was angry, and grateful. I'd begun to enjoy the ride and forget what I was there for.

Dawn, the first one without Iris, was bleeding in when I entered Glendowning's block. There were lights on in a couple of houses; coffee was percolating, someone was waking up under a hot spray, getting ready to fling himself against the same hard vertical surface all over again. Not Glendowning, though. The brick split-level was quiet, as dark and peaceful-looking as a dam at dead low tide. There were no police cruisers in sight, keeping the peace in their noisy obnoxious way with loud radios and stuttering strobes. The only thing moving in the immediate vicinity was the little painted wooden man sawing a log in the front yard.

I killed the motor, coasting to a stop in front, and toed down the stand carefully, being quiet about it. I was either early or way too late. I listened for the sounds of a neighborhood trying to come back down after a sudden violation of the night: dogs barking, babies yowling, Randolph Scott potting at black hats on the insomniac channel. Nothing. That was one race I'd won. I patted the Indian.

I leaned back against the sissy rail, propped up my injured foot on the handlebars, lit a cigarette, and smoked, waiting for the glowing tip to lose its hard ruby edge. I needed light for what I had in mind and I didn't want to slow down for wall switches.

Dawn spread with a glacier's eternal creep. Shadows slithered, seemed to pause, then slid away. I reached back to make sure the .38 hadn't slipped out of its holster during the ride; reached back a second time just for luck. I smoked and watched the light spread, and when I couldn't see the glow of the tobacco without turning the cigarette around to look, I snapped it toward the gutter and put my foot down and got off the bike.

I was still being quiet. If I thought my ankle would take the strain I might have slipped off my boots and crept across the grass on the balls of my feet. A mourning dove hooted, like wind in a bottle. I wanted to shush it.

The lawn ornament was anchored to the earth by a wooden stake opposite the paddles that activated the sawing man when the wind blew. I worked it loose, lifted with both hands, twisted my trunk, and hurled the ornament through the picture window in the redwood wall next to the front door.

The safety glass exploded inward in kernels the size of molars. Down the street a dog started yapping frantically, without warmup. I swept the barrel of the revolver around the molding, clearing away the jagged edges, and stepped over the low sash, pivoting when my feet crunched down, with the gun in a two-handed grip. There was nothing to shoot at but bottles. I was alone on the riser looking into the sunken living room with the same newspapers on the sofa, the same butts in the ashtray with a new colony well along on the table next to it, and fresh empties on the furniture and floor. The place had begun to smell like the inside of a keg.

I checked all the rooms on the ground floor, moving faster than I had the first time, but not so fast I entered any ahead of my weapon. Another squalid stratum was settling atop the previous layers. Whatever had turned black and bubbling in the refrigerator had made its presence known throughout the kitchen. Ants spilled out of pasteboard containers and pizza boxes on the table and stove and joined a forced march past the pantry and under the door leading to the garage. Nothing had entered the den except a greater accumulation of dust. No one and nothing new in the bathrooms either, on both levels. At a glance, little Matthew's room had not been used. The bed was still made. The grownups' bedroom looked the same as well, even down to the pattern of the tangled sheets. I'd wondered how long it would be before Glendowning gave up going to bed and started sleeping in his clothes in the recliner downstairs.

On a hunch I tugged open the drawer in the nightstand that had contained the nine-millimeter Beretta tricked up on a .45 frame. No gun. There was a light oil stain on the paper lining where it had lain. I checked the other nightstand, but it hadn't migrated there; just a litter of bottles of nail polish and an old copy of *Woman's Day.*

Back in the living room I scratched my temple with the muzzle of the .38. My ankle was throbbing from all the walking and climbing and my neck hurt. With those things on my mind it was a couple of seconds before I realized there was a part of the house I hadn't searched.

On my way through the kitchen I used the gun to root among the teeming food boxes, not expecting to find anything except more ants. I was getting too cynical. The black plastic oblong of a key tag lay on the table with a key attached to the ring, its tab insulated in more black plastic. It was right where it would have skidded to a halt when whoever had used it last had tossed it. I scooped it up and opened the door that led down to the garage.

Something crunched when I put my foot down on the first gridded step. It might have been stale breadcrumbs. I switched on the light in the stairwell. The trail of ants that had started in the kitchen continued across the step, down the side onto the next step, and on from there. One, daunted at first by the obstacle of my foot, pulled itself up over the lip of the sole and trekked across my toe. Others followed in a straight line, as determined as private detectives to move on to the next step. I wondered what the attraction was. I shook them loose and went on down.

Glendowning's white Dodge Ram pickup stood a couple of feet over from where I'd first made its acquaintance, encroaching on the half of the garage where his wife had parked when she was living there. I heard a metallic tick and then a few seconds later a little hissing sigh, as of an engine cooling slowly. I grasped the handle on the passenger's door, tightened my grip on the Smith & Wesson, and swung the door open. Both seats were vacant.

I glanced inside the box behind the rear window. A full set of fat snow tires on titanium wheels lay on their sides in the bed, one to each corner. The extra weight had enabled the truck to hold the road at 120 on I-75. I let the door drift shut, not quite latching, walked along toward the front, and laid a palm on the hood. The metal was warm. It must have been scalding when he'd parked it after the drive back from Trenton. Without moving from the spot I glanced around the garage, then turned to go back upstairs.

Something crunched. I'd forgotten about the ants.

At the base of the stairs they formed again into a straight line on the concrete floor. The line extended beneath the pickup. I walked around the truck and looked at where the line continued on the other side. Glendowning lay in a heap in the center of the floor, wearing the same blue twill shirt and old jeans he'd had on when we met, and which from the look of them he hadn't had off since. His feet were still shoeless, the socks even blacker than before and worn through at the soles. One arm sprawled across the dark patch where Constance Glendowning's Chrysler had leaked oil. It wasn't all oil anymore.

His head angled down from his shoulder onto the concrete, his one visible blue eye glimmering with a flat shine, like paint on tin. The blue was darker now, the white around the iris no longer bloodshot. The blood had settled somewhere else. His mouth was open.

I squatted on my heels and felt his throat. The skin was stiff and cold, colder than Iris's had seemed. I made a face, reached out, lifted the hand at the end of the sprawled arm, and let it go. It lifted all of a piece with the arm and came down with a clunk like dry wood.

His spiky hair was matted at the temple where the bullet went in. The ants were busy there. The hairs close to the wound were blackened. I leaned close and sniffed. Then I blew out to clear my nostrils.

"That's the part I can't get used to, that burnt stink," said a voice behind me, ringing in the mostly empty garage. "Like scalding a hog. That's why I left the farm, and here I am, still scalding hogs. Now slide the gun across the floor and stand up, slow as the mail."

# CHAPTER

# EIGHTEEN

MILITARY TRAINING IS CLEAR in situations like that: Swing and shoot, and dive for cover while you're jerking the trigger. But it had been a long time since the military, there was a chance I'd be shooting at some kind of cop, along with everything that entailed, and anyway my neck hurt. I laid the revolver on the floor, gave it a push, and rose slowly.

"Smart boy. Now turn around, not too fast. You ain't Tonya Harding."

I did that, keeping my hands clear of my sides. There was a shallow alcove this side of the pull-up door, with a step-up for storing lawn mowers and garden equipment and creepers for the amateur mechanic. But the untidy human factor had kicked in, and junk had accumulated atop those items: dusty cardboard boxes, broken chairs awaiting repair or more likely some future trash day, odd scraps of lumber, a rusted charcoal grill. There had barely been room for him to stand back around the corner where he wouldn't be seen until it didn't matter, and from the looks of the jumble he had cleared it himself.

He was standing near the edge now, a middle-size slab of casual muscle and serious flab in a corduroy sportcoat, white Oxford shirt buttoned to the neck without a tie, wine-colored slacks, and brown wingtips. The sportcoat was mousy gray, worn smooth at the elbows, and the scoop neck of a white undershirt showed through the cheap shirt. The slacks bagged at the knees. His face was large and pitted and also wine-colored. The biggish nose was broken, not recently but often, and he combed his nearly white hair straight down all around in bangs like Moe Howard. His hairless right fist was wrapped around the handle of what appeared to be David Glendowning's modified Beretta.

He looked like a strikebreaker, which he might have been once. When I knew him he'd been a Detroit police inspector, and later assistant chief of police in Iroquois Heights; a position from which I'd helped get him busted. His name was Mark Proust.

"You remember me, I guess." His voice had a rough burled edge, as if he was used to shouting. "I remember you. I think about you sometimes."

"I think about you, too," I said. "You're usually in jail denims."

"Never did a day. They let me resign." He laughed, apropos of nothing. The sound reminded me of Carla Witowski's dog. Someone sometime had poked him in the windpipe with an iron bar or an elbow, but hadn't finished the job. "When I see Cecil Fish I'll tell him you said hello."

"I heard the voters flushed him out of the city prosecutor's office finally."

"Recall. Where a malcontented minority subverts the will of the majority."

Now I laughed. "Every thug and screwup out of a job knows that one by heart."

"Anyway he landed on grass. He's a paid lobbyist, tells Mayor Muriel to sign next to the *X*. Soon as the election fallout clears he's going to get me an appointment at City Hall. Head of security."

"When Chernobyl stops glowing, maybe. You stunk up the place."

"I got a grandson in Minnesota, my daughter bought him a book. *Everybody Poops,* it's called. So everybody does it, but I'm the only one got pointed at." He'd stopped laughing. "That's what I think about when I think about you."

"Come on, Proust," I said. "If it was just that, you'd have come for me before this. Who's paying your freight?"

"Generous Motors; pipe that, will you? Biggest fucking corporation in the world, employing little old Mark Proust from Elk Rapids. I stop company property from walking out and mad bombers from walking in." He clamped his mouth shut then, as if to stop the flow. That was habit. I wasn't going to leave that garage and repeat the conversation to anyone. I wasn't going to leave that garage, period.

I needled him. I'd begun to get the idea, but I wanted to hear him say it, and the more he talked, the less he shot. "No kidding, they give you a whistle?"

"I'm the one gives out the whistles, smartass. I drill the troops and check 'em for missing buttons. It's just one plant, but I got more men under me than I had when I was with the city. GM's got big plans for the place."

"Which plant would that be, the Stutch plant?"

"Still the detective, I see." He waggled the gun in the direction of Glendowning's body. "Care to detect what happened to Davy, there?"

"I nailed that one in two seconds. You let yourself in while he was passed out in his recliner and shot him with his own gun. You'd have brought one anyway, but as long as he wasn't stopping you, you frisked the place and found the Beretta. It made the suicide angle play better."

"It *was* suicide. You smelled the powder burns. Poor little Davy got all weepy over what he'd done, running a car off the road with his wife and kid in it and killing somebody, and decided to stop the tears. Just like a drunk."

"What about Matthew?"

He looked blank for a second. "Oh, the kid. Wandered off, the little shit, the way kids do. I guess we'll all get a flyer in the mail someday with his picture on it, toss it out with all the rest of the junk. Too bad."

"Uh-huh. Who's got him, really?"

"What's it to you? You're part of the suicide now." He raised the gun a notch.

"I get it. He shot me, then used the gun on himself. I came here all hotted up over Iris and we had it out. You put that together just since I broke the window?"

"Before. When I found out you were coming I hauled Davy out here where you wouldn't see him from the window and staked him out. You took your own sweet time. We both of us got stiff waiting." He laughed wheezingly. "Iris, that her name? You fuck her?"

"You knew her," I said. "You worked the Shanks case back in Detroit."

"Christ, how many years ago was that. But the name wasn't Iris. It was Marla something. Old Ben Morningstar's foster kid. Wait, there was a heroin whore, a nigger. Wouldn't be her, would it? You like the dark stuff?"

Now it was him twisting the needle. Either he needed the excuse to shoot or he wanted to prolong the moment. It was a moment he'd been waiting for since long before Glendowning or the job at the Stutch plant.

He didn't need the excuse. He hadn't needed one to press the muzzle of a pistol against a helpless man's temple and pull the trigger. He'd been living with the pain of a rotten tooth so long, and now he was probing with his tongue at the pulpy socket.

I made an infinitesimal turn to the left. The hour hand of a clock never moved more slowly. I talked; whether to distract him or myself from what I was doing, I wasn't sure. "The angle doesn't play," I said. "Not if you want to tie it into the other thing. Rigor mortis takes four hours to kick in, minimum; not nearly enough time for Glendowning to have run me off the road near Trenton and make the turnaround and get back here and shoot us both."

"It won't matter. You'll both be stiff as doors by the time they find you. Davy don't get many visitors these days."

"That's about to change. The cops will want to talk to him about what happened on I-75."

"They'll just ring at the door. When he don't answer they'll get a warrant. That takes time."

"You're forgetting the window I broke. That's probable cause for a search."

He thought about that. I turned a little more, trying to place my right side between him and my left pants pocket, where I'd put the key to the pickup. He moved a shoulder. I stopped.

"Cops like a pretty frame," he said. "One little crack won't hurt."

"These are Michigan state troopers. They'll have Toledo cops with them. They don't do things the way you did in the Heights."

"Cops are cops. Quit fidgeting or I'll shoot you in the belly."

"My ankle's killing me."

"That makes two of us." He showed his Dutch teeth. "Go ahead and lean on Davy's truck. He won't mind if you scratch it."

I did that, turning to plant my left shoulder against the door, and lifted my bad foot, letting it dangle like a broken wing. My left hand slid into my pocket.

"Well, I'm due back at my desk at eight. No rest for the working man, right, Walker? Except for you." He leveled the Beretta at my chest.

The key tag had three raised buttons on it. I didn't know which operated what, so I pressed them all, squeezing hard with my fist. I hoped they didn't cancel one another out.

The Ram flashed its lights and blasted its horn in short staccato bursts, to warn everyone in the parking lot its owner was under attack. Proust jerked that way, firing spasmodically. Something clunked against the side of the truck. I was moving, pushing myself away from the door and diving across Glendowning's body. I struck the floor shoulder first. A blue light snapped in my brain—pure pain from my neck—and I blacked out for an instant, but I must have rolled according to plan, because when the light came back on in a stunning burst, I saw my .38 right in front of my face. I seized it, threw myself over onto my back, and fired from a two-handed grip. I didn't aim. I was just pushing lead in Proust's general direction. He returned fire. The slug twanged off the firewall and then off a steel joist and then the floor, changing chords with each hit as it lost shape and passing close to my right ear with a wobbling buzz.

My first slug punched a hole in the garage door. A round spot of daylight opened in one of the wooden panels like a furious eye. I took aim the second time, concentrating on Proust's thick midsection, but I was panting, from panic as much as from effort, and pain blurred my vision. Blood plashed straight out from his left knee in a powdery spray, like dust from a blown tire. He yelled and went down hard. The Beretta jumped out of his hand.

I clambered up and lunged and kicked away the gun before he could recover it. I needn't have hurried. He was rocking from side to side on the floor with his knee drawn up to his chest, gripping it in both hands and cursing in his rough burled voice, an octave higher than normal.

My ears rang. An enclosed space like a garage is no place to discharge percussion weapons. I holstered the revolver, bent over Proust, and held him by one corduroy lapel while I slid my other hand under his left arm and released a plated automatic from its clip. It was a Glock, the Budweiser of personal firearms, same caliber as the Beretta. I went over the rest of him for good measure, then pocketed the Glock in my Windbreaker and shuffled over and sat down on the step where he'd stood among the other rubbish. It felt good to take weight off my ankle, and for a couple of minutes I sat with my head down and my forearms resting on my thighs, listening to my lungs filling and emptying and Proust blaspheming.

I raised my head and looked at him. "Sure it hurts. You ought to have expected that, being an ex-cop. That's why they teach you to swing your stick at their knees when they try to make a break."

"I'm crippled," he said. "Oh, Jesus Christ. Fuck me. Jesus H. Fucking Christ."

"You're still three-quarters of a man. You want to try for half?" I slid out my .38 and took aim at his right knee, swinging the barrel from side to side like a metronome as he rocked.

"What? What's that? Oh, Jesus." His eyes fixed on the gun. His face was gray beneath the congestion, slimy-slick. He stopped rocking.

"You weren't listening before," I said. "Bad habit. Among a couple of hundred other things, it's what made you a rotten cop. I told you Glendowning had been dead at least four hours. That's why he couldn't have been driving his truck when it ran me off the road. Who paid you to kill him and then come after his wife and kid?"

"Who what? I need a hospital."

I fired at the floor between his feet. The slug knocked a chip out of the concrete and buried itself in the Sheetrock lining the outside wall. His voice went up another octave and he scrambled backward on hands and heels. His wine-colored trousers were stained black at the left knee. Splinters of white bone clung to the torn cloth. He was going to need a new kneecap, if anyone thought the rest of him was worth the investment. "You're a psycho!" he shrieked.

"Psychos don't have this much fun. Knick-knack on the other knee next time. Who picked up the bill?"

He was silent, except for some wheezing breaths. I leveled the barrel.

"It was Thorpe! Connor Thorpe! Jesus God, don't shoot me again!"

"Right answer. I guessed that when you said you worked security at the Stutch plant. How about me? Was this your bright idea or Thorpe's?"

"Thorpe's. He said we might as well take you down too, avoid a second front."

"Right again. He was the only one who knew I was coming here, except Constance's mother, and she didn't fit the frame. What did he mean about avoiding a second front?"

"I don't know."

"Final answer?"

"What?" His eyes had lost focus behind a film of pain and fear.

"You know the rules: No lifelines. No fifty-fifty, no poll-the-audience, no phone-a-friend. If you miss this one you leave here on a gurney."

"I'm telling you I don't know. I was just a hired hand. He knew I had a mad on against you and he said this was my chance to blow it out. He didn't say what his end was. Men like him don't. They just put in the order."

That disappointed me, because I knew he'd answered right again. The .38 was still aimed at his remaining kneecap; comically, he unclasped the one I'd shattered and covered that one with both hands, as if that would lessen the damage.

"Okay, you're one question away from the million," I said. "What did you do with the boy?"

No hesitation this time. He could see I was hoping he'd get it wrong.

"I took him to Thorpe. I don't know why he wanted him. He didn't at first. He said do Glendowning and use his truck so it looked like it was his thing. After that piece-of-shit Cutlass went off the road I pulled over and poked around inside. Everybody looked dead, especially the—I forgot her name."

"Iris."

"Yeah. I could see she was dead for sure, not having a head anymore. The boy was okay. Screamed like hell and tried to take a bite out of my hand when I unsnapped him from the kiddie seat. I had to give him a smack to quiet him down. Thorpe was sore as hell I didn't do more, but he said bring him to the plant. Your call came in while I was there. That made him madder. He said I should have torched the car."

"You called him before you went over?"

"Yeah, why?"

"Not important. I wondered why his line was busy at that hour. Keep telling it."

"Your call came. That's when Thorpe told me to go back and wait for you here, and that thing about a second front. That's the shebang. Jesus, it's cold for April." He was hugging himself, shivering. He was going into deep shock.

I didn't need the .38 anymore. I put it away, took out the Glock, removed the clip and ejected the shell from the chamber and put them in my pocket, and laid the automatic on the step. I retrieved Glendowning's Beretta and went upstairs.

Another of the many reasons Mark Proust had been a lousy cop was he had no imagination. I knew what Thorpe meant by avoiding a second front even if he didn't. Learning he had the boy at the Stutch plant gave me that.

I found what I wanted in the belly drawer of the midget rolltop in the den. David Glendowning's address book was a cheap one bound in brown vinyl, but it was rich with names and numbers. The first name I recognized was all the reinforcements I needed. I put down the Beretta to transfer the data to my pocket pad, then returned the book to the drawer and picked up the gun. In the living room I smeared it between my palms and dropped it on the rug next to the recliner. If the Toledo police were on point, they'd run a carbon test on Proust's hands to find out if he'd done any shooting recently. My prints on the gun that killed Glendowning would just confuse them.

Proust's teeth were chattering when I returned to the garage. He was too far gone in shock to protest when I put my hands under his arms and hauled him out of the way of the pickup. I selected an eight-inch-wide oak plank from the scrap lumber in the storage area—it was only six feet long, short but serviceable—and tossed it into the box. I found the switch that operated the garage door, started the Dodge and backed out, closed the door using the remote clipped to the sun visor on the driver's side, and drove up the steep incline to the street. I parked in front of the house, got out, flipped down the tailgate, and slid the plank back until it tilted to the ground, creating a ramp. I tested it for spring, then started the Indian, rode it to the corner, turned around, and gunned it, getting a running start. The front tire jounced up over the end of the plank, then the rear. I throttled back as I climbed and coasted onto the bed. There I cut the power and got off and laid the bike on the two fat snow tires resting in the front and rear left corners.

So far as I could tell I did all this without witnesses. If anyone had heard the picture window breaking, he must have thought he'd dreamt it and gone back to sleep to wait for the alarm. The shots had taken place in an insulated garage, built into the hill that supported the rest of the split-level. The architect had been considerate, a good man to have next door. The neighborhood was just coming awake, lights going on in windows not facing the rising sun.

The pickup was fully loaded—more fully than when it had left the factory—and I knew what it could do. I needed the transportation, Glendowning didn't, and I'd promised Dollier I'd have his bike back in time for work. The cops wouldn't have a tag out on the Dodge until after they'd talked to the owner. I would put all the miles on the odometer I needed by the time they found out he wasn't talking.

I was going to leave then, let the cops deal with Proust when they came to see Glendowning about his missing son, but that might take hours, while shock turned a crippling wound fatal. I didn't give a damn about that, except it was something Proust would have done. I went into the house and called 911, then hung up. The operator would trace the call, and send a car when no one answered.

Before I left, I circled the block, purely out of curiosity. Proust had to have driven some kind of vehicle down from the Heights on his way to kill Glendowning and borrow his pickup. I spotted it parked around the corner, a late-model caramel-colored Chevy I'd seen before. That explained a number of things.

# NINETEEN

I-75 WAS IN THE HORROR of rush hour, and I didn't get back to my house until nearly seven-thirty. Dollier, sitting on my front step, looked up as the pickup swung into the driveway, then got to his feet when he saw who was behind the wheel and trotted over, carrying his helmet. He'd discarded the black T-shirt for a white one reading PLAYS WELL WITH OTHERS. The face above the goatee was a stack of worried inverted V's; he'd spotted his motorcycle lying in the bed.

"Laid it down, didn't you?" he said. "I told you it wasn't a mountain bike."

"It still isn't." I got out and gave him the key. "Thanks for the loan. There isn't a scratch on it."

He hopped up into the box to confirm that. I put the ramp into place and between us we got the bike up on its wheels and guided it down to the pavement. He looked it over closely on both sides, pulled out his handkerchief to eliminate a smudge not visible to the naked eye of a non-owner, and strapped on the helmet. "How'd everything go in Toledo?"

"Bang-up job." I leaned against the pickup and lifted my bad foot. "Do you wear some kind of badge into the Tech Center?"

"No badge. Just show my ID at the gate."

I asked if I could see it. He hesitated, then produced a tooled-leather wallet with western stitching from his hip pocket and took out a laminated card. I took it from him and studied it. It had "General Motors" on it and his name and DOB and description, with his picture in the upper right-hand corner.

"I need another favor," I said. "I need to borrow this today."

"What for?"

"Did you ask Connor Thorpe what for when he told you to bring the Indian here?"

He scratched his chin-whiskers. "They won't let me on the grounds without the card."

"Take a sick day."

"I'm not sick."

I lit a cigarette. It spared me from setting fire to him. "Nice morning. Weatherman says it's going to be like this all day. There must be a place you can ride a great bike like yours on a day like this." I hadn't heard a weather report. If the rain held off two more minutes I had a shot.

"They'll can me."

"They won't know where I got it. Nobody's going to get that long a look."

He frowned at the bike. "There's a swap meet in Flint this weekend. They're setting up today. I wasn't going till Saturday."

"First day's always the best." I got out my wallet and removed two twenties and a ten. I put his ID card in the wallet and pocketed it. "Put that toward a pair of saddlebags."

"Never use 'em." But he took the bills. "Nobody'd buy that's you in the picture."

"I'll grow a beard."

He was holding the money in one hand and his wallet in the

other. I grabbed his hands and helped him stuff the bills into the wallet. "You get fifty more when I give back the card. That's for not telling anyone we had this conversation. Including Thorpe."

"I really don't like that part. Why don't you get the clearance from him?"

"Takes too long." I looked at my watch. "If you're going to say no, you'd better do it now. There's a back-up on 75 north to War-ren." I hadn't heard a traffic report either; but here I was on safer ground. The odds that there wasn't a back-up were about the same as winning the lottery.

That made his decision. Nothing makes a Detroiter turn pale faster than a freeway snarl on the way to work. He put away the wallet. "My old man never missed a day on the line in forty years. He'd be pissed at me if he wasn't dead."

"Don't sweat it. Come tomorrow, no one at GM is going to remember you weren't at work today."

After he roared off I went inside and sat down and propped my foot up on the ottoman, but I didn't take off the Windbreaker. I didn't want to get too comfortable. When the Toledo cops found Glendowning and Proust and compared notes with the state troopers from Michigan who were looking for Glendowning's son, I was going to have visitors, and I wasn't up to entertaining. First I called Henry Ford Hospital to ask about Constance Glendown-ing's condition. The nurse or receptionist I was eventually handed off to told me her condition was stable but that she hadn't regained consciousness. There were no broken bones or internal damage. She might have been talking about a car up on the hoist. I thought about having Carla Witowski paged, then decided that would take too much time. I rang off and called the number I'd copied from David Glendowning's address book. The name that went with it was Ray Montana.

A thousand years ago I'd had dealings with Phil Montana,

Ray's father, who a thousand years before that had battered out the American Steelhaulers Union with his bare fists and a couple of hundred thick-skulled fellow truckers. Some of them had had those skulls bashed in by rented muscle, including whole police departments employed by the steel mills, but the gaps closed quickly, and after consolidating its gains the ASU had gone on to organize the entire transport industry. Phil was dead, but a succession of mob puppets in the president's chair had forced the Justice Department to take it away and offer it to Ray in hopes the magic of the family name might prevent the rot from spreading. He'd finished out that appointed term, then carried the next election in a landslide. Justice was pleased at first, then alarmed; the creature had assumed a life independent of its creator. Under Ray, ASU had expanded its operations to represent taxi drivers, airport luggage handlers, food concessionaires, computer technicians, school bus mechanics, messengers, and golf caddies. If the job involved wheels, Montana was on it. Although a campaign to organize prison work gangs backfired when police officers threatened to bail out of the union, the message was clear: The Steelhaulers were standing still for no one. When Ray's aggressive management of the union pension fund proved more successful than the government's handling of Social Security, congressional hearings were suggested to determine whether any RICO laws had been violated. It was the kind of meddling talk that only increased Ray's standing among the rank-and-file. There were truckers, some of them former draft dodgers, who would take a bullet for Ray Montana.

The functionary who answered the telephone—a medium, velvety voice, sex unknown—got my name and Glendowning's and asked me to wait. I spent the time hoping things went better with Ray than they had with Phil. We hadn't parted company with anything like a firm handshake and a slap on the back.

"Ray Montana." A light voice, lacking his father's raspy baritone. He'd never stood on a loading dock bellowing above the grumble and peep of forklifts. These days a cell phone call or an e-mail from the Detroit headquarters carried farther than a speech backed up with blackjacks.

"Amos Walker, Mr. Montana. I'm a private detective, working a case involving one of your union representatives. David Glendowning."

"Shop steward in Toledo. Go on."

I paused. "That's impressive, if you don't mind my saying so. Like Patton recognizing the name of a corporal at Fort Bragg."

"Glendowning's on the short list for president of the local. I make it a point to keep track of the good men coming up."

Not to say the competition. But I'd learned a thing or two since Phil and held my tongue. "He's dead. Shot in the head to look like suicide, but it wasn't."

"I hadn't heard." No change in tone.

"It isn't public knowledge. You can confirm it with the police in Toledo. They ought to be filing their reports about now. They have a man in custody, a former Iroquois Heights cop named Proust."

"Iroquois Heights."

A man in public office, any sort of office, can say plenty with two words or nothing with two hundred. There was a whole book, very battered and read many times, in the way he pronounced the name.

I said, "Yeah," and one-upped him by a word.

"I'll call Toledo. What is your connection with this murder, Mr. Walker?"

That was impressive, too. I usually had to say my name twice before anyone got it, common as it was to the point of invisibility. I wondered if his father had ever mentioned it to him. "It tells pretty long, especially over the telephone. I'd like to tell it in person, if you're free."

"I will be when you get here. Mr. Reznick will give you directions to my house."

The velvety voice came back on and gave me an address in Beverly Hills; not the one in California, and not ever to be confused with it. I said I'd be there in a half hour. That gave me ten minutes to shower, which I did with my bandaged foot stuck outside the stall, put on fresh clothes and the same handy boots, and pack a bag. Hot water is a poor substitute for sleep, but it beats nodding off in the presence of a man who said he would "call Toledo" as if he could speak to the entire city on one dime.

# CHAPTER
# TWENTY

THEY CALL THEM bedroom communities, the endless string of schools and housing developments unwinding along the Mile Roads north of Detroit, and in their particular case the nomenclature has never been more accurate. They have no business districts, no industrial parks or museums or libraries, no strip malls offering everything for sale from maternity clothes to mortuary needs; just two-car garages and low-maintenance lawns and places to sleep and take on nutrition between eight-hour blocks at work and the twice-daily battle to get to it and away from it. Beverly Hills, identified only by a "Welcome to" sign dozing behind an unpruned limb, has few swimming pools and no movie stars; it doesn't even have hills. With the trees fully leafed out bordering Evergreen between Twelve- and Thirteen-Mile, it's possible to forget its homes even exist, tucked back as they are on streets with names like Plantation, Embassy, and Buttonwood Court. Some of them aren't even paved.

Ray Montana's man Reznick had directed me to an address on a curving two-lane blacktop belonging to a low red-brick house no larger than its neighbors, with a recently asphalted driveway flanked by lights stuck into the grass like garden markers. There was no gate, no wall or fence surrounding the property; no indication, in fact, that the man who lived there with his family was a public figure who bumped knees on a daily basis with industrialists, senators, and guys named Murray the Midget. Nothing, that is, except floodlights perched high in the mature maples planted on the four corners of the lot and a complete absence of hedges or any other foliage near the house, so that anyone approaching was exposed long enough for someone inside to empty a clip in his direction. Death threats came to Montana's door as regularly as the newspaper, hurled with greater accuracy, and the local police—Steelhaulers, presumably—had his children on a twenty-four-hour kidnap watch.

The man who answered the bell was small and dark, with buzz-cut black hair, sharp, intelligent features, and ears that came to a point. He looked like Kafka and dressed like Nureyev, in a black turtleneck and slacks, loose-fitting clothes that would allow him to move quickly and smoothly on his narrow feet, encased in black suede slippers like ballet pumps. He would rhyme *karate* with *latte*.

He didn't bow, although his soft expression left the impression that he had. "Good morning, Mr. Walker. I am Reznick. Are you armed?"

"I am."

"Thank you for your honesty. It won't be necessary to search you. Will you hand me the weapon, please?" He held out a small palm, shiny with callus along the inside edge.

"Not out here. I don't want to attract any more police attention than I have already."

"Are you wanted?" He might have been inquiring if I had a cold.

"Not yet, I hope. I expect to be popular later."

He stepped aside, far enough to get a running start at me if I decided to trip over the threshold. Inside a brief foyer with a ceramic-tile floor and a bronze bust of Phil Montana's bulldog head on a pedestal, I unsnapped the Smith & Wesson from my belt, holster and all, and laid it on the calloused palm. This time he did bow—his head, anyway—and led me around a corner and down a short flight of carpeted steps, carrying the revolver in front of him as if it were a tray of cocktails.

We turned before a bathroom with its door open and entered a small rumpus room, paneled in composition wood, with a low bar and a sitting area and behind the bar a mirror made up of peel-and-stick tiles. There was a little gym area with free weights and a punching bag, a pressboard bookcase full of children's books and recent bestsellers, and the sofa and chairs were covered with loose throws, the kind you use to conceal stains and worn spots on the upholstery. Feathered darts stuck out of a cork target on a wall covered with nicks from near misses. A tidy room, cheerily lit with table lamps and torchieres, and furnished for well under a thousand bucks. If any money was being made under the table, as Congress charged, not much of it seemed to be going to Montana.

"Mr. Walker," Reznick announced.

"Thanks. You can go now, and give him back his gun."

The little dark man turned and held it out on his palm. His face was unquestioning. I snapped the holster into place under my sportcoat. He went out, drawing the door shut behind him. It looked like an ordinary hollow-core door, but it was almost four inches thick. It would be soundproof. That made the domestic arrangement a blind for some high-level meetings far outside the fishbowl in Detroit where the union kept its headquarters; either that, or Montana was a noisy drunk.

He might have been reading my thoughts at that moment, because he said, "Make yourself a drink, Walker. Are you a morning man?"

Ray Montana was a couple of inches taller than his father, who had been called Little Phil in the days before he began cutting the steel barons down to size, but he wasn't tall. He had a compact build, running to middle-age fat now under a white dress shirt tucked into gray pleated slacks. At the moment, he was bent over an upholstered weight bench in the gym area, helping steady a pair of red barbells for a boy stretched out on the bench in a T-shirt and sweats. The boy was about fourteen, skinny but with definition in the arms, and in about fifteen years he would look like Ray. This would be his son, Philip. Philip's sister, Regina, was attending college somewhere in the East, unless that was just another blind to confound kidnappers. Dominick Montana, Ray's uncle and the first Phil's brother, had spent ten days bound and blindfolded in a barn in Livingston County forty-odd years ago during negotiations to end a strike at McClouth Steel. Who had bankrolled the snatch, and what it hoped to achieve, never came to light outside the smoky world of labor politics. Sheriff's deputies acting on an anonymous tip pulled Dominick's body out of the barn after he died from insulin shock.

"Just juice, if you have it," I said. "I forget when I ate last."

He told me there was V-8 in the refrigerator and to pour him one too. He held on to the weight bar for another second, then let go and stepped back. The boy drew the bar down to his chest, sucking in air, then blew out, straightening his arms slowly, until he was holding up the barbells at arms' length. Montana counted, "One, two," under his breath, then patted his son's shoulder and helped guide the bar into the brackets attached to the bench. Grinning, he squeezed the boy's shoulder, then pointed at the punching bag. Philip nodded, swung his feet down to the floor, and stood up. He mopped the sweat off his face and neck with a towel, then traded it for a pair of tomato-red speed gloves. He began hitting the bag tentatively, then settled into the drumroll rhythm of the professional pugilist. He had a better left jab than I'd seen on some experienced men.

"His school dropped boxing from the phys ed curriculum, would you believe it?" Montana came over to the bar and accepted his V-8, which I'd poured into a narrow glass from a collection on a shelf. "Somebody's parents took the district to court over little Timmy's shiner. We're breeding a generation of sitting hens."

"He needs to work on his right cross." I drank. The thick smooth stuff coated my empty stomach pleasantly.

"We're working on it. You box?"

"College stuff. I spent my first eight weeks in the army unlearning everything I'd been taught. Getting him ready for the union?"

"If he goes near headquarters I'll teach him how *I* throw a right cross. He can be a bum if he wants, hustle pool. Better that than he should grab his ankles for anyone's vote."

Ray had finer features than his father's, not as square. His eyes were the same shade of gray and set as wide, and the two men shared a pug nose and a long dimpled upper lip, courtesy of some Celt in the family woodpile. He looked as if he could handle himself—the elder Montana had probably seen to that, just as Ray was doing for his own son—but in Phil's case the training had been in the professional ring. It had come in handy in the urban battlegrounds of the Great Depression, but since all of Ray's fights took place in boardrooms and on platforms draped with bunting, the advantage was mainly psychological. It was a stretch to imagine him grabbing his ankles ever.

He sipped V-8, made a subtle face, and filled the gap with golden liquid from a square bottle that turned out to contain peach brandy. It wouldn't have been my choice for breakfast. "What's the name of the cop who killed Glendowning?"

I glanced toward Philip, going budda-budda-budda at the

punching bag. Montana shook his head. In anyone else I'd have called it a twitch.

"He's deaf. I'd appreciate it if you didn't noise that about. So to speak." He frowned at the pun he'd made. "It's the current fashion to parade one's disablements like a flag, but it's one luxury a man in my place can't afford. You don't know how much time my opponents spend looking for holes in my masonry."

Probably about half as much time as he spent plugging them up. Aloud I said, "If they get it, don't come looking for me. I can't work this town from the bottom of the river. The cop's name is Mark Proust. He was assistant chief in the Heights until they busted him a number of years back for staging fights in the county jail and cutting a slice of the action. Before that he was a detective inspector in Detroit. Before that I don't know. Losing his tail in some swamp probably."

"I remember the stink. The cops up there were nosing around the Steelhaulers, looking for new representation. We were dragging our feet. They were Stutch property, went around ticketing Japanese cars and tapping the phones of Ford and Chrysler execs who had the shitty judgment to live inside the city limits. Repping them would have been like handing Leland Stutch the combination to the safe at union headquarters. The jail scandal gave us an excuse to table the issue till it dried up and blew away. I was just one of the Indians then."

"That town's been for sale since Cadillac beached his canoe there to take a leak. It's off the block now, though. Connor Thorpe bought it."

"I know Thorpe." He pronounced the name the same way he'd said *Iroquois Heights* on the telephone. "Tell me how you know him."

That was as good a place to start as most. I gave him the whole thing while we leaned our elbows on the bar like a couple of movie cowboys, young Philip flapping away at the bag in the corner:

Rayellen Stutch, the inheritance, Carla Willard Witowski, my talk with David Glendowning, the shelter in Monroe, Carla's daughter Constance, the run-in with Glendowning's pickup on the interstate, Iris's death, little Matthew's disappearance, Proust's play over Glendowning's corpse in the garage in Toledo, and what I got out of Proust before and after I kneecapped him. Montana listened, sipping from his glass and showing no more emotion than a man listening to a ballgame with no money riding on how it came out. When I finished, he pushed away from the bar, went over and clapped a hand on his son's shoulder, squeezing it. Man and boy grinned. The boy mopped sweat off with the towel and let himself out the door. In a little while I heard water rushing through pipes behind the paneling. He was showering after his workout.

"I looked into organizing the private investigation business several years ago." Montana drank a little more, then filled the glass to the rim from the bottle of peach brandy. "Waste of time. The crooks couldn't be counted on to keep up the dues and the honest ones couldn't afford to. Anyway we couldn't regulate the overtime. A draft horse like you would price himself out of the market."

"Glendowning tried recruiting me," I said. "I hope his casket has a union label."

"I talked to the police in Toledo after you called. Your name didn't come up."

"They don't know about me yet. I dialed 911 and bugged out."

"Not smart. Cops talk to each other. Even if Proust clams, they'll tie you into Glendowning's pickup on I-75 and come knocking."

"I'll answer. After I talk to Thorpe."

"Asking why."

"I might get around to it."

"This Iris was a friend?"

"A good one," I said. "I don't have so many I can waste even the bad ones."

"Anything more?"

"Not more. Apart from. If it's any of your goddamn business."

He nodded. Said nothing.

I said, "I'll settle with Thorpe for Iris. That's my end, after I find out if the boy's all right."

"What's my end?"

"That's what I'm here to find out. Your name's in Glendowning's book."

"My name's in every shop steward's book between here and the Gulf of Mexico."

"I'm betting your home number isn't."

"He had potential. I won't live forever. One way to guarantee I won't would be to agree to back a stranger's play."

I finished my drink and got off my elbow. "I'll be pushing off then. Thanks for the juice."

He didn't move. "When I called you a stranger I thought maybe you'd mention knowing my father."

"It wouldn't be good politics. We didn't get along."

"He told me that, years ago. I got the impression it was his fault. He also told me you're a man of trust. He said I should remember your name."

I put my elbow back on the bar and took my turn at saying nothing.

"Glendowning had personal problems," Montana said. "Show me a trucker who's happy at home and I'll show you a man I'd rather not have making decisions for the union. I'm sorry about his wife, but that was between them and the agencies whose business it is to deal with that sort of thing. His people liked him. They respected him, which is more important. He was a man of trust. They won't like it when they find out what happened to him. If they find out Connor Thorpe is involved and I knew it and didn't do anything about it, they'll gas up their rigs and run them right through this house."

"That would be a waste of fuel," I said. "With Iroquois Heights so close."

"What do you want from me, Walker?"

"How about a splash of that brandy? I like to start a long day with fresh fruit."

He filled my glass and waited. The gray eyes held no expression.

I drank, and set down the glass. The stuff tasted like a cobbler gone bad.

I said, "I want a second front."

# TWENTY-ONE

THIS TIME OUT, no police pulled me over. That made sense, according to the standards in Iroquois Heights: The truck I was driving was on the BOL (Be On the Lookout) list in two states. At one point I sat at a stoplight next to a shiny new cruiser for three minutes, watching the two uniforms in the front seat watch an in-line skater in shorts and a halter top negotiate her way through the pedestrian press on the sidewalk.

The county records office shared a newish brick building in the civic center with city offices and the criminal court, behind which armored vans conducted a shuttle service between the back door and the county jail. I parked in the little visitors' lot—metered for one hour, against an average wait of two to three hours inside—stowed my Chief's Special in the Ram's glove compartment, and entered the building through a metal detector with a three-hundred-pound cop waiting out his pension on a stool next to it. His flushed and battered face looked as if it had witnessed its share of rubber-hose therapy sessions in the basement of the old city hall.

The clerk behind the counter in records was the grandmoth-erly type, if your grandmother moonlighted as a prison matron. The steel rims of her bifocals matched her hair, blown out as big as a racing helmet and sprayed just about as hard, and she tucked the end of her man's necktie inside her blouse like a top sergeant. When I told her what I needed she said I'd have to wait ten days for my request to be processed. I took out Connor Thorpe's letter of authorization and spread it out on the counter.

She read it, lips pressed tight as if to keep them from moving, then turned without comment and went through a door in back. I spent ten minutes reading a brochure on pet-licensing proce-dures, then watched her come back, wrestling a threadbare book the size of a drafting board around the edge of the door. Dust and weightless bits of paper wheezed out of the page-ends when she thudded it down on the counter. She pointed me to the reading room, a partitioned-off area just big enough for four job applicants to fill out their forms at student desks. I drew two of them to-gether, spread the book open across the kidney-shaped writing sur-faces, and leaned on my hands to study the pages I wanted.

The book was a bound collection of construction blueprints filed with the building permits office for the three-month period between April 1 and June 30, 1936. Such things weren't requested often, and no one had thought them worth the cost of transferring to microfilm. The carefully ruled lines in blue pencil had faded into the slate-colored pages, and I hadn't slept in twenty-seven hours. I had to scrub my eyes with the heels of my hands and play slide trombone with my neck in order to avoid seeing two of every-thing.

I spent an hour and a half studying the plans, breaking once to go out to the parking lot and feed the meter. I didn't care about a ticket, but I didn't want a cop writing down the plate and recog-nizing it from the roll-call list. I'm ordinarily good at reading blue-prints and can grasp the general layout fairly quickly, but the angle of reading while standing up aggravated my whiplash and I had to take frequent breaks, rubbing my neck, rotating my head, and hobbling around on my taped-up ankle. I felt like a car someone was trying to nurse through one more winter.

The Stutch Motors plant, later Stutch Petrochemicals and later still a division of General Motors, had gone up during the labor uprisings of the 1930s, and was consequently built to withstand a long siege. The main building contained the executive offices, with a glass wall overlooking the foundry on the ground floor where Leland Stutch could glance up from his desk and watch the steel being poured, like money into his mattress. There was only one door in and out—the local fire marshal must have rated at least a new car every model year to overlook that code violation—the walls were built of bricks pressed and fired on the site to a thickness of nearly two feet, the windows were triple-paned and sectioned off with titanium grids. The security offices were in the basement, with emergency living quarters in case it took the city police more than a couple of days to crack open enough of the strikers' skulls to turn the tide. A chainlink fence had been erected around the compound to repel saboteurs during the Second World War, with hoops of barbed wire on top for that cozy concentration-camp effect. When negotiations broke down, the suits had only to padlock the front gate, bolt the door, and wait things out, roughing it with domestic wine and tinned salmon. Strikers who managed to scale the fence without eviscerating themselves had to make their way through a maze of satellite buildings—glass plant, coke ovens, fueling stations, stamping and assembly facilities—and avoid tripping over three miles of railroad latticework just to get to the main structure. Along the way they would encounter guards with truncheons and Thompsons and a couple of dozen half-starved German shepherds. Casual Friday would be canceled until further notice.

In its heyday, the plant had had its own telephone system, independent of the city's and more sophisticated than those in most communities, its own generators, backup generators, and backups to the backups, each the size of a juggernaut, humming away in a building constructed just for them. An urban myth persisted that Stutch had commissioned a flag emblazoned with the company logo, to be run up a staff in the event of an armed labor takeover of the United States, declaring the place a sovereign nation. There were autoworkers still living, and Steelhaulers still active in the union, who would never be convinced it was a myth; they'd seen the tommy guns and watched the dogs savage one another over a hunk of bloody round.

None of these precautions had ever been put to the test, or perhaps the very fact that they were never challenged meant that they had passed it. Now, the grim lines and terse descriptions written on the sixty-four-year-old blueprints read like an archaeologist's report on a feudal ruin, something from a barbaric time familiar only to medieval scholars and buffs who walked around in clanking armor on festive weekends. The union execs who sat on the boards of all three major U.S. automobile manufacturers would scratch their heads over them between courses in the Grill Room at the Detroit Athletic Club. Most of the buildings were gone now or used for storage. When Antitrust ordered Ford to break up its sprawling River Rouge plant to promote competition, Stutch had turned the page. He sold the glass-making equipment, scrapped the dynamos, and farmed out the stamping and assembly operations, at a profit; always at a profit. He'd donated several hundred acres to the city—again to his advantage, but not one that would turn up in any ledgers—leased most of his rolling-stock to the Penn Central and B & O railroads, and consolidated his remaining operations in the main building, the gaunt, Gothic relic still brooding on its hill like Frankenstein's castle.

In his high nineties, the old man had cut back his management to two supercharged hours in the dead of night, during which a banker in Switzerland, a loyalist general in Chile, or a loading-dock foreman in Atlanta might expect to be rousted out of bed by a telephone call, and observed that schedule until his death at age 106, or 108, or 112, depending upon which biography one read. With him had passed an era dominated by wildcat semiliterates who had parlayed piles of old wagon springs, steam engine parts, and bizarre-looking new implements hand-forged in backyard shops into an industry that no one but themselves could have predicted. Only a few, like him, had lived long enough to see it pass into the white soft hands of business school graduates who had never busted a knuckle trying to remove a rusted bolt in their lives. His plant, ghost that it was of what it had been, was one of the handful in existence into which a time-traveling contemporary could wander and not feel lost among robot welders, computer consoles, foremen in white lab coats, and day care nurseries. It was as doomed as Tiger Stadium.

But *ghost* was misleading. This phantom had concrete feet planted twenty feet deep in solid bedrock. The materials were no longer available to contractors. Even if they were, government inspectors would never clear them, because buildings weren't supposed to last two hundred years with so many bricklayers and carpenters out of work. There was enough asbestos between the firewalls to wipe out the population of South America. When the time came to demolish it, the city would have to be evacuated for fourteen blocks around and the dynamite required would be sufficient to level the Mountains of the Moon. The preparation alone would employ more men working with crowbars and sledgehammers than the Berlin Wall, and it would take more trucks to clear away the rubble afterward than even Ray Montana could muster. It would be as hard to get rid of as a Christmas fruitcake.

There was nothing pretty about it, even in the architect's elevations that accompanied the floorplans. Albert Kahn, whose graceful Greco/Roman/Deco/Nouveau/Moderne setpieces had transformed the Detroit skyline throughout the first forty years of the previous century, had had no hand in the design. It was as utilitarian as a pipefitter's glove, as homely as a rich man's marriageable daughter, and no one who had attended the groundbreaking in 1936 could have imbibed enough champagne to think six decades of smelter-soot and pigeon filth would contribute to its charm. Its square blunt face and rows of windows intended only to save on electric light during the day shifts were things only a former backyard mechanic could love. It was plain from the layout that Stutch had loved it, as much as a working-class child of the nineteenth century could love anything. He could have established himself in one of the offices on the top floor, with a view of the city and soundproof insulation to spare him the ballpeen din, but he'd chosen instead a bleacher seat behind the dugout.

There was no telling what changes might have been made inside the building since the old man had grown too feeble to climb the stairs to his fishbowl above the pouring vat; but I was betting on the below-ground bunker where Connor Thorpe kept his tabs on his empire of cops, private and public, being the hardest nut to crack. That was what he had meant when he'd told Proust he needed to avoid a second front, the first being the authorities who would rattle the gate with warrants in hand when it got out he was holding a little boy inside. The interior walls were nearly as thick as the ones that held up the building, with the doors to all the offices—steel, or I was no judge—opening onto a single corridor. It was that paradox of bricks-and-masonry security, the impregnable fortress that was also an escape-proof trap. My trail ended there either way.

I was yawning fit to crack the hinges of my jaws when I closed the book. A cloud of dust and paper shavings curled out and lodged in my throat. I coughed. My eyes watered and I mopped them with my handkerchief. I was just beginning to realize how tired I was, and how many years had passed since I'd waited out a

V.C. sniper through twelve hours of the Cambodian night. I was no match for the walls of the Stutch plant wide awake, with a sound neck and two good ankles. In my present condition I couldn't open a cardboard container of mooshu pork. That made me think of Moo-goo, Carla Witowski's surgically silenced dog, which in turn made me think of Constance Glendowning, sleeping out a merciful coma in Henry Ford Hospital, unaware that her child was trapped somewhere in the concrete bowels of Iroquois Heights. I needed to follow her example or I wasn't going to be of use to any of them. Not even the dog.

I carried the big book back out into the reception area and slid it up onto the counter. Before I could thank the clerk in the helmet of steel-gray hair, she told me someone wanted to see me.

I turned around and there he was: just under six feet of muscle and hard fat in a blue suit, wire-brushed black hair, and aviator glasses with smoked lenses, smiling impersonally with small even teeth stained a uniform tobacco-beige. I didn't need to look at the shield he was holding. In a strong light it would show behind his features like a watermark. He said his name was Vivaldi, detective sergeant assigned to the City-County Building, and that Mayor Muriel would consider it a personal favor if I'd accompany the sergeant to his office.

I went with him without a squawk. That's how tired I was.

# TWENTY-TWO

"Any relation to the composer?" I asked Sergeant Vivaldi.

"My father thought so, my mother had her doubts. I dumped a bale of cash a couple of years ago on an outfit in Southfield that looks up family trees, to settle the point. All I got for my money was a shoemaker in Genoa and a couple of dozen relatives here in the States I was just fine knowing nothing about." There was rough humor in his tone, as personal as a form letter at Christmas. He would converse the same way with suspects in manacles and defense attorneys who were getting ready to tear him apart in the witness box. I sensed a retirement package in his near future.

We stepped off the elevator on the second floor and followed a gray-carpeted corridor lit through frosted ceiling panels and lined with framed certificates of community achievement. At the end we stopped before a prism-glass door with fresh shiny lettering on it reading:

ARBOR MURIEL

MAYOR

Vivaldi opened it without knocking and held it for me with a polite expression, well practiced to draw the sting from the fact that he was sealing off the only escape route. It was no wonder they'd tagged him for the city hall detail. I went in and he followed, releasing the door to its silent closer.

More gray carpeting and certificates, a wide window above an air conditioning vent with drapes spread to reveal nothing more interesting than the parking lot, a little sitting area with magazines (no one sitting in it), and seated behind a glass desk a short-haired female receptionist with makeup air-brushed by an expert and Vivaldi's same have-a-nice-day-asshole smile. She buzzed the mayor, got the okay through the little speaker, and rose to get the door. Vivaldi said he had it and swung it for me. It had glass prisms too, with nothing lettered on them, although there were tiny abrasions where something had been scraped off recently, probably PRIVATE. Muriel had won the election on the promise of an open-door policy; the bankroll General Motors had ponied up had just paid for stamps and paper clips.

It was a pleasant room as offices went. Some effort had gone into making it look like the private den of a businessman who worked hard during the day and painted birdhouses in his basement in the evening. Aromatic red cedar paneling gave the place the air of a mountain cabin. Again the carpeting was gray, but the office had just changed hands and it was imprudent politics to spend too much on renovations at the outset, even if the previous tenant had been obliged to drop out of the race when his wife named one of his unpaid volunteers as a co-respondent in her divorce suit. Muriel, or his image consultant, had hung the walls with Audubon prints. A settee and armchairs in the corner where he entertained the press were covered in tan Naugahyde to suggest seasoned leather, but not so loudly it might arouse the animal rightists. The desk from behind which he came to shake my hand was heavy and paneled, with a genuine leather top distressed to appear to predate controversy, a good reproduction of a partners table from the Woodrow Wilson era. Indirect lighting took the place of the sun through a window in back with its drapes drawn shut. If my sense of direction wasn't muzzled by sleep deprivation, it would look out on the Stutch plant.

"Thank you for making time for me, Mr. Walker. I'm always delighted to welcome visitors from the city to the south."

He had a firm grasp, naturally. He'd had time to bring down the swelling since the campaign finished and to get back into practice. Arbor Muriel was the kid who stayed after school to clean the erasers. His ears were big, with his graying temples trimmed close to let them spread out, and he had a slightly bulbous forehead, like a baby's. Beneath his round cheeks his jaws came straight down to a rectangular chin, a keyhole shape and not at all like a skull in one so lively. He wore glasses with tortoiseshell rims and plastered his black hair over to the side from a part that was broadening like the gap in the Red Sea.

He was in his shirtsleeves, tie a little loose, as if he'd been about to turn back his cuffs and dig into a little wholesome porkbarrel-cutting like he'd promised the electorate. Bad advice. His bony sloping shoulders needed the pads in the suitcoat that hung on the back of his ergonomic chair.

But then again, the gawky awkward message he put out may have been part of the homey tapestry, like that line about the city to the south. You just never know with politicians.

"I'm from Detroit," I said. "Not Biloxi."

He opened his wide grin to give that the hee-haw. "Now, we'll have none of that intra-urban rivalry. It never did either of us any good under the old economy. Now it's just pointless. Thank you, Sergeant."

Vivaldi took this dismissal out of the office without apparent rancor. He was a well-trained yard dog. When the door shut, the mayor and I went through the business of seating, the big desk between us like a fence, and discussion of refreshments. I said yes to coffee, on the condition that it was leaded and black enough to swallow a small galaxy. He put in the order over the intercom, thanking the air-brushed receptionist on the other end twice. He did everything but wag his tail and try to lick her face. He sat back, just far enough to make contact with the back of his chair, and rested his hands lightly on the arms. I'd heard he'd taught high school civics for twenty years before throwing his hat into the ring. He looked like an assistant principal, at that.

"I understand you're here on business for Mr. Thorpe," he said.

I smiled. "I'm impressed."

"I'm sorry?" His eyebrows went up, but the grin didn't slip.

"The clerk downstairs looks like a veteran to me. It usually takes a little while for the new boy in town to bring those petty warlords into the loop."

"If you mean Mrs. Patrick, she reported your visit, yes. I make it a point to get to know as many of the personnel as I can the first day. They seem to appreciate it. Connor Thorpe's been a friend to the people of this community. We like his associates to know we're flattered when they make use of our facilities."

"I'm not an associate, Your Honor. I'm just a fetch, like your man Vivaldi."

"A fetch? Yes." His brain pushed that around like a tongue. He was adjusting his approach to the station of the approachee. I wondered when that coffee would get here. I thought a cigarette might re-ignite my brain cells, but I remembered the voters in Iroquois Heights had passed an ordinance banning smoking in public buildings.

"Have you been working for Mr. Thorpe long?"

"Off and on for a couple of years. I'm a contract laborer. I don't work for anybody for long."

"I see." He didn't. "I imagine he's particular about whom he contracts with. That speaks well for you."

"Does it?"

He frowned. He noticed the pebbled gold cover on his appointment calendar was standing straight up. He flipped it down with an index finger. Then he made another pass. "May I ask what it is you do?"

"I'm in information services."

"Ah. Publicity." Now he was in friendly territory. Then he frowned again. For a man in his line he was as easy to track as a box step. "I shouldn't think a man in Mr. Thorpe's position would have much use for it. Security is usually pretty much concerned with achieving the opposite."

"I shouldn't think a man in your position would say 'I shouldn't.' The people who cast their ballots your way might think you're putting yourself above them."

"I'm afraid I don't understand."

"Better. Americans like their public servants good and ignorant. Ignorant, anyhow. It's the great leveler. Glad to have been of service. I'll be shoving off just as soon as I've had my coffee."

He got sore at last. I'd about given up. His round cheeks reddened, but just then the receptionist came in carrying two steaming mugs and he had to wait until she set them down and left.

"I invited you here in good faith," he said. "Mr. Thorpe has made many investments in this town's welfare on behalf of his employers. With a new engineering and design center going into the former Stutch plant, he promises to make many more. Naturally the residents are eager to know when. On the one hand there will be layoffs when the plant closes. On the other there will be jobs in construction, and more jobs later when the new facility opens. When someone carrying credentials signed by Thorpe asks to see the plant's original blueprints, it's not too far outside the realm of probability to assume preparations are under way to demolish the existing structure, get the ball rolling, or rather swinging." The frown this time was thoughtful. He was making a note to use the

turn of phrase later. "As mayor it's my responsibility to remain in-
formed upon such issues. It's a trust I take seriously. If you don't,
this interview has no purpose."

"I didn't request an interview, Your Honor. My preferences in
the matter weren't considered enough of an issue to ask. Sergeant
Vivaldi is a polite party, his ancestor worked an honorable trade in
Genoa, but I've been rousted by champions. I recognize all the
techniques. The last time I came here a couple of missing links in
uniform tried it the old-fashioned way, with cuffs and bruises. I
preferred that. It worries me when a gorilla behaves like a citizen,
the same way it worries me when a man of the people employs the
personal subjunctive as if he were addressing the House of Lords."
I paused to take a slug of coffee. It was that yellow-brown belly-
wash the vending machines spit out. It smelled like soap and tasted
like sewage. I'd swallowed enough to make the comparison.

"You were mishandled by officers of my police department?
What are their names?" He unclipped a gold pencil from the calendar.

I stopped in the middle of a sneer. I was pretty sure he was serious. That didn't line out with anything I knew about places like
Iroquois Heights. The people in Iroquois Heights empowered slick
crooks with good tailors, aw-shucks country boys with rumpled
hair and larceny in their hearts, big daddies in Stetsons, shriveled
rats in sharkskin, musty-smelling bookworms with two sets of
ledgers, petty thieves with holes in their mattresses, big-time
crooks with numbered accounts in Berne; carny guys, top hats,
born-agains, fallen reformers, sticky-fingered prudes, lechers in
French cuffs, loud liars, quiet chiselers, wardheelers and skimmers,
kleptos and kickback kings, brown-nosers and backstabbers—nice
men, sometimes, for the variety, soft on children and three-legged
cats, but rotten black inside. Men who knew how to make the machine run. They didn't elect idiots. They wouldn't get the chance,

because the men who choreographed the elections wouldn't give them that choice.

The easy explanation, that I was being hustled, sent me back for another gulp of the nasty stuff in the mug. It burned my tongue and dissolved some of the corrosion from my connections.

"I didn't get their names," I lied. "Anyway, what would be the point? Even if you stripped their blouses for show they'd just turn up in some place even worse than this. There's no place worse than this, so they'd probably just come back."

"Just what are you?"

"I'm a private detective. From that it should follow that the other thing you want to know is nobody's business but Thorpe's. I can't sell it to him and give it to you for free. In my little circle I'm considered an ethical character."

"A very little circle." It was his only good line and he didn't like it, being out of character. It tasted as bad as the coffee.

We were silent for a while after that. I was telling my leaden muscles it was time to exit when a door I hadn't noticed before opened in the cedar paneling to my left and Cecil Fish, Iroquois Heights' former city prosecutor, came in with a look on his face that said he'd heard every word.

Everything made sense then. Mark Proust had told me Fish was the one who told Mayor Muriel where to sign, but I hadn't put any store in it. Proust was the kind who told everyone he had friends high up, even if he was the only one he managed to convince. I should have given him the benefit of the doubt. This case seemed bent on tipping every one of my old monsters out of the closet.

# CHAPTER

# TWENTY-THREE

CORRUPT MEN ARE OFTEN SMALL. I don't know why. All the large, bluff Big Jims and Honest Johns who at one time ruled the nation's dirtier, more sprawling cities seem to have been repealed along with Prohibition, or demoted to used-car lots and midnight cable companies. The Napoleon complex is handy: The runt kid whose pants were always getting run up the flagpole at summer camp finds stature serenading the press from the top courthouse step or misquoting the Old Testament on television, and hasn't the patience to get there by the numbers. Or maybe the NFL and the NBA have snapped up all the greedy glandular freaks and all that's left are the half-pints. All I know is you could pack the dozen or so well-placed crooks I've had the happy fortune to know in the back seat of an Escort and still have room for the week's graft.

Cecil Fish was one of the dozen. His three-piece suit, dark brown, and the shine on his cordovans, Italian slip-ons with two-inch heels, called attention to his bantam build and George M. Cohan strut, and the razor-edge white handkerchief in his show pocket made him look like the little man on the Monopoly box, minus the monocle and handlebars. A new hairdresser and male-pattern baldness had gotten rid of his blonde bangs, but the gray was gone. It takes dedication to stay on top of the roots once you decide to tint, but he had the fussy temperament required. He strode in as if he were late for a plane, but stopped short of the desk and looked around, possibly for the flunkies who carried his bags. He was keeping a low profile these days and didn't have flunkies.

The sacrifice hadn't improved his attitude, or maybe he just didn't like what he'd heard. His gaze jerked past me and landed on the mayor. "I'll see to this, Arb. You've got that lunch with the county commissioners."

Muriel glanced at his watch, plain gold with a leather band. It had cost about as much as the clasp on Fish's Rolex. "That isn't for an hour."

"They'll want the reassurance of your smiling face when they drift in. You don't want to come in last: Too imperial. Too last administration."

That final addition made up Muriel's mind. He nodded, a short jerk of his rectangular chin, got up, and slipped on his suitcoat. The built-up shoulders made him appear more mayoral. He was one of the nice ones. He stuck out his hand for me to take. I went ahead and took it and then he was through with me. He paused before a mirror with a polished wooden frame hung near the door to reception, snugged up the knot of his tie, and then he was gone.

The atmosphere in the room changed then, but it had less to do with Muriel's leaving than with Fish's presence. Whenever he entered a place it felt as if someone vital had just stepped out.

Fish swung the mayor's swivel and slung himself into it as if it were his favorite easy chair in his own home. He sat sideways with his head turned to face me, hung one knee over the other, picked up the gold pencil from the desk, and held it with the blunt end against the desk's leather top. He was never at a loss over what to do with his hands, and what he did with them never seemed to have a point. The smirk on his face was as close to genuine warmth as his face ever achieved. It was a failing that had cost him the first couple of times he ran for office; he'd given up on getting rid of it finally and like all good politicians had found a way to turn the liability into an asset. The cocksurety was considered a plus in obtaining flashy convictions. The smirk was Fish's answer to the hole in Adlai Stevenson's shoe.

Speaking of which, the Italian cordovan on his right foot glistened like an oil spill. He glanced at it briefly, checking for scuff marks, then turned his blue eyes on me with the same speculative expression. "You look even worse than last time. The night life must be catching up."

"Nice shoes," I said. "Vivaldi?"

That threw him, but only for a second. He was too experienced a courtroom lawyer to display confusion. "The trouble with you Eagle Scouts is you think poverty is some kind of badge of honor. Some of us care about our appearance, budget a little more for clothes and food, a nice car, a steep mortgage. A nice haircut doesn't mean a wicked man."

"On the other hand it doesn't turn a rat into a poodle. I hear you're a paid lobbyist these days. Who pays? Same gang as before?"

His expression didn't change, although a muscle jumped in one cheek. There used to be a mole there, but if it was surgery they'd done a good job and left no scar. Maybe it had been just a wart after all. "I represent a number of interests. Everyone's entitled to a voice in this democracy."

"Some are louder than others. Those dead presidents can really yell." I drank more coffee. Either I was getting used to the taste or it had improved in contrast to the company. I was as wide awake as a hummingbird.

"I'm using a spare office here, with the mayor's permission. He's a good man, but he's new to government. I explain procedure and provide tips on how to cut through red tape. It's temporary, and strictly without portfolio."

"What's it pay?"

"Straight salary, no perks or benefits. The better I do my job, the shorter it lasts. I think even you would concede I'm no slacker."

"You never tried to turn an hour's work into a full day's pay."

He allowed himself to look surprised. "Thank you for that."

"You can shove your thanks up your boondoggle. I don't think you even like money. It's just something you ride, like the interurban, and change trains just before it derails. You've got a cockroach's flair for survival. Now you can thank me."

"Damn you, you shabby little saint," he said mildly. "What are you doing for Connor Thorpe?"

"I'm looking for a missing person, a small boy. It's got nothing to do with you." I watched him to see if it had anything to do with him. Nothing moved in his face, not even the muscle in his cheek.

"What's the boy's name, and why does Thorpe care?"

"Ask him. A little matter of a confidential investigation is nothing between a couple of close friends like you."

It was a gamble. The odds scared the hell out of me, like diving headfirst into a dark swimming pool. If he was in with Thorpe, or if he wasn't and called my bluff and asked him about the boy, the plant would be waiting for me with torches and pitchforks.

Fish retreated, with the tiniest shake of his head. The water was deep enough and not too cold. He changed weapons, more smoothly than Muriel. "Earlier this week you were detained by two officers of this police department for having a defective taillight."

"License plate light," I corrected. I'd wondered when he'd get around to it. Fish twirled the police like a pistol. His ability to win their loyalty was his steel core. They reported to him ahead of their watch captains.

"License plate light. You showed them a check signed by Leland Stutch's widow. Are you working for her as well as for Thorpe, or are the cases related?"

"I didn't say I was working for Thorpe."

"You said you were looking for a little boy."

"You asked what I was doing for Thorpe. I said I was looking for a little boy. If you assumed I was answering your question, it wasn't my job to set you straight. I'm not a paid lobbyist."

"So Rayellen Stutch has hired you to find this boy."

"If you like." I sipped coffee. I was starting to enjoy the conversation.

He banged the table suddenly. He'd forgotten the pencil was in his fist and he marred the leather top. He flung away the pencil to shake a finger at me, the way he'd shaken it at a hundred juries to put some animation in their oxlike faces.

"It's a mistake to think that because I don't have my name on a door in this building I'm harmless," he said. "Muriel never asks questions he doesn't want to know the answers to. When I shoo him out of the room it's bare knuckles. I couldn't use them back when there was some chance I'd be a senator. That's gone, and as I recall you had some small part in it."

"Was that you? I forgot. You had more hair then."

"I'll remind you. We went a couple of rounds over that Broderick killing a few years ago. I had you on the mat once, but I couldn't bring my heel down on your throat the way I wanted to, because people were watching. Well, the auditorium's empty. I've got free use of two hundred and fifty police officers. I had that before, but now I've also got a second team. Cops busted off the job because they did a little improv on the shift and got caught on video. Parole cops who have favors done for them by ex-cons they could bust back to prison at the scratch of a pen. Election toughs who started tearing down opposition posters, then graduated to caving in precinct workers' ribs in parking lots.

"There's a third team, too, that I don't even like to think about.

But I'm an attorney. I won't lose sleep forever." His face was bright. He might have been standing on a platform.

I grinned. "That's quite a half-time talk. Ever scare yourself?"

He went all ice then, as only the blue-eyed ones can. But he had the same control over his moods they say Houdini had over his muscles. For sure it had taken some kind of escape artist to turn a recall into an unofficial appointment as mayor.

"What were you looking for in the Stutch plant blueprints? What's it got to do with Rayellen Stutch and a missing boy? Is there a boy?"

"There's a boy. And I like to look at blueprints. The older the better. Blueprints, not boys. It's a hobby."

"Boys or blueprints?"

"Blueprints. The boy's a job. How about you?"

His mouth hung open for a moment, and I knew why they called him Fish-hook down on Boyle Street. Then he found his smirk. "You must like pain and hardship. Your résumé shows that." The smirk capsized. "What are you doing?"

"Violating an ordinance." I touched a match to the Winston I'd stuck between my lips. "You're all hide and horns, counselor. You can use my ears for ashtrays, all right. Only you won't, because Connor Thorpe's tougher. You bought-boys like to leer at the suckers who punch the clock and buy on time. You think they're afraid to take shortcuts. They'll never be as afraid as you. On the one hand you've got the reform crowd to worry about, the citizens' groups and the Eyewitness News hacks and the spooks in your own camp who will sell you out for a free dinner, because when you buy a jackal that's what you get. On the other hand you've got the guy who bought you to begin with, who knows you'll sell *him* out for the same free dinner. He'll also throw you to the 'gators when they froth up the water, because he's a jackal too. Those clowns I scared off with Mrs. Stutch's check will never have it as bad as you.

They're just maggots, any buck will do as long as it's dirty. You're a maggot with ambitions. You want to be Thorpe."

"You talk a good half-time yourself," he said. "Assuming you're right—which is one hell of an assumption, and slander besides—how does that make me worse off?"

"There'll always be a dirty buck to be made, but there's only one Connor Thorpe to a thousand bought guys like you. He controls the security budgets of the Big Three. By now he's used them to dig up enough on the men who deal out those budgets to nail himself tenure, followed by a tropical retirement. He's a corruptor, which is a whole different creation from the simply corrupt. You'll never graft enough to catch him."

"I'm not working for Thorpe." This came out on an automatic spring.

"Neither am I. But I'm the one with his letter in my pocket."

He found his smirk again finally. This time he'd had to scrabble for it in a drawer. "You won't always have a letter."

"Yeah, well, mine's bigger than yours." I tipped the cigarette, which I hadn't wanted anyway, into the mug on the desk and got up. I winced a little when I put weight on my ankle. Fish was too experienced a predator to miss it.

"Hurt yourself?"

"For once, not in the Heights."

Sergeant Vivaldi stopped gabbing with the receptionist and pushed himself off the desk when I came out. I swept on through and punched up the elevator. I should have taken the stairs. Just as the doors opened, Vivaldi came trotting out of reception. He asked me to hold the car.

I held it. He got in, said, "Ground floor?" and pressed a button. The doors rolled shut and we rode down in silence.

When the car didn't stop on the ground floor, I stepped back quickly to give myself swinging room, but my ankle was hurting and I was off balance. Vivaldi's right fist caught me just above the belt buckle. I doubled over; that was real enough, but before he could give me the two-fisted club from above I grasped hold of his crotch and twisted as if I were working the airlock to freedom. He said, "Jesus!" in about four syllables and grabbed for my arm. I reached up, clutched his face hard, glasses and all, with my other hand, and straightened my arm with a pop, driving the back of his head into the mirrored lining of the elevator. The glass dished in and starred.

The doors opened on a basement boiler room. I punched the ground-floor button. The doors took a week to close. The car took longer making up its mind to rise, but I didn't know my way around the basement or if there was an exit. Vivaldi, glasses gone and his hair in his face, remembered he had a gun. He stopped reaching for it when I stuck a finger in his face. He'd recognize that if he'd been fetching for Cecil Fish long.

"No holes in the merchandise," I said. "You folks sure do enforce the smoking laws up here."

It worked. He held that half-crouch, breathing hard, with pain lines on his face and one hand partly inside his jacket, while the car eased itself to an obese stop. When the doors opened, I stepped aside and held the button for a white-haired man in a rusty leisure suit pushing a wheelchair with a mummy in it wearing a silk dress and a blue wig. Vivaldi shuffled to the other side and hadn't made a move to come out when I let the doors go.

Out in the parking lot I glanced up at the second-floor window I figured belonged to Mayor Muriel's outer office. It was bullet-resistant Plexiglass, tinted, and I couldn't tell if Fish or anyone else was standing there. It didn't matter. He'd taken his kick at the sandcastle and wouldn't risk another. One thing you can depend on is a bought man.

He got in the last word anyway. A canary-yellow parking ticket stuck out its tongue at me from behind the windshield wiper of the Ram pickup. There on it was the plate number, penciled neatly in a left-hand slope, and no cops hiding in the box to jump out and grab me and hand me over to Toledo. Some coffee-sergeant inside had probably pinned up a notice offering an apartment for rent on top of the hot sheet on the bulletin board.

# TWENTY-FOUR

THE STUTCH MOTORS PLANT crouched on its hill like a gaunt spider, casting no shadow under a clouded noonday sky, vampiric. Even the smoke from its three stacks didn't appear to be moving, parallel rivulets dried to black crusts on zinc. The gridded window on this side reflected the buildings of Iroquois Heights. It wasn't giving up anything.

This time the angle was slightly different. I was looking out the window of Rayellen Stutch's art studio, a plain room with walls painted off-white in order not to distract from an artist's honest evaluation of her paintings, and which would look dirty yellow against the soft whites in the conservatory. Mrs. Campbell, as gray and calm as a bell moth, had installed me there while Mrs. Stutch was changing, then glided on out. I'd as much as called her a busybody to her face, but she was playing the faithful retainer and didn't curl a lip. Now someone was putting the baby grand through its paces in the room next door: Handel, I thought, although I only knew the old gentleman from long drives when the jazz stations went progressive and one more doowop on an oldies track would send me up onto the median. The housekeeper's left hand was wasted on the Germans. Someone ought to introduce Fats Waller into her repertoire.

Unframed canvases and works on paper leaned against the baseboards all around the studio: pastels and watercolors, oils and acrylics, and a train wreck of a charcoal sketch Mrs. Stutch might have done during a hiccup fit. There were still lifes and pastorals that reminded me of the rustic images on Mayor Muriel's walls, portraits and abstracts, one or two copies of old masters done with a twenty-first-century twist. I recognized the strokes from the framed costume prints on the hallway walls outside. On the drafting board, unfinished, Mrs. Campbell noodled the white piano's middle scale in three-quarter profile, surrounded by pencil sketches in long view and close-up fixed with pushpins to the board. Her expression, glistening in fresh oils, was serene.

The art was good, pleasing at least to my monstrously untrained eye, and I'd rather have spent the time looking at it than at the old plant. But since I was fated to while away a good part of the night inside I needed to scope it out. Also the room reeked of turpentine and my eyes were burning just fine without help. I raised the double-hung window eight inches and wedged an aerosol can of fixative under the sash.

Rayellen Stutch came in dressed in a shimmering copper-colored scoopneck top without sleeves, white pleated slacks with flared cuffs, and soft brown slippers with moccasin stitching. The slippers underscored her resemblance to an Indian princess. Her black hair spilled uninterrupted to her shoulders and her eyes were as dark as tamarack. She stopped when she saw me.

"You look awful," she said.

"Thanks. I feel horrible. Are you part Indian?"

"Dutch, I'm told. Stutch the Dutch." She smiled briefly. "All the blonde genes spilled through the hole in the dike before I came along. Please sit down. You look as if you're about to collapse."

I shook my head. "I'll just lean here. You'd have to pry me back up. The only thing holding me together is a whole lot of whiskey, a little bit of caffeine, and a quarter mile of athletic tape. Nice portrait." I tilted an eyebrow toward the oil on the drafting table.

"Just a doodle. If I could catch on canvas what comes out of the piano, well." She left it. "What in the world happened? Mrs. Campbell said you'd called to cancel lunch."

"An oversight. I haven't eaten in so long I forgot how to chew."

She was out of the room before I could put a period on it. The music next door stopped, voices murmured. Mrs. Stutch came back in. "I hope eggs and coffee are all right," she said. "I didn't dine here last night, so there are no leftovers. Mrs. Campbell was going to shop this morning, but that was when we were expecting guests for lunch."

I said eggs would be fine, ducking the implied question at the end. I asked her how the fundraiser went.

"I suppose it was a success. I don't like putting the arm on people. Becoming wealthy and staying that way is hard work, as I said, but I'm expected to make people feel guilty for not giving something *back*, as if they stole it or swindled it. Anyway, we don't need a new library, just more space for books. Instead we're going to have a media center."

"Was Thorpe there?"

"No. He never attends these things. About the most he does is pose for pictures in his office giving someone a check." She paused with lips parted. "Is there some reason that's important?"

"I wanted to see if you were backing his play. If you were, you might alibi him. Or maybe not. It would be easy to find out from someone else if he was there. But I know he wasn't, so I'm just spilling words." I took a deep breath and spilled some more. I didn't stop until I got to Ray Montana. Her skin paled beneath the tan. She drew the chair out from the drafting table and sat down. It was a tall chair. We were almost eye to eye.

"This Iris was a friend?"

"Why does everyone ask that?" I said. "And what's it matter? She's as dead as Pharaoh and David Glendowning."

"I don't believe Connor had anything to do with it. Murder and kidnapping. Why?"

"From the start he didn't like your looking for your husband's daughter and granddaughter. You said yourself he dragged his feet when you wanted to put him on it. He told me when he sent me to you he hoped nothing would come of it. I'm pretty sure he set those cops on me when I was leaving this house. He knew they wouldn't scare me off, being six feet and one inch of real man with assorted attachments, but they might rattle me enough at the out-set to take the fun out of the detail work. When that fizzled, he put Proust on me, to follow me around in that brown Chevy and find out what I found out when I found it out.

"Proust was a little rusty at first; I spotted him. After that he got better, or else he pulled a rotation on me. He'd still have con-tacts on the local force. They didn't have to know what it was about. When it came time to do Glendowning and then me, he went solo. Also the kidnap. That schnook Glendowning only got tagged because it had to be done with his truck. That was a shame, maybe. He was talking about getting himself straightened around." I didn't not believe it, but I didn't believe it, either. When someone's dead you're supposed to say something nice about him, and I hadn't liked his haircut.

"But what does Connor have to gain?"

"I'll ask him with this." I'd snapped the Chief's Special back onto my belt. Now I unholstered it and slapped it down on the windowsill.

She looked at it without recoiling. Well, she was born in Brooklyn.

"Where? Not in the plant." She glanced out the window in-voluntarily.

I folded my arms and said nothing. I was too tired to play it any way but out of an old melodrama.

She nodded then. "That's right. You said something about my backing his play."

"I got the phrase from someone this morning. Some things stick. Like who stands to gain the most if one of Stutch's heirs doesn't come out of the hospital and another vanishes from the interstate and is never heard from again."

"I hired you to find them, have you forgotten?"

"That was before you knew Cecilia Willard had a great-grandson. That's four of you splitting thirteen million a year. You might have to take in boarders."

"I could have let the thing stay dead and kept the whole thing. I would anyway. The bulk of the estate went to Leland's grandson. Most if not all of it will come out of his portion."

I picked up the revolver. She didn't move or react, just sat on the tall stool with her slim ankles intertwined.

"One thing my marriage taught me is the law belongs to the side with the most lawyers," she said. "If I had to, I could tie up the courts until young Matthew's reading *Modern Maturity.*"

That rang like coin. I holstered the gun.

"Where else if not the plant?" I asked. "He's always there."

"You won't get in. It's built like—"

"I know what it's built like. I know the footage and the stresses and the name of the architect. The reason it's built like that is the reason he's holding the boy there, if the boy's alive. It's designed to turn away a mob. Only I'm not a mob. A drop of water can sweat through a dam built to hold back a river."

"But how will you get out?"

"That's the part I'm still working on." I hadn't told her yet about my talk with Montana. I realized then I never would, although I trusted her far enough now not to run to Thorpe with the information. It wouldn't take more than an ounce of common sense to talk me out of what I'd rigged up.

She shook her head, sending blue shimmers through that fall of hair. "I didn't hire you for a suicide mission. I'd rather pull the plug than let you go in there alone. I don't go there myself, although ostensibly I own it. It's Connor's lair. What he has with the men under him is something I can't buy."

"It's a guy thing. You wouldn't understand."

"I don't have to." She wasn't smiling. "All I have to do is fire you."

"Go ahead. I fire easy."

"Will you walk away if I do?"

"Not so easy. The world's turned. My neck and my ankle will heal, expenses cover that. They don't cover Iris or Glendowning or Constance in the hospital or little Matthew, whose world is shot to hell and he knows even less about why than we do. If he's alive. Then there's the posthumous frame I was supposed to stick my head through in Toledo. I don't worry so much about myself, but I do care what happens to my corpse. Those things have to come out of Thorpe."

"Those things are what police are for."

"This town doesn't have police. The real police would have to clear jurisdiction through what wears the uniform here. That would be followed by a call to Thorpe asking what time would be convenient for a raid. I might as well call him on your bill and leave the taxpayers a little more to bribe the trash man with."

"I'm the town's richest citizen. I know a bit about money and power. I wasn't brought up in Walnut Grove, and I wasn't out diddling the pool boy while Leland was on the telephone, wheeling and dealing in both hemispheres. If it's muscle you need—"

"Knowing the vocabulary doesn't mean you speak the language," I said. "Hiring leg-breakers takes almost as much practice as breaking legs. You never know where they've been, for one thing. Around here they've probably all broken legs for Thorpe. When push comes to shove they might forget whose legs they're being paid to break this time out." I was talking too much about breaking legs. My own conversation was beginning to taste as bad as Muriel's coffee. "Anyway, I've got it covered."

"Covered how?"

I pushed away from the windowsill. "The less you know about that part of the operation, the fewer questions you'll be expected to answer when the authorities come around. And they'll come around, sure as winter. As a matter of fact, it'd be best if you fired me right now. That way everything I do from here on in I do as a free agent."

"If I fire you now, can I re-hire you later?"

"No comment. That might be one of the questions they'll ask." I waited.

She unhooked her ankles, hooked them the other way. "You're fired."

"What, no severance package?"

She smiled for the first time in forever. Then she became as solemn as an Indian; "as a Dutchman" didn't answer. "When are you going in?"

"As soon as I get some sleep. I've been running on fumes since sunup. I'm putting into a motel. I expect the cops at my place any-time. The real cops."

"Do you have a bag?"

"In the pickup."

"Bring it in. I'll have Mrs. Campbell make up a guest room while you're eating."

I'd forgotten about eating. I hoped I didn't nod off with a wad of eggs in my throat.

"I've been here too long already. If someone spots that pickup, I'm finished."

"Pull it into the garage."

"You'd be harboring a fugitive. There's a buzzer out on me in two states."

"Don't fight me on this one," she said. "You're too tired to win twice in one afternoon."

I didn't try. Lead was creeping into my extremities and darkening the edges of my brain.

I'd parked the Ram behind the house, where it wouldn't be visible from the street in case some prowlie had read his sheet, but that wouldn't stop a neighbor from coming around to borrow a cup of money and going away to spread the word the Widow Stutch was entertaining a visitor. One of a pair of electric doors opened in the garage with almost no noise at all and I parked next to a bratty European sports job with a maroon finish that went down a block. There was a row of gleaming hoods beyond it, another roadster and a stretch Cadillac for show and a Land Rover Defender standing tall on tires the size of Volkswagens, in case a safari broke out. I wondered who took care of them all. Mrs. Campbell, maybe, when she wasn't playing the piano or moving furniture. You just didn't know what the house contained at a glance; including its owner, who painted portraits and offered to raise an army of muscle. Old Man Stutch had recognized a bargain when he saw it.

The door thrummed shut as I scooped my bag from the narrow space behind the seat. No garage door I'd ever seen moved half as fast with so little fanfare. Mrs. Campbell took the bag away from me at a side door. I followed her through a pantry the size of my living room into an acre of bright kitchen hung with copper utensils like mission bells, and sat down at a painted country table that belonged in Mt. Vernon, set with china and six forks.

The eggs were omelets, golden brown, stuffed with peppers and onions and cheese, smothered in a cream sauce. I yawned my way through two helpings and half a pot of coffee. After that I floated off on someone's arm—I think it was Rayellen Stutch's—to an upstairs bedroom done in mauve and silver, with a tall bureau and a big oak four-poster festooned with some kind of netting, or maybe that was just my vision beginning to cloud. At least the window looked out on a part of Iroquois Heights that didn't include the damn plant.

I'd torn up the road back and forth between two states on three different sets of wheels, been in an accident, had a gun stuck at me, been sassed at by three different kinds of crook and caught one in the breadbasket from a fourth, stumbled over a corpse (first of the year), and managed to lose three people under my protection, at least one permanently, since the last time I'd closed my eyes. Just another day in the life of a self-employed screw-up. I needed twelve hours. I told whoever helped me to the bed to wake me in four.

I was left alone to undress and unwind the tape from my ankle, which I did without worrying what I would substitute in its place. The ankle was striped violet and purple and a gay shade of yellow, but the swelling didn't look any worse for all the time I'd been spending on it. Those ambulance boys were worth more than what they were paid, an epidemic condition in our booming economy. I tossed the coils onto the nightstand next to my revolver in its holster. My neck was stiffer than ever. I would need that brace soon if I didn't want to walk around like Ed Sullivan for the rest of the year, but where I was headed it would just be in the way.

Naked, I slid between sheets as crisp and cool as dry snow. Just before I coasted off into dreamless black, I thought I heard the grumble and cough of diesel engines barking to life, from as far west as Green Bay and as far south as Louisville. I caught a glimpse behind my eyelids of tall silver stacks farting balls of black smoke in Grand Rapids and Columbus, down logging trails north of Buffalo and along the banks of the St. Lawrence; a dense fleet of eighteen-wheeled heavy cruisers thundering onto freeways on every side of the big mitten, smashing gears and blasting the same harsh note out of their air horns that Ray Montana used when he pronounced the name Iroquois Heights.

# CHAPTER

# TWENTY-FIVE

THESE THINGS I KNOW:

When it comes to sleep, four hours is not as good as eight.

Sometimes, four hours is worse than none at all.

I might have kept myself alert unloading and cleaning my gun and reloading it, practicing my fast draw, or rotating the Ram's tires and changing the oil. Instead I was still coasting downhill through the Black Forest and nowhere near the bottom when my engine started knocking. It was someone's knuckles, Rayellen Stutch's or Mrs. Campbell's, rapping on the guest room door. Before I could answer it I had to brake, turn around, and begin the long climb up toward the light. The trip took more out of me than the one down, and by the time I cleared the bricks of the Stutch plant off my eyelids and blinked up at the gray mesh between me and the ceiling, I was sweating and a heavy fog filled my head, thick enough to roll sluggishly when I turned my head against the needles in my neck, like one of those tilting-wave toys that take up more room on an executive's desk than a day's work.

Someone had lashed a Chevy short block to each of my feet,

but I managed to swing them out from under the top sheet and down to the floor. The pain from my injured ankle took the Overland route to my brain, down arroyos and over mountains and around Apache country, but it arrived fresh and full of fire just the same. When I bent down to rub the swelling, the glutinous mass shifted toward the front of my skull and I began to black out. I jerked my head back up, lighting up all the pain-points in my abused tendons but cutting through the fog.

Whoever was out there was still knocking. She'd been knocking for a month. I looked up at a robe hanging from one of the bedposts, a dressing gown with martini olives floating on a burgundy sea and a lining of dark red silk. I stood carefully, dragged it on, and tied the sash. It was old—not worn-old, but of a quality that had gone out with mahogany dashboards and steamer trunks. The sleeves came short of my wrists, the hem just to my knees. The garment would have fit Leland Stutch. It seemed gaudy for a man who had bought his pinstripes and Homburgs in the same store where Herbert Hoover shopped. It had probably been a gift, which explained its bandbox condition. A vintage clothing store would have traded a bundle for it, but for me it was just something to wrap around my nudity.

There were no slippers. Stutch's size fives wouldn't have supported a sparrow hawk. I waded barefoot through silver pile to the door and cracked it. Mrs. Stutch smiled through the gap.

"I brought coffee. Are you hungry? I sent Mrs. Campbell to the store."

"Thanks. I'll stay hungry. I'd rather have the circulation going to my brain. Is there a shower in this zip code?"

"The house isn't that big. I bought it to avoid just that kind of joke. Bathroom's across the hall. May I at least set down the tray?"

I swung the door all the way open. She sidled around me, carrying a heavy silver tray with a tall matching coffee pot shaped like a hookah and a pair of white china cups on saucers. She smiled at the sight of me in the dressing gown. "Sorry I didn't have anything in your size. Leland told me he used to have a bodyguard at the time of the strikes, a big good-looker who stood in for Johnny Weissmuller. People were always trying to shake his hand. They thought the little man with him was one of Leland's clerks."

"It's the little yappy dogs that bite. What time is it?"

"Twenty to six. You've got a couple of hours before dark. Are you sure you don't want to sleep a little longer?"

"I'm sure I do, but I've got arrangements to make. Do you have any kind of athletic tape in the house?" I was gripping a bedpost to keep weight off my ankle.

"Miles. I'm a fitness junkie, remember? Would you like me to wind it on?" She set the tray on an upholstered bench at the foot of the bed.

I said I'd manage. She went to get the tape while I showered.

The bathroom was Nile green, with French-milled cakes of emerald soap in the shower and in a little jadeite tray shaped like a coiled asp next to the sink. The towels were striped green and white, and Cleopatra trolled her fingers over the side of her barge inside a green baize frame above the toilet, to put the fine point on it. It was a nice house, what I'd seen of it when I was awake, except someone had let a decorator run riot in it.

I'd brought in my bag, and from it I took my electric travel razor and buzzed off the top growth. I pulled out a dark gray jersey top and a pair of crushable khakis, well-crushed, and put them on. Back in the bedroom, I sat on the bed and let Rayellen Stutch watch me tape my ankle from the roll she'd brought, drinking coffee in a mauve satin wing chair. She was wearing the outfit she'd worn previously and looked as fresh as if she'd just put it on; fresher anyway than me. I rolled on thick black wool socks and stuck my feet inside the elastic-sided boots. They felt clammy inside.

"Shouldn't the whole outfit be black?" she asked.

"In a Hitchcock film. These urban nights never get dark enough. I'd stick out." I took the .38 from its holster and spun the cylinder. Then I stood and put the works on my belt. I stuffed my sportcoat into the overnight bag. I'd left the leather Windbreaker in the pickup. It wasn't any more practical but it went with the look. When they found my carcass I didn't want Mr. Blackwell clucking over it.

I grasped the bedpost to pull myself up and fetch my coffee from the bench. She made a noise of protest and started to rise, but I propelled myself onto my feet, ignoring the jag of pain, and beat her to it. I poured a cup and drank, trying to lean against the bed-post in such a way that it didn't look as if it were standing in for my starch. Otherwise she might do me the favor of calling for back-up after I left. For all I knew, Thorpe had a tap on her line.

She read my mind; the last part, anyway. "I've been thinking about Connor. I know what he's up to."

"Me too. You first."

"He worked for Leland a long time. What if Leland promised him a legacy, back before I came along? Then along I came, and Leland forgot. Connor sucked it up then, but this business of additional heirs set him off. He's holding the boy for ransom."

"Did Leland ever discuss his will with you?"

"We never talked about money."

"Interesting marriage." The coffee in my cup hadn't grown on the same slope as the stuff downtown.

"People who never get sick don't talk about their health," she said. "What do you think of my theory?"

"It makes sense. It made sense when I came up with it. If there's anything in it, you should get a call."

"It hasn't been that long. Should we wait?"

"That would be prudent."

She smiled without warmth. "If you were in favor of waiting, 'smart' would be the word you'd use. 'Prudent' is for spinsters and presidents."

"There's a time factor. Unless Proust has used his one telephone call on Thorpe, he doesn't know that I'm not dead in Glendowning's garage in Toledo. I don't think Proust was in any shape to call. Giving birth might be a bigger deal than having a slug taken out of your knee, but I've never heard of anyone carrying on any sort of conversation during either procedure. The longer Thorpe goes without getting word, the more suspicious he gets. I need to get in before he decides to shore up the security or worse, fly the coop. If it's cut-and-run, he'll get rid of the boy. He'd just slow him down."

"Then what are we waiting for?"

"What do people usually wait for under these circumstances? Dark."

She sat back, fingering her cup. "You're a funny sort of detective. Do you go off on crusades often?"

"The crusaders didn't go off on crusades. They're not cost effective. It so happens I've knocked a hole in the criminal code, and if I don't dig up someone to stuff into it, the people who keep the code will use whatever's handy. Whatever's handy being me."

"It wouldn't have anything to do with your lady friend getting killed."

"She was beheaded," I said. "It was a damn good-looking head, too."

We talked a little more, Mrs. Stutch trying to find out what my plans were for leaving the plant, me changing the subject to the décor in the house. It turned out Mrs. Campbell had done that, too. She was a frustrated aunt. After that we went back down to the studio, where I borrowed an X-acto knife Mrs. Stutch used to trim paper, cleared the drafting table, and sliced young Dollier's photo out of the corner of the General Motors security ID I'd borrowed from him. I cut my picture out of my investigator's license, rubber-cemented it to the GM card, and secured the works behind the window of my pocket folder. It looked cheesy in the room's electric light, and no one was going to believe I was twenty-four years old. I was counting plenty on its being dark enough at the plant to bluff my way past the gate.

"Take the Land Rover, why don't you?" Mrs. Stutch asked, as I swept away the scraps and put the folder in my pleated hip pocket. "If you're right about the pickup, you might be stopped before you make it to the end of the block."

"I'd rather take the chance no one sees the plate. White Rams are as common as carjackers. There's only one Stutch Land Rover, and I look even less like you than I do the kid who belongs to the card. Anyway, using Glendowning's ride appeals to my sense of justice."

"I didn't realize you were so poetic."

"It's not an asset in my work. I'll call you when it's finished." I didn't add that the call wouldn't be necessary if it finished the way I had planned. Everyone in Iroquois Heights was going to know there were doings up on the hill. I slid off the stool.

"It's not dark yet," she said.

"I've got someone I have to see first."

She got up from the chair she'd been sitting in. "You didn't tell me that part."

"I don't tell anyone everything. It's a habit."

She stood very close in front of me. I smelled scented soap on her skin. It wasn't the green stuff from the guest bath. It would be engineered to remove all traces of the heavy exercise she liked, with something added that wouldn't be available to the general run of health maven. "I've forgotten your first name."

"Amos."

"I like it. Old Testament?"

"It's not getting any younger. Don't fall into the habit of calling me by it. When the cops come visiting I'm just a hand you hired for some legal legwork."

"Don't worry. I have the advantage of not having been born with money. A better education might have made me think I'm smarter than them." She put a hand to her throat. "It's been a long time, you know."

"Since Brooklyn?"

"No." She was breathing shallowly. Her nostrils quivered. "Being Mrs. Leland Stutch is like being the most popular girl at school. All alone Saturday night because everyone assumes she's spoken for."

"It's longer than that. Old Man Stutch died before Viagra."

"So you can see my situation."

"I bet you were popular, at that."

There was a little space during which Mrs. Campbell, back from the store, sounded out the opening bars of a nocturne in the next room, or maybe it was Count Basie on Valium. Then the mistress of the house went up on the balls of her feet and kissed me. Her tongue pried at my lips. I let it. After a while I grasped her upper arms and pushed her back down on her heels.

A hard red light flickered in the brown of her eyes. "Maybe I'm not Dutch enough for you."

"Brunettes are okay. My mother was a brunette. Field hands don't mesh with boss ladies. No future in it."

"Ethics, is it?"

"To start."

"I fired you, remember? We're just two people."

"I'm just one person. You're the navy and the marines and the New York Philharmonic. Bad arithmetic. Leland's dressing gown doesn't fit. I'm getting out before you order one in my size."

"That's reverse snobbery. I'm not in the market for a kept man."

"That's okay, because I don't keep any better than yogurt. This is just juxtaposition and adrenaline. I need the adrenaline for later."

She tugged down the hem of her blouse. "You're in mourning, is that it?"

"If you like. There's no future in it either way."

"Don't flatter yourself. I wasn't thinking of anything permanent."

"That's the hell of it," I said. "I'm in the kind of work where the landscape keeps changing. Permanence is the only thing that might buy me."

She'd stopped rearranging herself. She hadn't gotten that disarranged to begin with. She looked Indian again, as impassive as the head on a can of baking powder. "Someday, some woman— not me—will make you that offer. I hope for both your sakes you won't be too busy looking back over your shoulder to listen."

"The thing is I was." I picked up my bag and got out of there.

# TWENTY-SIX

THE LAND ROVER had tracked a mixture of sand and red clay into the garage. For a moment I thought about moistening a handful of it with water from the sillcock inside the door and smearing it over the Ram's license plate, but vetoed the idea on the grounds that even an Iroquois Heights cop might be familiar with the gag and move in for a closer look.

The clouds were turning a deep eggplant color in the west when I backed out. I thought for a second I saw the red light of the sun on the lip of the land, but the overcast was complete. The angry copper glow belonged to a stream of liquefied steel pouring from the ladle into molds behind the east window of the Stutch plant. When the building came down in a year or so and the engineering and design center went in with its computer stations and fluorescent midnights, the inner workings of the automobile industry would be hidden from the unprivileged eye, cosseted behind soundproofed and heat-resistant walls and cricketing keyboards, and cloaked in mystery overall, like a conjuring act in Atlantic City. For now, the plant was the dead last place on earth where one could witness the flexing of the naked muscle that turned the crank that worked the gears that made the Industrial Revolution revolve.

Twenty years ago, in the midst of white flight from Detroit, the Iroquois Heights citizenry had become alarmed that over-development might deprive the place of its small-town charm. Never mind the fact that it was as charming as Black Rock. They voted to float bonds for the construction of a greensward in the southeast corner to serve as a quarantine line between themselves and the festering metropolis at their feet. Matching federal funds gave the city council authority to condemn twenty-eight privately owned acres, including a number of historic storefronts and a res-idence under construction. Dozers carved the flat landscape into enchanted hills and mysterious valleys, sod was laid, trees were planted, and nature walks and bridle paths installed withal. There was a bandstand and a duck pond and a scatter of picnic tables and wrought-iron benches chained to concrete footings. Six months after the ribbon-cutting ceremony, the mayor, the city treasurer, and the private contractor who had bid low on the project retired. Another two years went by before someone noticed that the band-stand was tilting a few degrees to the left. When city workers at-tempted to jack it up and introduce a ton of fresh cement to the foundation, the jack sank out of sight. A private environmental group conducted tests and reported that the park was built on the site of an old landfill, richly contaminated by battery-acid spills and the leakage from oil drums, which had rusted through finally and caused the earth piled on top of them to collapse. By this time, the poured slabs beneath the tables and benches and the comfort station had begun to crack apart and a brackish swamp had opened on the south end of the pond. Of the three individuals responsi-ble, one was dead, one was under indictment in Florida for laun-dering Colombian drug money, and the third was living in a country with no extradition treaty with the U.S. They called the place Victory Park.

I drove the Ram between a pair of stone posts where a gate had been before the city gave up charging admission and followed the crumbling composition drive to a parking lot in the northwest corner. There was only one car in the lot, a navy or black four-door Oldsmobile nosed into a low brick retaining wall with a view beyond of the city lights cast out like bits of colored glass on black felt. I pulled in beside the car, leaned over, and rolled down the window on the pickup's passenger side. The tinted window on the driver's side of the Olds whirred down at the same time. Ray Montana looked out at me with his hands resting on the wheel. There was a block of shadow in the passenger's seat.

"Is that Dave Glendowning's truck?" Montana asked.

I said it was.

"You like to take chances."

"Nope. All my pillows still have the DO NOT REMOVE tags. I needed wheels and didn't have them. Glendowning had them and didn't need them. Around here they arrest you for walking to the mailbox."

"I could've lent you a car."

"Everyone's offering me transportation. Where were you all at two this morning? Who's that with you?"

"Personal security." As Montana spoke, the shadow moved, leaning forward into the last gasp of light from the shrouded sun. A shaved blue-black head with a gold loop gleaming in one earlobe showed above a matching dark shirt-and-tie set. The face was familiar. I'd seen it on TV, either during one of Montana's press conferences or in a documentary on Easter Island.

"Where's Reznick?"

"He's the day man," Montana said.

"I thought bodyguards did the driving."

"Everyone thinks that. That's why they shoot at the passenger."

"What good's personal security with a bullet in its head?"

"What good is he if it's in mine? Anyway a head's a hard thing to hit."

"Can we continue this conversation in your car? I've got a touch of whiplash."

At the end of a brief murmured conference the bodyguard got out. He wasn't as big as he looked sitting. He had short bandy legs and a heavy torso, an authentic Chippendale. At that he was big enough. His suitcoat was a size too large: a .44 magnum long. He was still standing there when I climbed down from the cab and came around to his side. He smelled of gun oil and clean sweat.

"It's okay," Montana called from inside the car. "Get in the back."

"He's armed." The man's voice was a light tenor. Elephants are keyed a little high too.

"Who isn't? Get in the back."

He got in the back. I slid into the bucket seat next to Montana's. The car had that new-toy odor of fresh rubber and molded plastic. The CB radio in the dash was the first I'd seen in years, but they'd never gone away, really; just ebbed back to their source. Truckers called home on cell phones but kept in touch with one another over the citizens' band.

Montana's profile was sharp against the window on the other side. The reflected glow of the lights beyond the wall gleamed in his cornea. "Looks clean from up here."

"Not really," I said. "You can still see it."

"Everybody's got one Iroquois Heights story. What's yours?"

"I'm greedy. I've got ten. I left two teeth on Pioneer Street and three full sets of fingerprints at the county jail. The last time that happened they threw me in a pit with a black inmate twice my size and laid bets on which one of us came out. Those are the big-ticket items. I won't put you to sleep with the small stuff. What about you?"

"Nothing, personally. Being the son of a famous man has some perks. My father had a story. He wasn't born famous. You know about this park?"

"The gift that keeps on giving."

"Before that. That was comic relief. I mean back when it was a dump. Steelhaulers were on strike, blocking roads and gas pumps to discourage the scabs. The old city racket squad parked a seven-passenger growler crossways on the street that ran past the fence, and when my father stopped his gas rig like a citizen they pulled him and his partner out of the cab and dragged them behind the fence and gave them the Louisville Massage for about five minutes. Long time."

"Baseball bats?"

"Get your eyebrows off the headliner. Where do you think *we* got the idea?"

"I didn't mean that. I thought the cops preferred saps and truncheons."

"Not then. Greenberg and Gehringer were in the lineup and the whole country was horsehide-happy. Anyway my father curled up on the ground, the way he'd learned to do in the scrapyards when a pickup fight went sour. They broke his jaw and his arms in six or seven places. I guess you don't count ribs. He was in traction for eight weeks while my mother cleaned houses on top of her regular waitressing to pay the rent and the hospital bills. She probably cleaned house for at least one of the cocksuckers who passed down the order for the beating. Dad's partner didn't know to curl up; he was raised in a good neighborhood. He didn't move anything below his chin for nine years. Then his head stopped moving too and they buried him."

"Stutch's order?"

"Who knows? Those big chiefs used buffers on buffers. He could say he never knew about it, and I suppose he did say it, if he was ever asked. I don't remember because I wasn't born yet. That was back when Stutch had his name stamped on every bolt and washer that came out of his plant. He knew what all his bolts and washers were up to all the time."

The dim wash of light gleamed on bared teeth. I realized he was grinning. "The joke is, my father and his partner weren't on strike. They didn't even belong to the union then. They were scabs, delivering steel for Stutch. It was a random roust."

I looked out, thought I saw the pulsing white-orange of hot steel through the window of the plant. I decided it was too far up. I was looking at Betelgeuse. "You know the boy Thorpe's holding is a Stutch. Leland's great-grandson."

"I know. I've been thinking about it ever since this morning."

"Where'd you wind up?"

He turned his head my way. Strangely enough I couldn't see him as well then. It took his face out of the light. "My father did a lot for the Steelhaulers after he joined. There are men in the local who are too young to remember him. They cross themselves when his name is mentioned. They don't even know they're doing it."

"I saw it when he was alive. You don't see that kind of thing anymore. Too many microphones under too many beds."

"He was a good man once. Almost as good as he was bad later."

The dark oval of his face went silent. I was expected to say something.

"I wouldn't know," I said. "Maybe. I only knew him at the end."

"I do. And if I didn't, there are plenty of men still alive who could tell me. You don't get that unless you were a hell of a man once."

"Yeah." It was something to drop into the next silence.

"Maybe Stutch was good too, at the beginning. What the hell, he started this whole thing, just as if he stuck the key in the ignition and turned it."

"Twisted the crank would be more accurate, but yeah."

The impertinence bounced off the dark oval. "Well, I'm trying real hard to be Phil Montana from the time before anyone crossed himself at the name. Which was the time when it would have been appropriate. I don't know this kid Matthew, but I'm in no place to say he won't try just as hard to be like that other Leland Stutch."

"That's deep, man."

We both turned to look at the tenor in the back seat. Only his gold earring showed.

I returned my attention to the shadow behind the wheel. "What's the twenty on your guys?"

He chuckled softly. It's hard to tell in the dark if a man has a sense of humor. It can be faked, like a lunatic shamming sanity for the psychiatric review board.

"Someone's been watching *Smokey and the Bandit*," he said.

"Someone's had four hours of sleep in forty, and he wasn't a morning person to begin with. He wants to know if your people are in place."

"There were right around seventy of them last count. More on the way. Don't know where I'll put them. I almost had to stack the seventy. The payload alone's over two million pounds."

"How soon can we expect the rest?"

This time Tenor laughed. Montana didn't. "How the hell many do you need? You want to level the place?"

"Why not? You might get a commission from GM. A new car, anyway. You remember how much it cost Detroit to demolish Hudson's. They had to replace part of the People Mover."

"The plant's built even solider. Then there are gas lines and underground tanks. We could take down half the city."

"It'd be a start."

We sat there for a while as more lights came on below and the pencil beams of homebound cars on the main cut thinned out, turning down side streets and into driveways. The city grew quiet and we grew quiet with it. Montana stirred, creaking the vinyl upholstery, reached across me, and popped open the glove compartment. The dim yellow light shone on a flat pint of Bushmills. He took it out, slapped shut the compartment, and broke the seal on the cap. He tipped it toward me.

I took it. The sweet sting of the ferment made my stomach rumble. "What happened to the peach brandy?"

"That was breakfast."

I swallowed a mouthful and handed it back with a face. The heartburn kicked in immediately. Irish is a miserable drunk. They should have left it back home with the blights and leprechauns.

"I know," Montana said, and took a drink. "What can I say? Dago red gives me the runs. Have you given any thought to a signal?"

"The building was engineered to protect the suits and the equipment from the employees. The nerve center's in the security office in the basement. From there, whoever's on duty can throw on and off the outside floods in one movement. In the plans it's an old-fashioned knife switch, like in Frankenstein movies. Now it's probably a circuit board, but that would be the only change. Thorpe would have seen to that. The floods are always on at night. When they go off, that will be your cue to move in. Make sure your people understand that." I pointed to the CB. "Can the cops listen in?"

"They use a different frequency, but if they scan it, it won't mean anything to them. No bears or good buddies. We move with the times too."

In the back seat, Tenor said, "I could use a swig of that. I'm black Irish."

"Have some coffee," Montana said. "There's a Thermos on the floor. You're working, remember?"

"So's Walker. You let him have a swig."

"He's only got his own ass to worry about. You're supposed to worry about mine. You can't get good help," he told me, as the man in the back unscrewed a big metal cap.

I said nothing. After a little while I tipped up the door handle and put a foot out onto the pavement. Montana's face was expressionless under the dome light. "You right- or left-handed?" he asked.

"Right."

"Don't shake Thorpe's hand. He's a lefty."

I thanked him and got out and pushed the door shut.

# TWENTY-SEVEN

AND NOW HERE I AM, stopped in the middle of the lane on Factory Way a hundred feet short of the broad asphalt drive leading up to what remains of the old Stutch Motors complex, smoking a Winston down to the filter. I don't want to move because ironically enough it's almost the only spot in the city where the throbbing glow of the hot steel can't be seen; municipal hedges planted to obscure the community's bestial beating heart and the shoulder of the hill stand between us. I return to the moment in dreams, and so I always think of it in present tense.

The Ram's motor idles smoothly. The crickets are louder. A jet that is only a turquoise blue and an orange winking light crosses a hole in the overcast, rushing to catch up with the muted surflike roar of its engines as it heads somewhere that is a hell of a long way from here. I check the load in the .38 again. Now the bitter scorched-rubber stench of the filter igniting stings my nose. I snap the stub out the window and put the indicator in Drive. The dream ends there and then it's then again.

I rounded a squat concrete pillar with the defunct STUTCH

PETROCHEMICALS sign engraved in brass, a thing too pretty to be taken down by even GM's corporate raiders, cruising barracuda-fashion between the long gray columns of the stock reports in the *Wall Street Journal*, flipping their tails suddenly and streaking in at the first sign of a steep loss in the third quarter. Opposite it, perpendicular to the street and lit by ground floods, stood a long rectangular sign reading GENERAL MOTORS in fat, harmless-looking letters of robin's-egg blue on a white background, and below them, in letters one-third their size, IROQUOIS HEIGHTS PLANT second-billed in black.

I hadn't turned any too soon. In the corner of my rearview mirror I spotted the low wide front end of a city cruiser entering the block at crawl speed, swiveling its spots on both sides of the street in search of juveniles out past curfew. I held my breath and kept watching as it rolled past the end of the drive. I hadn't been seen.

I crept forward to avoid bursting a tire on the sharp edges of broken blacktop, crumbled like piecrust beneath the chuckling weight of inbound dump trucks heaped with iron pellets and out-bound flatbeds hauling steel coils stacked like silvery logs with their centers hollowed out. The raw earth was coarse sand streaked with red clay. Clumps of wild juniper had sprung up on either side of the drive, casting nasty shadows beneath the harsh white of the stadium lights mounted on twenty-foot poles twenty feet apart; under Stutch, the slope had been trimmed as neatly as any lawn in Grosse Pointe. A Chiricahua Apache could not have crawled up it undetected, much less a Fifth Columnist or a union lineworker striking for a cost-of-living raise.

Any thought that the premises were not locked down as tightly as they had been in the past evaporated when the old foundry hove into sight. It was eight stories of soot-blackened brick, blacker than the sky behind it except for stuttering flashes of the jewel-faceted glow of the hot steel through the window, and set back fifty feet from the gate in a cyclone fence. The fence was made of gleaming chainlink, indecently new and twelve feet high, with coils of razor wire on top, glittering under the floods and twenty times more effective than the barbed wire it had replaced. There were inmates recovering in the Jackson prison infirmary with yards of stitches holding in their intestines who thought they could clamber over smaller gauges of the same wire by draping it first with the mattresses from their cells. But they wouldn't get even that far here: Glass insulators showed at intervals among the chain links. A yellow metal sign wired to the fence warned visitors in black letters that the fence carried ten thousand volts, courtesy of Detroit Edison. I wondered if the carcasses of small birds scattered about the ground with their forked feet in the air had been added for emphasis.

Another sign attached to the gate told me to honk. I honked, and after ten seconds the gate drifted inward in two halves, propelled by a pair of torpedo-shaped hydraulic tubes. I pulled ahead and stopped in front of an octagonal sign. It was one of the old yellow stop signs, freckled with rust. A round-faced guard in an old-time postman's cap leaned out an open window in a painted plywood kiosk and asked to see my ID. I showed him Dollier's security card with my photo, holding it so that my thumb covered the date of birth. He looked from the picture to my face and nodded. "Uncle Jimmy sure is taking an interest these days. I seen more new faces in a week than I seen in four years."

Uncle Jimmy is GM. "You're telling me. I was just getting comfortable in Warren."

"You're early. Eight-to-four don't start for twenty minutes."

"I had to get out of the house."

He grunted understanding. He was a babyfat forty, with a Hitler moustache and satchels under his eyes. "Should of stayed a bachelor."

"Who, you or me?"

"Everybody. Ever notice how tomcats are always smiling?"

I said I hadn't thought about it. My knuckles were white and shiny on the steering wheel. I had to draw a philosopher.

"My relief, now; he's a happy newlywed," he said. "He's never early."

"He'll learn."

That hadn't occurred to him. Brightening, he waved me past with a pudgy hand wearing a gold band sunk in fat.

The compound was as bright as day. The lightposts painted with silver Rustoleum were as thick as trees and there was an old-fashioned round spotlight as big as a tractor tire mounted on a swivel on the old machine-gun emplacements on the factory roof. During the Second World War, when the place made tank turrets for Chrysler, and later, when the boys came back and bought tailfins in pairs like saddle shoes, both doors had stood open around the clock so as not to slow down the parallel streams of shifts coming in and going out. The place would have looked even more like a maximum-security penitentiary then. Now it looked like the Warner Brothers backlot, gloomily awaiting the return of George Raft and the prison flick.

I drove around a small one-story brick building, a miniature replica of the main foundry building with tin sheets replacing the broken window panes, plainly empty, and parked in an employee lot with more spaces than cars; backing into a space so the pickup would be pointed out. All the odds were in favor of a running exit.

The distant roar of the high jet was still audible when I stepped down to the pavement. I looked up, but the hole had closed and there was no sign of it overhead. I knew then it wasn't the jet I was hearing. It was the impersonal controlled rage of the blast furnace transforming tons of iron pellets into liquid steel. From that angle, looking up toward the window in the foundry, I saw only the reflected light flickering off the tarred roof of the smaller empty building that stood the length of a football field away. It looked like sheet lightning.

If the 1936 plans were still current, the security entrance was around the corner from the big doors. Walking that way, feeling under my Windbreaker for the Chief's Special, I smelled mildew, the dank desperate air of a dripping basement. Old mortar has its own kind of decay, not as offensive as animal rot and nowhere near as noble as wood, but pervasive and without hope; the smell of Alcatraz, or of a dungeon used during the Inquisition. Pain, sweat, anger, and worry seeped between the porous grains and pooled around the foundation. But then that might have been just the mood I was in. It probably smelled jolly to a foreman one week away from retiring with full benefits.

How it smelled to a three-year-old boy without his parents was something I was better off not thinking about.

It was a steel fire door, battered as a farmer's truck and unmarked, no handle. There was a white gutta-percha button set in a socket next to the jamb. I pushed it. I heard nothing.

The door opened inward and I rested my right hand on the butt of the revolver. Another guard in a butternut twill uniform and postman's cap asked to see ID. This one was ten years younger and fit, with blue-black beard gleaming like anthracite beneath his skin. He looked at the card, told me to move my thumb. I hit him with the .38.

I was holding it around the cylinder and when the steel backstrap tapped his temple he took a step forward and then the hydraulics went out of his knees. At that he managed to thumb loose the strap that held his sidearm in its webbed holster. I figured he practiced his quick-draw in front of a full-length mirror. I caught him under the arms, shuffled forward through the door, and sat him on a steel-framed chair with a copy of *Newsweek* folded to the Transitions column on the seat. "James Butler Hickok, security specialist for General Motors; pistol-whipped Friday, April 28." I took out his weapon, a cast Ruger P85, and put it in my left-hand slash pocket.

The guard made a guttural noise and stirred. I tapped him again. He went as limp as a sock and I had to hoist him up and hook his right arm over the back of the chair to keep him from sliding to the floor. I put away the .38, found the roll of athletic tape I'd borrowed from Rayellen Stutch in my right-hand pocket, and wound several yards around his ankles and wrists, securing him to the frame of the chair. I pulled his necktie off over his head, balled it up and stuck it in his mouth, and ran the rest of the tape around the lower half of his head to hold it in place. Then I saw the alarm button on the floor and had to drag him three feet away, chair and all.

We were in a cloakroom-size chamber with no ceiling of its own. The walls went up eight feet and then stopped, with nothing but air between them and the joists twenty feet up. Leland Stutch's windowed office, suspended from the same frame that supported a deserted catwalk, looked right down into the cubicle. There were no lights behind the glass. No one came out and no alarm was sounded during the minute I stood there with my hand on my revolver.

The ceiling troughs shed some light inside the little room, but it wasn't sufficient for reading and someone had brought in a domestic lamp with a flowered china base and a pleated shade and set it on a heavy scarred yellow-oak desk with magazines and a deck of cards on top. The only decoration was a bank calendar on one wall with a color photo of Picture Rocks.

Wild Bill in the chair had both eyes open. I didn't like the way he was looking at the button on the floor, so I unplugged the lamp, cut the cord at the base with my pocket knife, tied one end to a chair leg, and the other to one of the squat legs that held up the desk. He might have been able to scootch one or the other, but not both. He glared bullets at me all this time.

"You shouldn't have asked me to move my thumb," I said. "I'm sensitive about my age."

I couldn't tell if he'd heard me. The furnace was roaring steady as the debt.

I remembered something then and went through his pockets until I found a fistful of keys on a ring with a leather tab attached. I hated to do it, but I took out the Smith & Wesson and tapped him again. They were heating the last batch of steel for the day and I didn't know how soon the works would go silent. You can still make a lot of noise with a necktie in your mouth. He was going to wake up nauseated and seeing double. I hated to do it.

A door in the partition opened onto the plant floor. I ditched the guard's Ruger in a wastebasket to cut down on weight and went out slowly, holding the .38 down at my side. A dozen or so hard-hats were dotted about, coiling cables and sitting in forklift cabs watching the steel being poured, but, like them, I was just an ant in that vast room and they were used to people coming and going. They hadn't been put on alert, then. Thorpe was playing close to the vest.

The place was mostly automated despite its ancient exterior, so there weren't a quarter as many workers present as there would have been even fifteen years ago. Four times as many wouldn't have made the place look any less empty. It was big enough to hangar a 747, and that was just the charging room, where the steel was poured. Floor-to-ceiling partitions separated it from the smelter, where the raw ore was Bessemered and converted into pig iron, and the rolling mill next door.

My nostrils stung with the smell of hot metal. In the center of the room, above a set of rails on a trestle, a concrete ladle, reinforced with iron and burned blue-black, like the bowl of a pipe, collected a stream of white-hot molten steel from the furnace, releasing at the same time a thinner stream from a hole in its base into ingot-molds mounted in the beds of open rail cars. When the molds were filled the cars scooted on an electric charge through a portal into the next room, where rollers waited to flatten the ingots into sheets like cookie dough, which when cool would be coiled into long cylinders, to be transported for stamping and assembly elsewhere. The thick stream pouring into the ladle was liquid light, with smoke and steam rolling off it, and staring at it for any length of time without the protective goggles worn by the workers invited permanent blindness. I looked away quickly and still had to shut my eyes tight until the purple spots faded.

The heat in the big room was oppressive. I was soaked through beneath the thin leather Windbreaker. Most of the workers were in undershirts, stained as black as the ladle. This was the blazing Purgatory at the center of the American automobile industry.

According to the blueprints, an elevator and a set of fire stairs each led down to the basement from the southwest corner of the charging room. I chose the stairs. I stopped at a brick wall where the door was supposed to be. On close study I saw where the old wall left off and the new one began. They'd done a neat job bricking it up, but they couldn't get the same material; the color was slightly different. I followed the wall until I came to the elevator. It was all dark shaft behind an old-fashioned folding cage. There was one button in a brass panel next to the door. I thought about it. Then I pressed it. Here was where the element of surprise went out the window. I leveled the revolver and waited.

The car made as much noise as a fat man lifting himself out of a tub. It shuddered to a halt, a homely freight job with silver-covered Celotex between the studs and a plywood floor, corrugated like cardboard, and I folded aside the cage and stepped aboard. The cable groaned.

Before I pressed the down button, I reached up and loosened the bulb recessed into the ceiling, twisting it in quick jerks to avoid burning my fingers. The car went dark and I rode it down, crowded tightly into the far right corner on the theory that anyone waiting at the bottom with a gun would open fire on the center. I braced the Chief's Special for a hip shot.

No one shot at me. There was no door or cage in the basement. I stepped straight out into a corridor lit by recessed fixtures, shedding separate pools onto a linoleum floor with a swirled pattern.

I seemed to be in the middle of the corridor. It stretched out for at least fifty feet in either direction and vanished into darkness. The walls were plaster, painted a warm yellow to offset the subterranean gloom, but it was turning a mustard shade that only contributed to the sensation of interment. There were no pictures on the walls, just doors staggered on both sides. Each had a narrow rectangle of wire-gridded window and a no-frills steel knob with a cylinder lock. None was labeled.

The security offices, including the big one reserved for the director, were supposed to lie to my right, with the emergency living quarters comprising five rooms strung out in the other direction from the elevator. I hoped that hadn't changed. The disappearance of the fire stairs had me rattled. I turned left and crept along close to the wall.

The lights appeared to be on in all the rooms. I flattened against the wall, gripping my gun, and slid an eye past the edge of the first window. There was a twin bed, a camp-size refrigerator with a two-burner hotplate on top, a card table, and two folding chairs. The room was six by eight and I could see the whole thing. The mattress was rolled up at the foot of the bed. No one was inside.

Same story in the next room. The one after that was a community bathroom, with a stool and a sink and a shower stall and frosted glass in the window. I had a heart-stopping moment when I flung open the door and wheeled in fisting the revolver in both hands. I didn't disturb anyone.

Behind the window in the fourth door, Matthew Glendowning was sitting up in bed with his chin resting on his knees and his hands locked around them. His eyes were pink and swollen, but he wasn't crying. He looked bored. He had on the same clothes he'd worn the night before, but he was barefoot. No one was with him.

I juggled out the ring of keys. On a hunch I tried the knob first. It was unlocked. I didn't like that, not by half. But I opened the door and went in.

Matthew was off the bed in one motion, butting me in the stomach with his head of black hair. I jackknifed, emptying my lungs, but when he started around me I got a hand inside the neck of his T-shirt and twisted. He kicked me, and pain shot up from my shin, but he wasn't wearing shoes. I kept my balance and spun him and pushed him into a wall, pinning him by the shoulders with the gun still in my right hand.

"It's me, Matthew," I said. "Mr. Walker. Remember? I'm a friend of your mother's. I drove the car."

He stopped struggling then and stared. His mouth opened wide. I hugged him to my chest, to muffle the bawling mainly, then tightened my grip and carried him out.

I turned right toward the elevator and stopped. Connor Thorpe was standing halfway down the corridor. Beside him was a uniformed guard aiming a pistol-grip shotgun at my chest and Matthew's back.

"Steal from my boss, steal from me," Thorpe said. "Only this time I'm the boss. The gun and the kid, Walker. Put them down in any order you like."

# CHAPTER
# TWENTY-EIGHT

THERE WAS NO SATISFACTION on Thorpe's basset face, no clue in his slumped posture, hands in the pockets of his heavy-duty business suit, that he felt anything at all about bagging an intruder. It wasn't that he had control over his features, which he had to have had in the beginning or he wouldn't have come this far; he'd just been at it so long, living constantly two minutes ahead of the kind of person he'd been put in place to outwit, that he no longer felt anything at the climax, win or lose. His sad eyes and perpetual scowl meant nothing more than the smile on a sarcophagus.

The guard with him was cut from greener wood. He was young and pale, with the kind of gray eyes that always look as if they're staring through a sheen of tears, and his nostrils twitched. I didn't like that part. His shotgun, a utilitarian twelve-gauge stamped out of sheet metal with a plastic stock, lay at chest height with the hand holding the grip braced against his right pectoral and the other hand cradling the forepiece. The bore was as big around as a shot glass.

"How about we go to parade rest?" I said. "Your boy looks like he spooks easy."

"How about you do what the chief said?" The guard's voice was high and tight.

Thorpe said, "You're right about him, Walker. They shaved the trigger pretty thin."

Matthew's fingers dug into my sides, but I relaxed my grip and leaned over and let him slide to the floor. As soon as his feet touched down he scampered around behind me, arms locked around my left leg with his face peering past my hip. He didn't know I was no kind of shield against a shot pattern the size of my head. I lowered my gun hand and let the Smith & Wesson fall to the floor.

I said, "Not bad. Slick but not showy. The frame was to keep me in, not out."

"Anybody can get *in* anyplace." Thorpe sounded preoccupied. "The men who built this plant knew that. The main power switch is down here. Anyone who wanted to put the place out of commission had to come to the basement. Then all Security had to do was block the fire door, cut the current to the elevator, and starve them out. Getting rid of the fire door was my idea. Call me lazy. It eliminated a step."

"Maybe your predecessors were nervous about becoming trapped themselves."

"Oh, I rigged a way out in a pinch. One that didn't make it into a set of blueprints that any voting citizen could wander into city hall and gape at."

"Who told you I was coming, Fish or Muriel?"

His amber teeth showed, but the downturned corners of his mouth didn't move. It was only a smile if you stood on your head to look at it. "Fish is a wardheeler. You never piss off the money source, that's the rule. He wouldn't come to me over a letter of authorization with my signature. And Muriel would watch his own nuts burn before he'd yell fire if Fish didn't tell him to."

"That's no way to talk about your own property."

"This town has been spreading its legs for so long it's become a habit. I don't know why I still bother to grease it, unless it's to watch guys like Cecil Fish clap their flippers and bark. I keep thinking sometime they'll say no. But they never do." He swung his long face from side to side slowly, as if at some unrelated memory.

"You're expecting too much from guys like Cecil Fish." I kept my eyes on the guard. His nostrils were.the only things moving.

"Not without effort. When you do what I do for as long as I've done it, the easy thing is to think everyone's out for what he can get. Maybe it's this underground office. From down here all you see is dirty feet and crotches. It's why I like to have you around, to freshen the view. It's why I steered the Rayellen Stutch thing your way."

"That's not why. You knew Mark Proust and I had a history and you could count on him to finish me off when I became inconvenient."

"I wondered why I hadn't heard from him," Thorpe said. "You didn't kill him, did you?"

"I couldn't be sure he had a heart, so I shot him in the knee instead. Why'd you have him grab the boy?" Matthew's grip tightened around my thigh.

"I'm looking after him while his mother's in the hospital. He's related to my employer, after all."

"I guess you got so busy you didn't get around to telling her."

The guard broke in. "You want to call the cops while I hold him here, Chief?"

Thorpe jingled keys and change in a pocket. It was as close as he came to chewing his lip. "In a minute. Let's go in the office."

The guard stepped to one side and tilted his head up the corridor. The gray eyes stayed on me.

Matthew didn't budge when I tried to move my leg. I laid a hand on his shoulder and squeezed it gently. After a second he unlocked his hands and grasped a fistful of my khakis. I followed Thorpe past the elevator, the boy padding silently behind. The guard brought up the rear.

The office, behind another unlabeled door, this one windowless, was twice the size of the bed cells, which didn't make it big. The walls had been painted recently in shades of sherbet, to relieve the bunker atmosphere. It wasn't a success. The low ceiling and the presence of a gray steel desk, five matching file cabinets, and the dank smell of cellars everywhere contributed to the sensation of having been buried alive. Behind the desk, in a slanted console that had been built into the wall, was a row of brightly colored pressure-pads, including a large red one to the right, isolated from the others. These would control the electrical power throughout the plant, including the security floods outside. The red one had to be the main. It was a refinement of the old-fashioned knife switch but no less effective.

Thorpe settled himself into the oak swivel behind the desk with a little sigh. There was nothing on the desk but a telephone and a steel-jacketed microphone on a stand with a toggle switch in the base. He would summon his people over loudspeakers installed throughout the building. From a drawer he drew a homely black automatic with composition grips, a .38 Special, and laid it on top. "If you'd leave us alone, Andy?"

The guard hesitated in the doorway, then withdrew, pulling the door shut behind him. The latch clicked in the steel frame.

"Tell the boy to sit down," Thorpe said. "Children make me nervous."

I squeezed Matthew's shoulder again. He didn't want to let go of me, but he didn't struggle when I picked him up under the arms and sat him on a wooden upright chair that looked as if it had been there since the room was furnished. He fidgeted and bounced his legs, but he stayed put, scowling fiercely. He was as scared as scared gets. There were no other chairs, but I wouldn't have used one if one were available. You can't move as quickly from a sitting position.

"I'd offer you a drink, but I quit. Bad stomach."

I said I'd pick something up on the way home. He showed his teeth again. Then he got out his worn leather case and lit one of his thick black cigars. He flipped the spent match onto the linoleum, where it had company. The room smelled of generations of cheap cigars.

I got what I needed from his sad smile. "Am I going to make a break for it, or try for the gun? I don't guess Andy needs it to be any more complicated than that. He isn't in the game or you'd have let him finish it up out in the hall."

"Not necessarily. Have you ever heard a shotgun go off indoors? Some of us care about our eardrums." He tipped a cylinder of gray ash onto the desk. "Trespassing and illegal entry, Walker. A little bit of industrial espionage sprinkled on top, for the boys in the press. I can say Toyota hired you, give the nosebleeds in the State Department something to do with my tax dollars. It'll play. Tokyo's been jumpy ever since the Krauts bought Chrysler."

"Glad to see you're enjoying yourself. You weren't too thrilled about the project at the start." I shifted my weight on to my good ankle. I still needed Olympics sponsorship to make the leap across the desk.

"I thought Rayellen was borrowing trouble. The old man took care of the Cecilia Willard situation a long time ago. But I'm a company man, like you said. I follow orders."

"Who gave the order to snatch the boy?"

That stung him. He took the cigar out of his mouth and aimed a scowl at it as if the tobacco had been sprayed with an inferior grade of insecticide. "When the ball takes a bad hop, you go after it. Nobody was supposed to come out of that wreck. Proust let me down."

"Says who, Mrs. Stutch? You're saying she wanted the heirs found so she could take them out of the family album."

"You ought to improve your reading. *The Hound of the Baskervilles* is okay when you're ten. And I stopped working for her right after I handed you the baton. That's when I started preparing for retirement. You want to live? Go back and tell her she can have the boy for ten million."

"So a kidnap's all it is. Why not twenty?"

"Ten's all I need. I'm getting to be an old man. Anyway she wouldn't pay twenty. She gets thirteen a year. She can scrape by on three through Christmas: clip coupons, go to Aruba in the spring when the rates are better."

"When I leave the boy goes with me."

"I figured you'd say that. I had to ask." He picked up the automatic. He looked genuinely sad.

I said, "You're forgetting Proust. Prison's no fun for cops. He'll deal you like an ace."

"I'll buy him a good lawyer."

Matthew said, "I gotta pee."

"Go in your pants!"

Thorpe glanced away to say it. I scooped the heavy microphone off the desk and slammed it against the side of his head. The impact jarred the switch into the *on* position; feedback squealed through the building. The gun went off. I looked at Matthew. He wasn't hit, but when I looked back the muzzle was swinging around toward me; with one bad ankle I hadn't been able to put all my weight into the blow. I slashed down with the microphone and broke his wrist. His howl joined the electronic squeal and the gun fell to the desk. I missed it on the bounce and it went over the edge and clattered to the floor. I thought it went off again when it hit, but that was Andy banging on the other side of the steel door. In another second or two he'd use the shotgun to blow off the lock. I bent to scoop up the automatic and kicked it under the desk instead.

"Attention! This is Connor Thorpe! Security to the basement! Atten—"

Thorpe's voice rang everywhere. He'd reclaimed the microphone with his good hand and was shouting into it. I smashed my fist into his face. He stopped.

"On the floor, Mr. Thorpe! Stay clear of the door!" Andy's high-pitched voice was muffled by the door.

I lunged, snatched Matthew by one arm, and threw him to the floor. He started screaming. I dived headfirst over the desk, no time to go around it, and mashed both palms on the electronic console, hoping the main power control was among the pressure pads underneath them. I hadn't time to look.

The room went as black as any cave on the dark side of the moon; but not for long. A great concussion flattened the air, followed by another, less loud, but only because the first had deafened me. Orange light blasted the darkness, as bright as the hot steel in the furnace at ground level. The sulfur stink of spent powder ate up all the oxygen in the room. Hornets stung me in several places; I was on my way to the floor, but I couldn't fall fast enough to avoid all the pellets. I struck hard on one shoulder and scrambled toward where I thought Matthew was, to throw myself across him, but I'd lost all sense of direction. A wall stopped me. Under the ringing in my ears I tried to separate the boy's screams from Andy's shouting, in order to orient myself. Crawling, I put a hand down on a mass of leaking meat: Connor Thorpe's smashed face. He'd slid out of his chair and landed on his back. I recoiled, adjusted my course ninety degrees, and this time my hand closed on the automatic. But it didn't happen fast enough.

The room filled with light. Andy had found his way to the

main switch. I pivoted on my knees, raising the pistol. I was out-gunned. The bore of the shotgun was two inches from my face. It was as big as a water tumbler now.

Something exploded. I flinched—and wondered how I knew I was flinching when my face had been blown away. But this one was louder than the shotgun, loud enough to drown out all the shotguns in the world. Another came hard on it, a reverberating crash that went on twice as long, or that had joined with a third one just behind it. Something pattered on my head and went down under my collar, granulated dust that until a second ago had been plaster in the basement ceiling. I was bleeding in several places under my shirt and it made a grating mud when it mixed with the blood. The shotgun swung away from my face. The world was shaking apart; I wasn't important anymore. Andy turned, staring up toward the source of the explosions.

I shot him in the groin. He gasped and dropped the shotgun. I grabbed for it, mad to have it before he fell on top of it; but just then another blow shook the building and I lost my balance and toppled off my knees just in time to take all of Andy's dead weight across my body.

More explosions then, and with them the rumbling vibration of big motors and heavy wheels rolling through the smashed bricks littering the foundry floor above. Ray Montana's army of eighteen-wheelers had begun its assault on the Stutch plant.

# CHAPTER

# TWENTY-NINE

Matthew had run out of lung power for screaming, and took in his breath in sobs in the little silence between battering blows twenty feet above our heads. At those times the only other sound in the room was the sifting of plaster and old dirt from the ceiling joists. If Thorpe and Andy were breathing, they were being quiet about it, conserving their strength.

The hell with them. I worked my way out from under Andy and crawled around the desk, still gripping Thorpe's automatic. Matthew lay face down where I had flung him, his shoulders working. When I laid a hand on his back he jerked, turned his head my way, and opened his mouth, but nothing came out. It was the same deep shock I'd left Mark Proust in after I'd shot him in the knee. I ran my hand over the boy's body, but couldn't find any place where he was bleeding. Both shotgun blasts had come in at doorknob level.

I got to my feet and took his hand. He rose and tried to climb into my arms, but I told him to stay behind me and take hold of my coat. The leather tightened across my back when he tugged on the tail and I stung in three or four places where lead pellets had lodged beneath my skin. I dragged my sprained, stiff, and shot-up body toward the corridor with the boy hanging on.

I paused at the doorway, holding the automatic, and looked in both directions. Chunks of mustard-colored plaster strung together with horsehair lay on the floor like jigsaw pieces, and one of the recessed ceiling lights had blown out; a fog of smoke was still drifting out of the brass canister. There was no one in the corridor. They were all busy running for cover upstairs. Now I hoisted Matthew onto my left hip, told him to hang on, and headed for the elevator. I was ten feet from it when the building shuddered and eight square feet of plaster, insulation, and pieces of lath dumped onto the floor in front of me, followed by half a ton of coarse sand and red clay. Matthew let out a wail and buried his face in my side. I coughed out a lungful of dust, dragged my sleeve across my eyes, and swung back the way I'd come.

Connor Thorpe looked dead. His nose was all over his face, the lower half of which was all crusted blood, and his skin was gray-green, like his suit. I set Matthew down on his feet and let him cling to my thigh while I bent and slapped Thorpe's cheeks. The little bit of color that came into them after thirty seconds seemed hardly worth it. His eyes opened, all at once without a flutter. He looked right at me.

"Where's the way out?" I asked. "You said you had another way rigged besides the elevator."

"Go to hell." It took him two tries to say it. He had to spit out a mouthful of blood and mucus.

I stuck the automatic in his face and eased back the hammer.

"Go to hell," he said again.

"He's just a little kid, Thorpe."

"He's a pain in the ass. I told her he would be."

"Told who?" Another blow shook the building. A section of

ceiling bellied in and fell on top of Andy. He didn't stir. "Forget it. Where's the way out?"

"Go to hell."

I looked at him. I was as numb as a tire. "Tell Iris I'm not a Republican." My finger tightened on the trigger.

"Who?"

Just then the steel door came free of the wall, frame and all, and hit the floor with a crash. Matthew screamed. I elevated the barrel of the pistol and let the hammer down gently.

The best place for the boss's escape hatch was in the boss's office. There were no traps in the floor or ceiling and the walls were seamless. I told Matthew to stand clear, stuck the automatic in the waistband of my pants, pulled the nearest file cabinet away from the wall. There was nothing behind it except feathery dust and a yellowed file that had been lost since V-J Day. I moved two more cabinets and found a seam in the wall.

I pulled away the fourth, breaking loose a scab between my shoulder blades and releasing a trickle down my spine, and there was a recessed hand-pull at waist level. When I tugged on it, the entire panel came out of the frame. I leaned it against the cabinets and took a step forward to investigate what lay beyond. A fresh explosion jarred the telephone off the desk. Its bell rang when it struck the linoleum. I hoisted Matthew, pulled out the pistol, and stepped through the hole in the wall.

Beyond the trapezoid of light from the office the place was as black as deep space and filled with the potatoey smell of moist earth. The passage could have gone on forever or stopped ten feet in. Matthew whimpered; I wanted to join in. I groped my way forward, poking the automatic out in front to measure the depth. After a little while I could tell I was heading upward. The packed dirt under my feet graded gently. Another impact from above shook loose a stream of dirt onto my head. I stuck my hand up out of instinct and barked my knuckles against a four-by-four. The passage was shored up like a mineshaft.

Probing farther, I had to stoop to avoid hitting my head. The ceiling slanted at a shallower angle. Finally I had to let Matthew down. He moved behind me and took hold of my coat without having to be told; he was becoming an old pro. When another bang spilled more dirt down inside my collar I picked up the pace. My heart thudded in my ears and in all the places where I hurt. Of all my many nightmares the worst was being buried alive.

We went on for what seemed like miles. I wanted to light a match, but I thought I smelled gas. Ray Montana had said something about submerged gas lines. The racket from above was louder. A bell was clanging; either someone had activated a fire alarm or it had jarred into action all by itself. The sour smell of my own sweat joined with the dank subterranean stench.

I couldn't tell if my eyes were adjusting to the dark or light was coming in from somewhere. I could see my hand holding the pistol and the pale outlines of the timbers against the black earth. The air seemed to be freshening. Maybe my system was learning to get along with less oxygen. Then I saw a sliver of light lying across the path a dozen feet ahead.

When I got to the spot I looked up. The light was coming through a crack in the ceiling that extended from one wall to the other. I reached up with my free hand and felt boards. I pushed. They gave slightly. I told Matthew to stand back, stuck the automatic under my waistband, and pushed with both hands. A wooden hatch of some kind lifted out of a frame and light—or rather the absence of complete dark—hit me full in the face. I eased the hatch over to one side, sliding it against something that was not earth. The breaded edges of six inches of concrete formed a square around me. I took out the gun. It made gripping the concrete difficult, but I didn't know who or what might be waiting for me at ground level. I tightened my grasp and lifted myself high enough to peer over the edge. I looked around a large room with bulky objects studded about, lit only by a night that was not quite as black as the passage I'd come through. What light there was entered by way of a gridded window, with black squares checkering it where missing panes had been replaced with plywood or sheets of tin. It was the abandoned building I'd driven around to park in the employee lot.

Just then a shaft of white light swept across the window, pulling shadows around the room from great inert blocks of iron, decorated with massive flywheels and leather belts hanging in loose coils like lariats. Gears crashed and something as big and heavy as a brontosaurus rumbled on past outside, shaking the floor. Then darkness again. If anyone was in the room, he was hiding behind machinery. The air smelled of rust and rat musk and old oil.

I lowered myself back into the hole and leaned down to whisper in Matthew's ear. "Stay here. I'll come back for you. I need to check the place out."

"No!" He flung his arms around my neck. A bolt of pure pain shot straight up a tendon.

I laughed. After shotguns and pitched fights and raw terror, whiplash just wasn't in it. I put away the gun, took hold of him, and shifted him around so that he was straddling my back. "Okay, tiger, we go up together." I reached up and pulled us both out of the hole and into the sweet stale air of dead industry.

# CHAPTER

# THIRTY

I KEPT THE BOY behind me as I probed the shadows of that petri-
fied forest. The floor was a litter of broken pulleys and levers and
bolts the size of toadstools, sheared off and rusted to the concrete.
Except for a couple of hundred spiders dozing in webs as thick as
bridal veils and a bat that took off straight at my head when I startled it from its perch, making me duck and Matthew yell, the place
was uninhabited. I stubbed a toe on a fallen gear as big as a man-
hole cover.

The window was no exit. It was too high to reach and the drop
was too steep on the other side. The door was made of oak planks
two inches thick, with crossbars at top and bottom. It was locked
from the outside. Thorpe would have arranged another way out,
but I was tired of poking around in the dark. I found a steam piston-arm cloaked with dust on the floor, about two feet long and as
heavy as a sledgehammer, and had Matthew stand clear as I swung
it. The socket-end struck one of the planks with a dull clang I felt
to the shoulders. The plank moved out an eighth of an inch and

sprang back into place. When oak decides not to rot, it turns to iron.

On the fourth swing an eight-inch sliver separated itself grudgingly from the door. I took a breather, then went at it again. At this rate I would have us out in time for Bastille Day.

Light raked the window again. I felt a stinging vibration in the soles of my feet, an angry diesel drumroll rattled the panes in the window, air brakes chuffed as it slowed for the turn. The floor was shaking so hard I could barely keep my balance. I let go of the piston-arm, scooped Matthew off his feet on the run, and crouched with him behind a mammoth generator, Thorpe's ugly black automatic in my hand. It was as good against what was coming as a Popsicle stick.

The same crew that had installed the door had laid the bricks that made up that wall. The impact was as loud as a case of dynamite going off. The floor moved and I had to clap a hand against the generator to keep from falling over. The bricks started about an inch out of their courses, but they held. Mortar dust rained down.

There was a snort on the other side; a comment from a frustrated rhino. Gears groaned, the rumbling and vibration started up again as the thing backed away for another pass. I figured it went back twenty or thirty feet. A pause, then a couple of gunning snorts while the thing pawed the ground. Gears again, and then the high-pitched whine of the second charge. I hung on to Matthew with one hand and the generator with the other, the pistol pinned beneath my palm. Another case of dynamite went off, the wall fell down in a sheet, and the great square-gridded maw of a Freightliner cab came howling through, ten feet high and shedding whole bricks and pieces as if it were spitting them out. The wall, built as they hadn't built them for sixty years, had put a bad scratch in its bumper.

It didn't slow as it kept on coming. I wanted to move, but my feet were sealed to the floor. I might have been rusted down as solidly as the old machinery. I pointed the automatic at the radiator. It could have eaten the entire clip and still been hungry. Matthew was as frozen as I was.

Then the air brakes blasted, metal shrieked against metal, and the big front tires rolled to a crunching halt five feet short of where we were waiting to be punched through the brick wall at our backs. The smoke from the twin stacks rolled forward, mingling with the clouds of dust. I made out a head behind the divided windshield, but I couldn't see the expression on its face. It would have been comical. The driver had voided his insurance destroying an abandoned building. We waited, breathing shallowly and in unison, while the gears meshed again and then the truck backed out, sloughing more bricks as it unplugged a hole as big as a barn door.

I let another minute pass while the rig wheeled around, jackknifing its long silver trailer with THERMO KING block-lettered on the section that stuck up above the cab, then slid past the hole and out of sight. Then I straightened, holding Matthew's slick hand. The trucks were all on our side, but in a war without uniforms, friendly stragglers died as easily as the enemy.

There was a pile of jagged debris nearly as tall as the thing that had made it. I lifted the boy onto my back and climbed over the rubble, testing each piece before trusting my weight to it to avoid re-twisting my ankle.

Jurassic Park awaited us outside. Boxy vans, submarine-shaped tankers, flatbeds loaded with Earthmovers and coils of steel and concrete septic tanks, dirty orange dump trucks, and cabs without trailers streaked past under the floodlights and turned around and stood in place like wounded animals, panting smoke and steam with smashed windshields and dented grilles and headlamps broken out, one-eyed and deadly, like all casualties in the wild. A Mack Bulldog cabover swung past us belching blue flame from its stacks, its driver cranking the level steering wheel in both hands and letting it whirl the other way as he straightened out for another assault on the main building. Diesels whined, gears stripped, back-up beepers played the shower theme from *Psycho*. The earth had cracked open and hell had butted its smoking brimstone spires up through the fissure.

The foundry, the only part of Leland Stutch's heart that had continued to beat in the new century, was no more. The left side of the building had collapsed. Two of its three smokestacks no longer towered above the skyline of Iroquois Heights. One lay stretched out full length atop a pile of blasted bricks, one hundred feet of black iron pipe, still lisping smoke out one end. A stream of molten steel—dregs from the blast furnace—had carved a tunnel through the dust and rubble and eddied into a smoking quicksilver pool. Flames rose and fell wherever it had come into contact with something combustible. Insects clad in hardhats and filthy coveralls crawled over the piles and scampered for cover on the flat. The fire alarms, at least, had fallen silent, probably choked with dust or buried under wreckage. I wondered if anything was left of Connor Thorpe's underground bunker, or if it had caved in on him and his man Andy.

"Holy shit!" said Matthew. He'd been exposed too long to his father's trucker friends.

"Yeah." I hiked him higher on my back and loped off toward where I'd parked the Ram.

Matthew recognized his father's pickup. "Where's my daddy?"

I told him I didn't know, and strapped him snugly in the passenger's seat. Say what you like about what had happened that night. I was yellow after all.

The truckers were concentrating on buildings, ignoring vehicles and pedestrians, who nevertheless had to leg it to keep from being run down. I drove through the smashed gate and had to go up on the grass to make way for an International that needed both lanes of the drive to make up for lost time. Down the hill a scarlet Peterbilt 359 with yellow flames painted on its hood rested against a floodlight pole whose concrete base had proven more than equal to the blow. Steam gushed from the smashed radiator. I stopped the pickup in the middle of the lane and got out to check on the driver. When I climbed up and opened the door on the passenger's side, he lifted his bloody face from the steering wheel and stuck a squat-barreled revolver at me.

Thorpe's pistol was in my pocket. I left it there and raised my hands. "I'm not with the plant," I said. "You all of a piece?"

He laid the revolver in his lap, put his hand to the gash in his forehead, and took it away to look at it. He was a redheaded cowboy with freckles the size of silver dollars in a yoke-front shirt, skintight Wranglers, and lizardskin boots that came to lethal points. "I been worse in Juarez. How's my rig?" He wiped the blood on his pants.

"If it were a horse I'd shoot it."

"I knew it. It ain't paid off yet."

"Better get a tow down to Detroit and find a bridge abutment to lean it against. State Farm won't pay off on any claim within a mile of here tonight."

"I'm Triple-A."

"Same story. Did you know Dave Glendowning well?"

"Never heard of him before this morning."

I left him smacking his CB mike against his palm to get a crackle out of it and went back to the pickup.

Ray Montana's big Oldsmobile was parked around from the concrete pillars at the base of the hill a few feet from where I'd sat in the pickup an hour before, when I was twenty years younger. I pulled up onto the berm next to the car and got out and unstrapped Matthew and lifted him down. I brought him over to the driver's side and introduced him. Montana struck a grave hand out of the open window and shook his. "Good to meet you. I was a friend of your dad's."

"Where's my daddy?"

Montana looked at me. I shook my head minutely.

He said, "You look like you've been digging a mine."

"I missed the lode. Are there any trucks left on the freeway?"

"I know a hundred that aren't. I only put out a call for twenty. Truckers talk to each other. I wouldn't be surprised if some of them aren't even union. They've all heard stories about how Stutch treated Steelhaulers in the old days."

"Some of them probably just wanted to cut loose."

"You know it." The bodyguard on the passenger's side showed white teeth. "Couple of 'em couldn't wait till they got to the plant. Took out one whole side of Main Street."

"They're going to haul me on the floor of Congress over this." Montana sounded unconcerned.

"I want Mommy!"

All three of us looked at Matthew, thinking the same thing.

Montana opened his door. "Grandy, you're good with kids."

"Sure. Come on in, little fella. I'll teach you how to palm a jack." The bodyguard took a deck of cards out of an inside pocket.

Matthew squeezed my hand. I told him it was all right. Montana got out and held the door while the boy climbed under the wheel.

We turned our backs to the car. The labor leader handed me the pint of Bushmills. I unscrewed the cap and swigged. The whiskey lit up all the hot points, including the shotgun pellets I was going to have to have cut out. I felt like a subway map. I recapped the bottle and started to give it back. He held up a flat palm. I put the cap in my pocket and took another drink.

Montana's silence was a question.

"Nothing much," I said. "I got shot. Thorpe wanted ten million for the boy. I didn't have it on me so I caved in his head a couple of times and broke his arm. Things got various after that. Did I mention getting shot?"

"I take back what I said. You don't look so bad. What's the damage?"

"Not serious. Not funny, either; at least I'm not laughing. I picked up some strays from a twelve-gauge. I was going off at the same angle as the gun. If I were double-jointed I'd pry them out myself."

"I mean how much? Thorpe was an enemy of the union."

"I'm not a hitter. Anyway he's not dead, or he wasn't when I left him. I'm not so sure about the shotgunner. The point is I wasn't acting on your behalf. I never will, if you're the kind that tags a price on mayhem."

"I didn't mean it that way."

"Of course you didn't, Mr. Montana. The day started too early for all of us. It's not through yet."

"If you mean the boy, I'll see he has someone to take care of him until his mother gets out of the hospital. Unless he has other relatives?"

"A grandmother. She lives in Melvindale." I gave him Carla Witowski's number. He got out a pocket memorandum book with folded scraps of paper sticking out of it and a ballpoint pen and wrote it down. "I'll deliver him tonight."

"She might be at Henry Ford Hospital."

He put it together then. I couldn't remember if I'd given him Carla's name earlier. Four hours of sleep was not enough. "Think he's the old man's great-grandson?" he asked.

"He didn't fall apart when everything around him was. I wouldn't make book against it." I drank. "Thanks for taking him. It wasn't the only thing I still have to do tonight."

A black-and-chrome Kenworth hauling a Roadway box approached, down-shifting to make the turn into the driveway. Behind the windshield a face under an Aussie bushman's hat glowed greenly in the reflection from the dash lights. Montana took a step into the beam of the headlamps, stuck up a palm, then curled in the fingers and jerked the thumb back over his shoulder. The driver recognized the president of the Steelhaulers. He released his brakes with a whoosh. His engine bawled, accelerating. He shifted shudderingly into second and thundered on past without turning.

"I don't know what else there is." Montana's voice sounded muffled after the racket. "You said Thorpe confessed."

"Thorpe's a company man. He hasn't done a thing on his own since he went to work for Old Man Stutch."

"Who gave him his orders?"

"That's the thing I was talking about. I have to find out."

"Where?"

"Where else? Iroquois Heights." I twisted on the cap and gave him back his bottle.

# CHAPTER

# THIRTY-ONE

A LINE OF CITY SQUAD CARS passed me speeding toward the Stutch plant, followed by three hook-and-ladders and an acid-green emergency van, flashing their lights and yowling and blatting their assortment of sirens, the later the louder and more conspicuous. I didn't pull over for them and I didn't worry that they'd recognize the Ram from the daily BOL sheet. The hot pain from the pellets in my back and left hip had spread, connecting the dots. I was wondering how much time I had before the infection put me out for the quarter. Also I missed Matthew's company. He'd been good about saying good-bye at Montana's car, had understood, and had even given me a quick hug. I'd felt like a weekend father going back to his divorced digs.

I made one stop, at a Shell station, and placed a call. While it was ringing I played detective, eavesdropping on the locals gathered near the counter of the convenience section.

". . . right through the 7-Eleven and out the other side. Never stopped, just kept on rolling. Looked like they dropped a bomb on the joint."

"Anybody hurt?"

"I heard somebody yelling inside. I don't speak the language so I don't know."

"Someone said they tore up the lawn at the Civic Center, ran over the sculpture in front."

"Good. I never could make head or tail of the thing. I don't know what was wrong with the fish fountain they had before."

"What I can't figure out is if these truckers got a beef with Stutch, why they took it out on the town. This is a nice place to live, got us a new school going in for three million, mandatory alcohol testing for convicted drunk drivers. We even charge 'em ten bucks a pop, so it's free to us taxpayers. Nice safe community."

"Hopped up would be my guess. All them long-haulers are on pills and shit."

Mrs. Campbell came on the line. She said Mrs. Stutch had gone to bed.

"Don't wake her," I said. "Can you have the garage door open for me? I have to get the pickup out of sight."

"Of course."

I reached for a cigarette. My pack was missing. I must have dropped it dodging scatterguns. "I guess Mrs. Stutch told you all about the pickup."

"As I said, we don't have any secrets." She put her chin in her tone. Then she took it out. "Can you tell me what's going on? I've been watching news bulletins all night. No one seems to know anything."

"Look out a window."

"There are red and yellow lights flashing on the hill. I heard sirens, and I thought I saw flames earlier. Is there a fire?"

"You can get it from Mrs. Stutch after I tell her." I reminded her about the garage door and hung up.

I stopped at the counter to buy cigarettes. The woman behind it, a native by the look of her, glasses with swoop frames and just enough peroxide to turn her hair the color of mud, looked at me, then glanced out the window to see if I had a rig parked out front. I'd wiped my face, combed most of the dirt and dust out of my hair, and shaken out my jacket, but the stink of battle takes a long time to wear off. She slapped down a pack of Winstons, took my money, and gave me change.

The locals, who had moved off to watch me in silence, started up again as I hit the door.

"So far they're leaving the residential sections alone. Whoever their fight's with it ain't us."

"I don't figure to take that chance. I broke out the collection and armed everyone in the house. Tim Junior's got the .22. Any gear-jammer aims his bucket at my place is gonna get a windshield full of lead."

"If you're that worried, what the hell you doing down here?"

"We're out of beer."

Rayellen Stutch's house was dark except for a light in the kitchen window and the overhead bulbs burning in the garage. Mrs. Campbell had opened the door on the left side, as before. I drove the Ram inside, got out, took the automatic out of my pocket, and stuck it down inside my waistband in front. I didn't go to the side door. Instead I walked around to where the Land Rover was parked.

It hadn't been moved. The chunks of dried mud and clay that had fallen off one of the rear tires still lay on the concrete, preserving the tread in relief. I crouched, picked up one of the pieces, and crumbled it in my fist. I sniffed at the granules. The dank potatoey smell put me back in the escape shaft between Connor Thorpe's office and the abandoned plant building. When crushed, the grains of sand separated themselves from the hardened clay. I dusted off my palms and straightened. Rayellen Stutch was standing in the side doorway.

She wore a long black dressing gown that shimmered like her hair, which hung loose about her shoulders Indian-princess fashion, and the toe of one black velvet slipper stuck out under the hem where it rested on the threshold. The light coming from behind her showed off her slim athletic build. The cleanly curving lines were like something shaped by human hands and baked in a kiln and then enameled. "Hard-fired," she'd called herself. I'd seen the same body in boxing trunks and a halter, but that was daytime, and we hadn't been alone, and there had been no black satin present.

"Amos? Are you all right? You look worse every time I see you."

"I was buried alive for a little while. I can't recommend it." I didn't tell her about getting shot. I didn't feel like answering unnecessary questions. "I got the boy out. He's okay. He's on his way to his grandmother's, like Red Riding Hood."

"What about Connor?"

"I had a little trouble there. I may have killed him. I'm pretty sure I killed one of his security men. The plant's gone, too. I didn't do that, but it was my idea, kind of. I wasn't expecting anything so thorough. They took out part of the city while they were at it. Not enough, but then the Romans left some of Carthage for the archaeologists. What we really need is a good old-fashioned flood." I was babbling. I reached up to push my mouth shut. My hand got as far as the automatic and rested there.

"Come inside."

"Not yet. I like the fresh air. Tonight I added claustrophobia to my little shop of horrors."

"You can't live without sleep."

"I'm not sure you're right. Not having slept got me through this night. When you're too tired to think you become all senses and instinct. You see things you might overlook otherwise. Smell smells you might not have noticed. It's like quitting smoking, or starting cocaine. Or so I'm told. I'm thinking of trying one or the other."

She touched her throat. It was entirely the right gesture, and the timing was in place. All it needed was a locket on a tiny gold chain; a gift from a lover's dead hand. "Amos, why did you come back?"

"To get the dirt." I snickered, but gave it up halfway through as a bad job. The pitch was a little high, for one thing, borderline hysterical. But I'd needed the laugh track. "Earlier tonight you told me you never go the Stutch plant. Did you mean that as in not ever, or as in 'I never watch television'?"

She said, "Leland took me there once, just after we were married. Of course he wanted to show me off. That was the only time. Everyone was very polite. Subservient, actually, like tenant farmers groveling in front of the landlord's new lady. He ran that kind of shop. I've never felt more out of place in my life. It wasn't an experience I cared to repeat. Why did you ask me that?"

"The Heights may be right out of Yoknapatawpha County, but the streets are all paved; never mind that the asphalt's cheaper than what's on the books. The only spot in four square miles you can get serious mud on your tires is on the driveway up to the plant, where the heavy trucks keep breaking through the crust. It's built on a hill made of clay and sand, with no little thanks to the glacier that cleared the land for this mistake. You ought to have someone hose down the Land Rover's tires more often." I still had some dirt on my hand. I wiped it on the front of the Windbreaker.

She realized she was stroking her throat. She let the hand drift back down to her side, like a leaf. "I—I never use the Land Rover, except when there's snow. When I drive I take one of the roadsters. On special occasions I ride in the stretch."

"Who uses the Rover?"

"I do."

I knew who was speaking before I turned. You know you're

tired when you start asking questions you know the answers to. Mrs. Campbell, looking grayer than ever in her jail matron's uniform with her silvering hair pinned back as tight as a bathing cap, stood on the concrete pad outside the pull-up door. The harsh light from the ceiling bulbs inside carved black hollows under her eyes and at the corners of her unpainted lips. Something glinted in her right hand: a small, nickel- or chrome-plated revolver. There are guns in two out of three households in metropolitan Detroit. They run prettier and more expensive in the better neighborhoods, but they make the same ugly holes.

"Keep your hand where it is," she said.

It was still against the front of the Windbreaker. I didn't move it.

"Mrs. Campbell—" Rayellen said.

"Please be quiet. It's like when I play the piano. I have to go back and start from the beginning when I'm interrupted. That's why I left the Detroit Symphony. They were renovating the Hall and we were supposed to rehearse right through the jackhammers. Fortunately, I had a fallback job."

"Working for Mrs. Stutch," I said.

"*Mr.* Stutch," she corrected. "There was no Mrs. then. I worked for him since I was very young. He was very supportive when I left to play professionally. Not at all condescending when I came back to fluff and fold his sheets, stinking of old man as they did. And the salary was generous. He even put a provision in his will to keep me on after his death, with regular raises and a bonus at Christmas. I make more than most headwaiters."

"Not as much as five million, even if we're talking Tavern on the Green," I said. "Or was the split better than fifty-fifty? Usually the one who maps out the job takes the bigger cut."

"Thank you for that much, at least. Most men would think Connor was in charge."

"Not if their name was Borgia or Barrow. Thorpe didn't have

the imagination required. Also he had nothing to gain on his own from eliminating a fresh crop of heirs. That's why I couldn't figure out why he was against tracking them down from the start. It had to be a partnership, and the partner had to have a stake. That's why I suspected Mrs. Stutch."

Rayellen took in her breath. "I thought we settled that before."

"We took it as far as it could go as of then. Later, when Thorpe said Matthew was more trouble than he was worth, he added, 'I told her he would be.' Okay, so I misplaced the object of the feminine pronoun; then wasn't now. I don't take jobs to flush out quail for the shooting, so I decided that story about doing right by Cecilia Willard after all these years was just a blind. If so, it worked. I tracked them down."

"It wasn't a blind," Rayellen said. "A wrong was done."

I said, "I'm glad to hear you say it. You're not as hard-fired as you like to make out, even when you're trying to seduce the bloodhound. That bit about DNA changing the dynamics of the paternity suit, and throwing a lot of money now at a problem that might clean you out in court later, made you look a little less like the gooey all-day sucker a woman in your position can't afford to be taken for. That's what all this New Age cynicism gets you: Shylock for a role model, Attila chairing the Dream Team. But I think writing your housekeeper into your will is taking things too far the other way. Especially this housekeeper."

Mrs. Campbell made a noise in her throat. It was like a clump of earth striking a coffin. "Is that what you think it was about? Sweepings from thirteen million annually, out of a billion-dollar-a-year enterprise? How do you justify charging a fee to act as anyone's detective?"

"I validate parking."

I didn't like the theory either. It had more holes in it than a hip-hop band and gave me a headache besides. I didn't try to defend it. The Dodge key with the panic button was in the Ram's ignition a dozen feet away, and anyway you can't work a pin like that twice, even in different garages. She was going to need the opportunity to talk if it would keep her from remembering the pistol in my waistband.

"As a matter of fact, I have arranged for a substantial allowance," Rayellen said.

"That's funny, too," said the housekeeper. "An allowance from my stepmother."

And this time she opened her mouth and laughed. Even the crickets shut up. They thought a hungry owl was hooting.

# THIRTY-TWO

I WAS JUST EXHAUSTED enough to take everything in with an un-real clarity, as through reflecting waves of heat in a desert, transmitting close-up details of fauna and flora in an oasis ten miles distant. I could see the cross-hatching in the skin of Mrs. Campbell's face and the way the shadows exaggerated its stern lines, like a Greek mask designed to drive home the character's state of mind for the dimmest spectator in the back row. I wondered who Mr. Campbell might have been, and if he'd ever seen her in that light. Maybe there never was a Mr. Campbell. I never found out.

"My mother balanced the books up on the hill forty years," she said. "They never exchanged a word during the first sixteen. Then Mr. Stutch came to her hot little office in the smelting room to discuss a change in the entry system. It was like Mount McKinley paying a visit. She never told me if anything happened that time. Probably nothing did. Mr. Stutch would have assigned his lust to its own department, somewhere between the power station and the glass facility. Whenever it started, it lasted twenty years. I came along after ten.

"Mother never complained. According to the way she looked at things, she had nothing to complain about. She retired at fifty-eight with a full pension, and she died knowing her daughter had a place in the Stutch household, assisting the cook. I was fifteen—I said don't move!" Light starred off the revolver's shining barrel.

I returned my hand to my chest, a couple of inches south of where it had been. In another hour I'd be close enough to grab the automatic and pick up a bullet on the way.

She went on in the old tone. "I may be the only person still around who remembers the original Mrs. Stutch. When she was younger she avoided publicity, and when she got old and sick, no one saw her except her husband and children and her doctors and the servants who brought her meals to her in bed. I was one of the servants. She asked for me in particular. We never talked about anything but how she wanted her eggs cooked—she liked the yolks firm and would send them back if they were runny, I remember she was quite ruthless about it—but she followed my every movement with those sharp eyes. I would see her looking at me when she was talking about eggs, and know that she was studying my features and coloring and comparing them to her husband's. I'm certain she knew. I'm just as certain it was she who arranged for me to take piano lessons. I was fascinated with the Steinway in the front parlor and when I wasn't needed in the kitchen and Mr. Stutch was out I would climb onto the bench and try to pick out notes; she probably overheard me and found out who was playing from one of the other servants. I have no doubt she was the one who persuaded Mr. Stutch to arrange an audition with the Detroit Symphony when I turned twenty-one. He wouldn't have considered refusing. Giving in was easier than discussing the truth. For all the talk about being a fearless pioneer and a savage competitor, he was a coward when it came to the really important things.

"Old Mrs. Stutch died before I could disappoint her with my failure," she said. "I suppose it was out of respect for her memory that Mr. Stutch welcomed me back to the staff. He never said a word about the time and money that had been wasted on me, never gave me cause to believe the thought ever occurred to him. I hate him more than any other man who ever lived."

"I shouldn't wonder." Rayellen spoke sympathetically, without pity. "You were old enough to understand when Carla Willard was born and the press covered Cecilia's suit against Leland, and you must have known about the arrangements he made to support Carla after the case was dismissed. If it weren't for his first wife, he'd never have done a thing for either of you. He supported you both, but he never gave you his name. What he gave you came from guilt, not love. Why didn't you tell me? I'd have—"

"You're as bad as he was. You both snatched up a fistful of cash, and neither of you had the courage not to feel guilty about it. So you decided to write checks until you felt better. You think just because you've hiked the price you're some kind of hero. That's just inflation.

"Well, I'm not much better," she continued. "I want more. You can keep the name; it's ugly, and I've never liked anyone who had it, including the first Mrs. Stutch. I'll take the fortune. And I won't feel guilty about it."

I said, "You forgot something. Your lever's safe with his grandmother."

"I'm reasonable," Mrs. Campbell said. "The situation's changed again. I'll settle for the ten million Connor proposed. He's a better bargainer than he is a lover. All those wives just wore him down in bed. Rayellen—I'll go ahead and call you Rayellen, since we're related—you can set me up an account in the Caymans. I've watched you do it for yourself on the computer. Aren't you glad we don't have secrets? You could close it out later, of course, when my gun and I are gone. It wouldn't be a smart idea. You can ring yourself with guards, all the new relatives, too. One day a guard will be pushing little Matthew on a swing and he'll come down without a face. It wouldn't matter much to him what happened to me after that. Ask Mr. Walker. His friend was sitting right next to him and his gun when she lost her head."

I heard Rayellen's nails scratch the doorframe. She'd staggered and caught herself against it. The movement attracted Mrs. Campbell's attention for an instant. I lowered my hand six inches. It still wasn't far enough, and just to make it interesting my hand had begun to shake. Fatigue, loss of blood, and stress of the post-traumatic and present variety were kicking in like a triple hangover. I would have one shot, if I didn't drop the gun first.

"Messy picture," I said. "You should stick to the piano and leave the artwork to your boss. Maybe set it to music for when you come back for another ten million."

"I'm not sorry about your friend. Why should I be? I didn't know her. No guilt, remember. As for my coming back, we'll have to wait and see. Connor told me his end of the ten would be as much as he needed to finish out. I'm younger. I want to travel. I wasn't with the symphony long enough to go on tour. Concorde tickets and five-star hotels can really kick a hole in a girl's budget. Also I'll need a whole new wardrobe. The first thing I'm going to do is burn these gray rags. I won't need to wear a disguise after tonight. Now put that hand back where it was." Her face had gone smooth and tight. The shadows slid away in a sheet, leaving behind skin as white as polished bone. I did as she said.

The garage shuddered delicately. Overhead, the pull-up door began sliding forward, its rubber rollers making almost no noise at all in the tracks. Rayellen had pushed the button next to the side doorframe.

Mrs. Campbell was standing directly underneath. She stepped back reflexively and pulled the trigger, but the bottom edge of the door struck the end of the revolver; the bullet plucked at my jacket and whacked the back of the Land Rover. I jerked out the automatic and fired five shots practically in one piece, like a movie cowboy fanning his hogleg. The door was halfway down, only Mrs. Campbell's lower half showing underneath. All five slugs tore through the bottom panel in a group no bigger than my fist. Her feet did a foxtrot, but I couldn't tell if she'd been hit or if she was just backpedaling. The door touched down without a sound.

I backed around the end of the Land Rover, jerked open the door on the driver's side, and rested my forearms on top of it with the pistol steadied in both hands, using the door as a shield. I shouted to Rayellen to open the garage door. Then my hands began to shake for real. I forced myself to breathe and they settled down. I'd fired six, counting Andy at the plant. I didn't know how many the gun carried. The next one would have to count.

There was a pause, then the building shuddered again and the door lifted. My skin twitched. I ground my teeth to choke off the tremor before it got to my hands. Nothing would ever raise itself more slowly than the door of that garage; not the *Titanic* nor the lost city of Atlantis nor the Tigers' pitching staff. It rose like the curtain on the last act of *King Lear*, operated by a crew that didn't care for Shakespeare. But it rose, and it wasn't two feet off the floor when I relaxed my shoulders and straightened.

Rayellen sobbed once, softly. I couldn't tell if it was relief or grief or her ironbound guilt returning. Mrs. Campbell lay half on her side on the concrete with the soles of her sensible shoes showing and her revolver lying a foot away from her outstretched hand. She wasn't moving.

I came around the open car door, lowering the automatic but not all the way, taking away my left hand so I could bring the gun up fast. I wasn't shaking now that I couldn't miss. I stepped over quickly and kicked away the revolver, harder than I'd meant to; it scraped across the concrete and went into the cut grass that bordered the drive. I leaned down and laid the fingers of my free hand on the big artery at the side of the woman's neck. It throbbed once and then its work was over. The front of the gray dress below her breasts was black under the light spilling out of the garage.

I heard slippers scuffing the floor behind me and rose. I moved too fast.

"Amos?" Rayellen Stutch's voice echoed like Chinese bells in the blackness. I fell away from them.

# CHAPTER

# THIRTY-THREE

I WOKE UP as they were loading me into the ambulance. I don't re-member, but they told me later I wouldn't put my head back down until the paramedics promised to take me to Detroit Receiving and not the hospital Leland Stutch had endowed in Iroquois Heights. The chief surgeon was being sued for leaving a putting glove inside a gall bladder patient and the board of directors had voted six to four in favor of letting him practice until the case came to court. I do remember seeing a fat cop in uniform walking past the van with Mrs. Campbell's shiny revolver in a Ziploc bag, holding it by the top between thumb and forefinger like dog droppings. Then I went back to sleep and stayed that way for fourteen hours.

My surgeon, a blonde stunner with blue eyes and a Malibu tan, incongruously named Rosenberg, pried sixteen pieces of lead shot out of my back and hip. She came in while I was propped up in bed eating breakfast and showed me the pieces in a disposable cardboard drool cup. They were the size of the peas they serve at banquets. She asked if I wanted them for a keepsake. I told her to distribute them in the charity ward.

She pouted. "I don't know why the men in your line are so flippant about this kind of thing. A few more degrees to the left and we'd have had to remove a kidney."

"A few more degrees to the right and they'd have missed me completely. Call me an optimist."

It was my first morning rightside-up. I'd been on my stomach for days with stitches and patches on my back, listening to the news reports on television because it still hurt my neck to look up at the set bolted to the ceiling. At the end of three days the Eyewitness News team had the fracas in Iroquois Heights pegged as a wildcat strike by a number of truckers who were dissatisfied with the last contract the Steelhaulers had ratified with General Motors, in particular having to do with working conditions at the former Stutch plant. Ray Montana appeared on *Meet the Press* to disavow any foreknowledge of the event and promised an internal investigation. The U.S. Attorney General announced that she would make no decision regarding the appointment of a special prosecutor until she had "read and re-read the reports of investigators engaged by the Department of Justice."

Connor Thorpe, recovering in a private room at the hospital in Iroquois Heights from injuries sustained in the raid on the Stutch plant, was unavailable for comment. He was one of only five people reported injured that night. Two were truckers.

The death of Myra Campbell, longtime housekeeper to Rayellen Stutch on the night of the assault on the plant, was under investigation by local authorities, who did not believe it was related to the rest of the evening's events. Mrs. Stutch herself was on vacation in Florida and could not be reached.

Some reports claimed more than a hundred tractor-trailer rigs were involved in the destruction of some eighty million dollars' worth of public and private property inside the Iroquois Heights city limits. More conservative estimates placed the number of vehicles at sixty. The Stutch plant was declared a total loss and the date for its demolition was moved up one year. In addition, heavy trucks had destroyed a 7-Eleven near the downtown freeway exit, most of a strip mall on the main drag, including a cut-rate drugstore and a Harley-Davidson boutique, and the entire east side of the old main four corners. On that pass, one $150,000 Marmon hauling a double-bottom tanker took out a Real Estate One, two video stores, a Hallmark, and the Shogun Massage Emporium; it was a century-old brick block with common walls that had survived two fires. The driver was being sought for reckless driving, malicious destruction, and leaving the scene of an accident, as well as violating a ten-year-old Michigan law banning double-bottom tankers on the grounds of their abysmal safety records.

Small-change damage included a half-dozen street signs pretzeled by rigs cutting corners and a honey locust that had been planted the previous spring in place of a statue erected to commemorate an old victory over the Iroquois. Local protesters—not an Indian among them—had gotten the statue scrapped and the tree dedicated to Native Americans. It was in the corner of the downtown park and whoever had knocked it down had to have taken aim. A Kenworth with Texas plates was suspected.

A White dump truck got stuck on top of a twisted hunk of bronze commissioned from a Japanese-Swedish sculptor on the lawn in front of the City-County Building. The driver fled on foot but was cornered by prowlies in an alley and placed in custody. The sculpture was named "Unchained Thought" and hadn't looked all that less twisted before it was run over.

Mayor Arbor Muriel issued a long rambling statement to the press decrying the "wanton vandalism," promising "virtuous redress," and proposing that a new community center be build on the site of the shattered downtown block. Of all those solicited for comment, he spoke the longest and had the least to say. Cecil Fish, who had no official capacity in local government, was not heard from.

I'd slept through Iris's funeral. Ms. Stainback, the Cerberus who guarded the gate at the shelter in Monroe, had made all the arrangements, and the procession had been long enough and sufficiently populated with well-known figures to make the papers. There was no mention in the obituary of the Detroit hookshop where Iris had worked for eighteen months twenty years ago. She was identified as a Jamaican native who had come out of an abusive marriage to found a shelter for battered women and children and died in an automobile accident while transporting a client and her young son to the home of a relative. A Catholic bishop known to the Vatican, the physician in charge of a drug rehabilitation clinic where Iris had put in many hours of volunteer work after her own recovery from heroin addiction, and the president of the local chapter of the National Organization of Women had been among those delivering eulogies. Iris would have been flattered by the first two and kept her comments to herself regarding the third, remembering the husbands of professional feminists she had entertained in the days before she'd reformed. Her ashes were interred in a Monroe cemetery and in lieu of flowers, mourners were requested to make donations to the Iris Chapin fund, proceeds to be used to improve and maintain the shelter. Lying on my stomach reading the account of the funeral, I made a mental note of the P.O. box where donations were to be sent.

I greeted more visitors in three days in the hospital than I normally did in a month at my office.

After Dr. Rosenberg left with her cup of lead, Sergeant Vivaldi of the Iroquois Heights Police Department bulled in, smiling with all his tobacco-tinted teeth, eyes hooded behind his smoked glasses. When he turned his head, a patch of white bandage showed where his wire-brushed black hair had been shaved. I wondered if Maintenance had gotten around to replacing the mirror in the elevator of the City-County Building.

"Heard you got yourself shot," he said. "Too bad his aim stunk."

"Mine, too," I said. "The guy who shot me's in serious condition on the fifth floor. He still had some blood left."

"Busy night. I heard you killed a woman."

"If you talked to Mrs. Stutch, you know that was self-defense. I was defending myself all over town that day, starting with downtown. How's your head?"

"I can still think with it. I won't need my Miranda card to haul you down when they spring you from this meat shop." He went out on this gem.

The next cop in the box was Loggins, the hefty female sergeant from the Juvenile Division of the Michigan State Police. She had on a slate-gray business suit that fit her better than the bolero jacket she'd worn to the scene of the accident on I-75. The shoulder bag was the same: too red, to match her lipstick. She'd brought along a male stenographer with the long sad face of a professional pallbearer. She asked me if I was feeling well enough to make a statement, in a tone that said she didn't care what the answer was. I told her the missing boy was with his grandmother and gave her Carla Willard Witowski's telephone number in Melvindale. I gave her some details I hadn't before. She said shock made people forget. If there was any sympathy in the remark, she'd masked it well; but then a person only has so much, and the store had to be conserved for her younger subjects. She made sure the stenographer had it all and we parted company on terms somewhat more cordial than when she'd entered.

Just to relieve me of the company of all these sergeants, a detective lieutenant from Toledo Homicide dropped by, a well-dressed black named Boncour, tall enough to have played a lot of basketball in college. He wanted me to pay him a visit after my release to tape a video statement in regard to the David Glendowning killing. He said I'd have to answer questions about leaving the scene and that a transcript of the tape would be sent to Lansing, where they review private investigators' licenses, but his disapproval was strictly professional. Mark Proust was talking from his hospital bed under heavy police guard, and Boncour was on his way to Iroquois Heights with a warrant for Connor Thorpe's arrest for conspiracy to commit murder. I said he'd have to fight it out with the authorities in Michigan, who were waiting to charge him with abduction and child endangerment, to start.

While I was dressing, waiting for the hospital paperwork, I took a telephone call from an attorney named Swammerdamm, who said he was senior member of the firm that represented Rayellen Stutch. He said he'd been in touch with the police in Iroquois Heights and that no arrest warrant would be issued if I agreed to surrender myself voluntarily for questioning at the station. Swammerdamm would be present at that time. His fee had been taken care of.

I took a cab home, poured myself a tall Scotch, and carried it and my mail into the living room. I was getting along with an Ace bandage on my ankle. The house smelled shut up, as if I'd been away a month. I opened a window and sat down in my easy chair and looked around, like Odysseus back in the palace at Ithaca. My little library of no value to collectors, the rack of LPs, even the permanent ring on the little side table where I placed my glass with the precision of a pilot landing on an aircraft carrier, were objects of wonder. In the hospital I'd tried to picture it all and had failed, like a little boy trying to recall the features of his dead mother.

That made me think of Matthew. I looked up the number of Henry Ford Hospital, called and finally got a nurse familiar with Constance Glendowning's case, who told me she was awake and expecting a visit from her mother and son. I thanked her and hung up without leaving my name.

The only thing in the mail that held my interest long enough to open the envelope was a check from Mrs. Stutch, without a note. It bore a Miami postmark. It covered my fee, with a bonus twice as big to cover expenses.

I called around until I found the garage in Trenton where my Cutlass had been towed and made arrangements to tow it from there to the garage I did business with in Detroit. Without an estimate I figured the repairs, including a new bumper, hood, windshield, and upholstery to eliminate the bloodstains, would leave me with just enough to pay my monthly bills.

The bills could wait. Next morning, after eight hours in my own bed, I uncharacteristically made breakfast, enjoying the novelty of cooking my own eggs and brewing coffee the way I liked it, letting it steep on the hotpad until it could stand on its own. I took a thirty-minute shower, shaved close, broke a new white shirt out of plastic, and put on the suit I wore to weddings and funerals and client visits in Grosse Pointe. In place of a necktie I Velcroed on the snappy blue cervical collar they'd given me at Receiving for my whiplash. I called a cab and had the driver wait outside my bank while I cashed Mrs. Stutch's check. I kept out a hundred in cash, put the rest in savings, and rode to the MGM Grand Casino.

What looked like the same seniors in the same pastel sweats were sawing away at the slots with the same look of no hope on their faces. At the cashier's cage I bought two fifty-dollar chips. I waded through the sea of jangling and bing-bonging from the machines, with the odd clink of silver dollars trickling into the trays, stopped at the roulette table, and put down a chip on the black seven. When the wheel stopped at sixteen red, I put the other chip down in the same place and turned away.

"Seven, black," said the croupier, a smooth young black woman in a stiff formal shirt and red bow tie. "Fifteen hundred to you, sir."

The other players applauded politely.

I asked the smiling cashier to make out a check to the Iris

Chapin Fund. Outside, I climbed into the first cab in line and gave the driver the address of my office.

"Any luck, mister?" he asked.

"A little."

His eyes crinkled in the rearview mirror. "Lady smiled, huh?"

"All the time."

And in a little while, I did too.